THE TH... DRAWN TOGETHER . . .

Nicola knew as soon as he touched her, such a gentle stroking warmth on her face, arms, shoulders, that she wanted him as much as he wanted her. Not, this time, sex with a stranger. The difference that affection makes.

David undressed her slowly. . . .

"You are very beautiful," he said softly, coming at last to lie beside her.

Then he froze. She heard it seconds after he did. The sound of a car coming up the driveway. Instinctively, Nicola rolled under the light sheet, pulling it up to her chin, a cold fear swamping her. David was at the window in moments.

"Barbara?" asked Nicola in a whisper.

Barbara, her bitch-beautiful stepmother. David's patroness, lover, keeper. . . .

"Hi, kiddies. . . . Been balling around some?"

David had everything to lose. For Nicola, the choice was easy as a clean breath in the night. There was a certain life-style to be enjoyed here, she realized. An escapist, hedonistic life which possibly, just possibly, she could grow accustom to.

A life-style to get lost in . . .

Bel-Air

Mary McCluskey

PINNACLE BOOKS   LOS ANGELES

BEL-AIR

Copyright © 1981 by Mary McCluskey

An original Pinnacle Books edition, published for the first time anywhere.

First printing, March 1981

ISBN: 0-523-41158-8

Cover photograph by Brian Leng

Printed in the United States of America

PINNACLE BOOKS, INC.
2029 Century Park East
Los Angeles, California 90067

Bel-Air

ONE

Nicola was in Florence when she heard that he was dead. That shadowed day began like any other of her vacation: a sun-lit stroll through the cobbled streets near the cathedral, then coffee in a sidewalk cafe where the air was spicy with the perfume of hot pastries and the colognes of the breakfasting businessmen. Nicola always left before the tourists arrived.

When she returned to the *pensione* on the *Piazza Mentana*, Steve and Janey were finishing breakfast in the sunny dining room.

Nicola took a clean cup from an empty table and joined them. The door that led to the terrace had been opened and a soft breeze rustled the linen tablecloths and the leaves of the many plants in the room.

Janey ran her fingers through her curly chestnut hair and yawned.

"Today will be a nice quiet day," she stated. "No galleries. Absolutely no galleries."

The three had been in Florence one week and with greedy enthusiasm had tried to see too much, too quickly. Steve, a trainee lawyer with a professional love for organized detail, had compiled a geographical list of galleries: they had been working through it.

"I don't care if I ever see another picture as long as I live," said Janey. "Not a masterpiece, in any case. God, my kids' stuff will be a positive relief after all this."

They laughed. Janey taught art at a London grammar school.

1

"When Felix gets here we'll have to start all over again," said Nicola.

The other two groaned.

"Felix," Steve said firmly, "can go it alone."

Their friend Felix was flying from Nice that evening to join them. He had spent the first half of his vacation in Provence, preferring, he claimed, an abundance of red wine, olives, and garlic to a diet of old masters.

"A week in Florence will be long enough for me," he had said, "to try every kind of pasta. Oh, and maybe glance at a few pictures."

Janey finished her coffee in a gulp.

"Why don't we just lie out on the terrace and get browned. We can't go home looking like half-cooked spaghetti."

"Good idea," agreed Steve. He glanced at Nicola's doubtful face. "Come on, love," he said, touching her cheek. "Don't burden yourself with guilt. It will all be here tomorrow."

Nicola grinned.

"All right. I'll get my bikini."

Later on, however, bored with the sun, they visited the Pitti Palace. Nicola felt contented as they sipped vermouth in the Palace gardens and watched the setting sun. The changing light caused the uniform colors to deepen. Florence—burnt sienna, tinted gold—became a magical sandcastle city, baked by the sun.

But as they strolled arm-in-arm into the *Pensione Katerina* for dinner, Signora Signorelli was waiting for them.

"There has been a telephone call for you," she said to Nicola. "You must call back. I have the number."

Nicola stared at her.

"For me?" She frowned, puzzled, a thread of fear as always at the unexpected.

"Felix," said Janey. "Sure to be."

Nicola nodded her head.

"He's missed his plane," she sighed.

"No," said Janey. "He's missed the bus to the airport to catch the plane."

Steve looked from one to the other.

"Both wrong. He caught the plane but it's the wrong one and he's landed in Beirut and he's wondering where all the pretty palaces are."

The girls laughed. With Felix even that was possible.

"I do not think it was your friend," said the Signora very quietly. "It was London. I will dial for you."

"London? Probably the *Chronicle* wanting me to do some stupid story," Nicola said crossly.

Steve was watching the kindly *pensione* owner as she dialed and for a moment their eyes met. The middle-aged woman shook her head.

"Not the paper, love," he said and fumbled in his pocket for cigarettes. Surprisingly, there was little difficulty getting through to London, and Nicola barely had time to accept and light the offered cigarette before the Signora was handing her the phone.

"Nicola. I'm afraid . . ."

She did not recognize the voice. Worse, she could not understand what the voice was saying. Then, suddenly, she heard a sentence with terrifying clarity:

"He is dead, Nicola. I'm sorry."

"Who is dead? Who is dead?" she screamed.

The line crackled, seemed to echo her own words back to her. The voice said "Jenson." Nicola finally recognized the voice of Mrs. Jenson, her father's housekeeper. Then a dark fog of fear clouded her mind.

"I don't understand."

Her voice was on the edge of hysteria and she realized that Steve had taken the phone from her.

"Hello," he said. "Will you tell me what has happened and I will explain to Nicola."

There was a pause while he listened. Nicola was aware of Janey holding her shoulders, of the Signora handing her a small glass of amber colored liquid. She sipped it, watching Steve's closed face. He glanced at her once and looked away again quickly.

"Yes. When? Yes, I have that. Will you give me all the details you have?"

There was silence while he listened attentively.

"We'll organize her flight for her. Thank you. I am sorry."

Nicola knew then. Knew before he put down the phone and turned to look at her sadly, knew before Janey, seeing his look, held the glass of burning liquid to her. Knew that her father was dead. They didn't tell her then, that he had killed himself.

TWO

It was Mrs. Jenson who told her that the death was suicide. He had taken a bottle of pills on top of a large quan-
tity of scotch.

"It could have been an accident," she said, wanting to
believe it. "He could have been drunk."

Nicola studied the plump, gray-haired woman sympathetically. She had been Nick Graham's housekeeper for
ten years and had loved him.

"A *whole* bottle of pills?" asked Nicola, softly.

Alone, she walked up to her father's studio. The house,
Nicola's childhood home, was in Arlington Square in now
fashionable Islington and, like so many in the area, Geor-
gian and three stories high. Nick Graham had purchased
the property for a song when Islington was still mostly
working class, long before the trendies moved in. He had
converted the top floor into a light, bright studio, set in
new windows, sky-lights in the roof. But this day, the studio smelled musty, had an abandoned, dusty look.

Mrs. Jenson had always been banned from this room,
except to bring cups of coffee and food. Her attempts to
tidy it periodically had incurred Nick Graham's wrath.
Once in a while he would sweep the floor himself, throw
out empty paint tubes and unsatisfactory canvases. He
hadn't done that for some time, Nicola thought sadly. The
floor was littered with twisted metal tubes and old newspapers. His easel stood where it had always been, but there
was no canvas on it. A stack of barely begun, abandoned
paintings rested against the wall. Nicola looked at each

one, hoping for a clue to her father's state of mind, but they were sketchy and said little. Only one of Mrs. Jenson hanging out washing as the wind billowed her skirts, had some animation, some reality to it; the rest were unsure outlines, lacking her father's former authority. Crumpled in a corner, Nicola found a canvas that revealed a stormy sky, blackening with ominous clouds. It hinted of a depressed or fearful mind, but she had no idea when he had painted it.

"Had he been working?" she asked Mrs. Jenson when, downstairs in the neat kitchen, they had tea together. Mrs. Jenson sipped from her cup and was silent for awhile.

"Not much," she said at last. "He really hasn't—hadn't—been doing anything much at all. Drinking mostly. By himself in the study," she added.

Nicola could imagine how much that must have hurt the housekeeper. Nick Graham had been a sociable man. On the rare occasions when he stayed home all evening he would talk, laugh, and entertain Mrs. Jenson with stories and memories. He had never been solitary. Nicola guessed that although Mrs. Jenson had cheerfully tolerated his many mistresses, his wild nights out, his crazy parties; she would have found the unusually silent man difficult. As if reading her mind, Mrs. Jenson nodded.

"I didn't like that. It was so unlike him," she said. "It worried me."

"Did he have any new women?" asked Nicola, thinking that the question was probably irrelevant as her father had never allowed a woman to hurt him much. Certainly not enough to cause him to kill himself.

"Not since that actress," said Mrs. Jenson, sadly, as if this too had worried her. "And he threw her over because she started nagging him about his drinking and him not turning up when he said he would. You know what he was like. Well, he told her to get lost. I think she was quite upset about it."

Nicola nodded. Another broken, though no doubt quickly-mended, heart to add to the list that stretched right back through her father's past.

Mrs. Jenson got to her feet and began bustling around the kitchen making more tea.

"Did you ring the attorney?" she asked, over her shoulder.

"Yes. He wasn't very helpful. There isn't much of an estate."

The older woman turned, the teapot in her hand.

"You must have expected that, dear," she said.

"Yes."

Nicola was silent for a while, waiting until Mrs. Jenson sat down again before she told her the rest of it. According to Sedly, the house would have to be sold before the estate could be settled. Nick Graham had no more than a few hundred pounds in the bank. He had left no will.

"Mrs. Jenson," she began awkwardly.

"Yes, dear, I know. He was in debt."

"Yes, and . . ."

"You've got to sell the house and give me notice."

Nicola looked at her sadly.

"I want you to have half of anything left over from the house sale."

"Not at all," said the housekeeper, firmly. "I've been happy here. And I'll stay on until you're straight again. Then, well, goodness I can always get another job."

"God, it won't be much," Nicola cried, "but I want you to have half. Please. You deserved it."

Mrs. Jenson was silent for awhile.

"All that work," Nicola mused unhappily, remembering her father locked in his studio for days on end. "All that work for nothing."

"He had no money sense," Mrs. Jenson said. "I've seen him sell pictures—big ones, too—to some little dealer or other just for the price of a bottle of whisky. He was crazy sometimes. Well, not crazy," she amended quickly, lest she offend Nicola. "But . . . you know."

"I know."

The two women sipped their tea.

"We must talk about the funeral, dear," said Mrs. Jenson, gently.

"Yes, we must."

7

THREE

Nick Graham had been terrified of cremation.

"What if I'm not really dead! What if there *is* resurrection of the body? I don't want to spend eternity looking like a dirty ashtray with all those pretty angels around. It's barbaric. I want a proper funeral. And—are you listening Nicola—I want a pretty carved stone, with an appropriate chunk of verse—some Bryon, perhaps, or Keats. What about . Herrick . . . Gather ye rosebuds while ye may. And on top of that, an angel. A sexy, carved angel with a shy smile."

"Dad, for Christ's sake."

"For *my* sake, thick-head. And you put flowers on the damn thing, would you. Once a year will do. On my birthday."

As the wind whirled her coat around her and Nicola shivered, she wished for a moment her father had been less emphatic. Though perhaps he had been joking that crazy day years ago. It was rarely possible to tell when he was serious and when he was not.

It had come to the moment when the coffin was to be lowered into the ground, and Nicola felt Mrs. Jenson's hand on her arm. She squeezed the cold, trembling hand slightly. The vicar's voice was almost lost in the whistling wind. The cemetery, high on Muswell Hill overlooking London, was the coldest, bleakest place Nicola could remember seeing.

The coffin was lowered and she swallowed hard, telling herself that it was not her father there. Not really what had

9

been her father. Whatever death was, whatever it meant, the bones and rotting flesh in that wooden casket had nothing to do with the man he had been.

They were burying him in the plot beside Nicola's mother. But that first funeral had been many years ago. Nicola had been five years old and she had not been allowed to attend. Her memories of her mother were now vague: a quiet lady with soft skin who moved quickly, lightly; a graceful shadow; a soft voice; a warm hug. That was all.

Mrs. Jenson was sobbing. So, surprisingly, was an elegant, middle-aged woman Nicola had never seen before. Dressed completely in black, even to her veiled, thirties-style hat, the blonde woman stood a little way behind the vicar. She held a handkerchief to her face and her shoulders were shaking. The actress? Another mistress from years ago? A few friends of Nick Graham stood behind the woman: one, James, a prominent art critic; the others, drinking companions. His oldest friend, Jack Dunstable, stood next to Nicola. Jack and her father had gone to Paris together as young men—to paint and learn about women, they claimed. Jack had come back after a year, had joined a large manufacturing firm as a clerk and was now managing director. Her father had stayed in Paris to pursue his dream.

How disappointed he would be at this, thought Nicola, glancing round. No more than twenty people, not one of them a fellow artist. Nick Graham, ten, fifteen years ago had been a member of an exciting circle of British talent, had been noted as the best of them by many critics. But as the others developed, his style changed little. And successful though he had been, he had never rejoined that group. Rarely taking chances, he had painted good pictures, but only those he knew would sell. And they had sold—very quickly. But her father's nature was such that he spent money as fast as he made it, and always needed more. A famous pauper.

The ceremony was over at last. Nicola and Mrs. Jenson took the first car back to the house. Nicola had invited no one. There was to be no wake, no boozing, no endless reminiscing. She had spoken briefly to Jack and Angela Dunstable, then left. There was nothing she wanted to say to the others.

"Thank God he wasn't there to see that," she said in the car. "He would have been so disappointed."

Then suddenly, without warning, she began to cry, a harsh sobbing that made Mrs. Jenson hold back her own tears and clasp the girl's shaking shoulders.

"Good," she said. "I hoped you'd cry soon. I've been so worried about you."

Ted Sharp, news editor of London's *Evening Chronicle*, was reading *The Times* when he saw Nicola walking briskly down the large editorial hall towards him. He had read her father's obituary minutes before, and felt slightly embarrassed now. He had never been good at expressing sympathy—never knew what to say. Besides, he liked Nicola. And it was his habit with anyone he liked, not to show it.

She had stopped to talk to Lilian Hill, the women's editor, who was making exaggerated gestures of sympathy—hand-patting and the like. Lilian's large, gold earrings swung from side to side as she shook her head.

Ted studied the two women: Lilian was dark with far too much of everything—make-up, jewelry, breasts, and buns; Nicola was slight, slender, her long blonde hair tied back today with a clasp. She usually wore it loose. He sighed. A pretty kid. He went back to his *Times* and the sports page.

Minutes later Nicola was looking over his shoulder.

"Ah, just what I wanted. Is that the library copy?"

"It is not. It's my copy. But—you can read it." He handed it to Nicola with a quick jab at a smile.

"Thanks, Ted. I'll bring it back in a few minutes."

"They've said some nice things about your father," he said, awkwardly. Nicola stopped then at his desk and flicked through to the obit page.

"I hoped they would."

11

She had begun reading and Ted decided to wait until she'd finished before offering his sympathy. She took a long time, probably reading it twice.

"Well," she said, finally. "Not bad. Thanks, Ted. I'll get a copy later."

She had put his *Times* back on his desk, smiled at him and was gone before Ted Sharp could say a word of sympathy. He was relieved and also annoyed with himself. He started reading through the copy on his desk, got down to work in earnest.

All day Nicola attempted to side-step people with expressions of sympathy. The awkward euphemisms for death embarrassed her and they were stammered out with such obvious discomfort.

"I was sorry to hear your father passed away, Nicola," said the young sports reporter, blushing. Nicola blushed, too.

"Thank you," she said. An inadequate response, she thought, but what else can I say?

Only her fellow junior critic, Jonathon, seemed relaxed and himself. Nicola was grateful for that. Jonathon critiqued the theatre that the cranky and established theatre critic didn't want to cover. Nicola covered the small art exhibitions that the equally cranky art critic couldn't be bothered with. The shared feeling of being understudies with little possibility of ever having lines to say, gave Nicola and Jonathon an empathy that, though it never stretched to out-of-office socializing, made their workday more fun.

"I saw the Wicked Witch trying to tear your arm off," said Jonathon cheerfully as Nicola settled into the desk opposite him, far away from the lady he referred to— Lilian Hill.

"She was saying how terribly, terribly sorry she is," said Nicola, relieved at his tone, copying it.

"How sweet," he said cynically. "Also that froggy creature known as the Art Critic . . ."

Jonathon looked up at Nicola, raised an eyebrow.

"Jeremy?"

"The same. He has been snooping around here this morning looking for you. The *Chronicle*, it seems, is to do a piece on your dad for tonight's edition. And so they should. Dear frog-face Jeremy has written his piece—from the clippings, of course. He thought, though, that you might give him a little "Inside color." I think he called it that. What color are you inside, incidentally?

"I told him," concluded Jonathon with some satisfaction, "to please piss off."

"And did he?"

"He did indeed."

"Thanks, love."

"My pleasure. Anything else I can do?"

His voice was now serious and Nicola looked up at him, noting the sympathy in his eyes.

"Take me to lunch?"

He grinned.

"Delighted. I'll even change the habits of a lifetime and pay for both of us."

Nicola, about to protest—they had always gone Dutch—swallowed the words. It was a gesture he wanted to make and she must let him make it. Jonathon accepted her smile then went back to work. Nicola began sorting through the notices from galleries, arranging them in alphabetical order, then subbing them down for the weekend "Guide to Galeries" section.

Junior art critic indeed, she thought. A ten year old with a knowledge of the alphabet could do today's work. I wanted to be a painter like Berthe Morisot, she told herself ruefully, and here I am mumbling my ABCs like a filing clerk with a bad memory. Her father hadn't been too impressed with her choice of career she remembered. Maybe he was right.

"An art critic!" he had bellowed, two years ago. "God's teeth, child, you don't need an education for *that*. All those years of study, all that time at the Slade. The very *best* art school in Britain. The best outside of Paris, in fact."

"Because you were there . . ."

"Even so."

"Dad, as any of my teachers would have told you, if you

13

would ever have listened to anyone: I have no talent. Adequate, good, even—but not good enough."

"Hmm," he said, eyeing her. "Possibly, possibly. No originality, perhaps."

Nicola bristled, despite herself.

"But there are other things: illustrating, teaching . . ." he paused, groaned. "An art critic! Oh my God."

Nevertheless, he had helped her get the job.

"You will regret it," he had said darkly when she accepted the *Chronicle* offer. "What's more, you'll hate every damn minute."

She didn't hate "every damn minute." It was only on days like this . . . L M N O . . .

"You're muttering again," said Jonathon.

"It's the alphabet. I can't remember it otherwise."

"Can't you just mutter it in your head?"

"No."

"Good Lord," he said, teasing. "Call yourself an art critic."

"Funny, that's just what I was thinking."

FOUR

"Good grief, I can't understand why you don't *want* to go," shouted Felix from the kitchen.

In Nicola's small apartment, he was concocting another of what he called his Creative Food Parcels. Tantalizing cooking smells wafted through to Nicola as she sat staring stupidly at the letter. She picked it up, then put it down again, waiting for Felix to finish cooking so that they might eat then discuss it further.

"It's not that I don't want to go. I'm just not sure."

"Very clear," said Felix sarcastically, and returned to his chopping board.

It had been three weeks since her father's death and Nicola, though still prone to occasional nighttime tears, was picking up the threads of her normal life again. She would not have believed she could miss her father so much. She had seen him rarely, had lived her own single life, but she missed his exuberant telephone calls and the occasional long lunches—mostly liquid for him, but a splendid treat for her. Always, he would urge her into extravagant choices:

"All civilized people love oysters, sweetheart. Why deny yourself."

And even when she was dieting:

"Come on now, Nicola darling. Smoked salmon is perfect diet food. One calorie to the pound."

She may have seen him rarely—but he had always been there.

Her friends, after her repeated refusals to join them in the pub or at parties, had taken to dropping in on her. Usually bringing a bottle of wine or gin. Nicola was grateful but she was especially grateful to Felix: always one to go a step further than the crowd, Felix would bring the ingredients for whole meals which he would settle down to cook with dedication. He was convinced, he said, that she wasn't eating enough. He was right. Earlier, when Nicola had opened the door to the tall, smiling figure clutching his bulging bag of groceries she had grinned with delight.

"You're pleased to see me," he said, suspiciously. "Why?"

"I want your advice Felix."

"Advice?" Felix managed to look both flattered and slightly nervous. "Good Lord, I'm the last person to ask advice from. Look what a mess I always make of things."

Felix, at twenty-eight, had established himself as a well-respected lecturer in ancient history. His Cambridge education had prepared him for that. It had not, however, prepared him for modern day realities. Perplexed by the fates, Felix moved helplessly from crisis to crisis. His checks bounced because he often forgot to deposit his paycheck, he would find himself in restaurants, penniless; he left his briefcase in taxis with monotonous regularity; his personal life was fraught with misunderstandings and broken dates. Despite all this, he was enormously popular and Nicola, like many others, delighted in his company. She considered Felix her closest friend.

"This is quite a simple problem," she said.

He set down his purchases on the kitchen table, removed the theadbare black velvet jacket he wore everywhere and turned to her.

"Ask away then, before I start my creative bit."

Nicola handed him the airmail envelope.

He studied the Los Angeles postmark for a moment then read the letter inside. He was quick about it and grinned immediately.

"Fantastic," he said. "Great. Just what you need. So, what's the problem?"

"Do you think I should go?"

16

"Of course you should go. When again will you get a chance to see L.A. or whatever the natives call it?"

"But I can barely remember Barbara!"

"So what? The exhibition should be good. She must be quite an interesting woman. What was she . . . your dad's third wife?"

"Second. My mother was first. Barbara was my stepmother for six years."

"Well, there you are then. And look where she lives. Christ, Bel-Air. You have it made, nut-head. Mustn't miss it."

But Nicola was still unsure and as Felix prepared their meal, she turned the question over and over in her mind.

She had been fond of Barbara, an elegant, attractive blonde, with an air of sharp sophistication that had fascinated the young Nicola. Barbara had been full of fun, had made Nicola laugh. She had never tried to be motherly or overly affectionate. Instead she had offered companionship, had brought laughter and music and delicious meals into the Islington home that had been quiet and lonely for Nicola since her mother's death. Her father had been so busy then, so preoccupied. Barbara filled Nicola's need for a confidante, and too, because she was imaginative and enjoyed games herself, a playmate.

But, thought Nicola, it had been a long time. She had been twelve when Barbara and her father divorced and there had been no contact since. She remembered her father saying that Barbara had married again—once? twice?—and married rich men.

It seemed that Barbara was now involved in the art world. Nicola could not fully understand why an ex-wife would bother to put on an American exhibition of her father's work. Perhaps she felt he hadn't had the recognition he deserved? Perhaps she still loved him? Her letter had been sweet and sympathetic, saying that even after so many years, she too felt a great loss. That he had been a great artist. Nicola sighed and Felix, as if on cue, emerged from the kitchen.

"No sighing. Steak Pizzaiola is ready for the eating."

17

He set out the food quickly, trying, with a swift efficiency, to hide his pride in the way the meal had turned out. Nicola sat down and gazed at the steaming dishes admiringly.

"Felix, you should have been a chef."

"Why do it for a living when you can do it for fun," said Felix airily. "As Fanny Hill might have said. Now, when have you got to be there?"

"Goodness, I haven't decided to go yet."

"Of course you have. Anyway, Janey and Steve will be around later—I invited them for a drink and I know you don't really mind, so don't pull that face—let's see what they say."

"They'll say go."

"Of course they will."

They enthused even more than Nicola had expected.

"You'll love it Nicola. It's a real fun place," said Steve, draping his long legs over the arm of the chair.

"But I'm not really a fun-person. I'm basically a serious person," protested Nicola.

"Nonsense, darling," said Janey, as briskly and dismissive as ever. "You could be a fun-person for a month. Anybody could. And in Bel-Air! Think about it: the richest, the most famous, the biggest and best of everything." She giggled. "Deliciously vulgar."

"I don't know anything about the place."

"It's hardly a place," said Felix. "More a state of mind. The Holy Grail to those who aspire and acquire."

Nicola forced a smile. She couldn't explain her reluctance to herself, though she felt it was probably her natural cowardice. A shyness at facing the unknown, meeting strange people, managing without the safety and security of her quiet social circle.

She looked around at the anxious faces of her friends.

"The office won't give me any time off. I've used up all but a week of my vacation."

Three voices loudly challenged that.

"You'll be covering the exhibition, you nut," said Felix. "Pay your own fare and they'll be delighted."

18

"They might," said Nicola doubtfully. "I suppose I could do some other stuff, too."

"And it'll be warm, remember," said Janey.

"But I like the autumn here. October's lovely."

"Come *on*, Nicola," groaned Steve.

She looked around at them, defeated.

"I suppose it will do me good," she said.

"Of course it will," said Felix.

The evening before she was due to fly to Los Angeles, Felix arrived to stay the night at her place, claiming that if he did not he would oversleep and not arrive in time to take her to the airport. Nicola looked at him steadily for a few moments with false cheeriness.

"Don't worry. I'm not going to seduce you."

Nicola laughed.

"Good. And I promise not to seduce you."

Nicola and Felix had slept together once two years before. It was an accidental coming together, happening when both were romantically involved with other people, and because of this it had been saddening and unsuccessful for them both. They had never tried it again, preferring, without ever discussing the question, the easy friendship they managed to retain. Both, over the last two years, had been infatuated with others, had enjoyed affairs, but their friendship remained firm. Nicola felt intuitively that if they became lovers their relationship would soon fizzle out, leaving them with nothing. There was an undercurrent of sexuality in their relationship, as in all close male-female friendships. She found him attractive, enjoyed the casual cuddle he would give her, the warm arm around her shoulders. But the small flicker that shot between them at times, usually after dinner and wine, was not strong enough to last long before burning out. She liked things as they were. She believed he felt the same.

The night before her flight he seemed restless, a little on edge. She cooked for him for a change, they drank a lot of wine, he read for awhile as she finished packing then they sat listening to music. Felix, she could tell, was not concentrating.

"What is it, love?" she asked finally. "What's wrong?"

He looked at her hard for a moment, as if she were angry.

"I'm thinking about sleeping on *that*," he said, pointing to the sofa bed. "While you're in your bed. I'll go crazy."

Nicola was amazed.

"But, Felix? Well . . . look, go home, stay at your own place."

"I want to stay here," he said stubbornly. "I want to sleep with you. I've wanted to for ages."

"We did once. It wasn't any good for either of us. We're happier as we are, surely. Good friends."

"It's possible to be sleeping-together good friends," said Felix, smiling. "Sorry. I meant to keep my mouth shut. It's the thought of you being away for a month too, you know."

"Will you miss me that much?" Nicola asked gently. She would miss Felix, she knew, but not in a desperate way, not in a deep sense. She had imagined he felt as she did but this was obviously not so and she knew that to sleep with him feeling as she did would be the greater cruelty. They were both silent for awhile. Felix refilled their glasses.

"Love, I think you had better go home," said Nicola with difficulty. "I'll call you in the morning. Early, so you don't oversleep, and you can take me to the airport.

"And when I'm gone," she added, "I think you ought to go out on the razzle and find yourself a dynamite redhead."

Felix downed his wine.

"I don't want a dynamite redhead," he said wryly. "I want a skinny blonde with soft, blue eyes and the sexiest mouth in the world.

"However," his voice stronger now, humor returning, "the name of the game is compromise, so yes, I'll go home and yes, tomorrow I'll go redhead hunting."

She walked with him to the door and he held her for a moment, kissing the top of her head.

"I have a big mouth," he said. "Sorry."

For a moment he held her close, his breath on her cheek, then he was gone. Nicola closed the door as he left, feeling sad and uncertain. She half wished he had stayed to ease

20

the tension she felt, her nervousness about the flight, about Los Angeles, and Barbara.

"New Experience Nerves," she said to herself firmly. "Cut it out!"

She prepared for bed.

In the flurry of tickets and baggage check and the ordered chaos that seems more obvious at Heathrow than any other airport in the world, Nicôla and Felix had little time to talk of anything more intimate than whether she needed the usual traveler's props: newspapers, magazines, chocolate, cigarettes, coffee. She had been horrified at how long before the flight they had to be at the airport, but the two hours passed quickly. Before she realized how late it was, her flight was called, and she was standing at the departure gate saying good-bye to Felix.

"You'll write?"

"Of course. Just you write back."

"And you'll take care of yourself? Eat properly, all that stuff."

She smiled, moved by his concern for her, her throat tightening.

"I promise."

She hugged him quickly and followed the other passengers through to Passport Control. When she turned, Felix had disappeared in an ocean of faces.

FIVE

From the air, Los Angeles looked like a sprawling mess to Nicola. She had expected it to be more centered, more together. Instead, it stretched carelessly across an enormous valley and reminded her of a child's model racetrack: giant roads curving around plastic buildings. A cluster of skyscrapers looked out of place, as if thrown down there simply to keep up with conventional ideas of progress.

The plane was making its final descent. Nicola wiped her face quickly with a cologne soaked tissue, trying to wake up. She felt as if she had been systematically force-fed during the flight—three cardboard meals in twelve hours—and she had slept little. Her palms were damp from nervousness.

It took an hour to get through customs and immigration and by the time Nicola stepped through the automatic doors into the bright arrivals hall she felt ragged and terrified. How would she know Barbara? How would Barbara know her? It had been fourteen years since Barbara had walked out on her father. The twelve-year-old Nicola had woken up to find that she was late for school and the house was silent. No smell of bacon frying, no sound of Barbara singing in the kitchen. Simply a note on her dressing table . . . "I have to leave, sweet Nicola. But I'll see you again one day, I promise you that." Signed with love and kisses.

Nicola had found her father still in bed, his clothes in a heap on the floor.

"Where's Barbara? I'm late for school."

"Hello, chicken," Nick Graham said, stretching. "Barbara has gone back to the Land of the Free."

"Why?"

"Why? Because, my love, she could not stand the heat in the kitchen."

Nicola puzzled over this for a moment.

"Is she coming back?"

"I don't think so. No, I should say probably not."

"Who's going to wake me for school? Who's going to cook dinner?"

Nick Graham climbed out of bed and put his arms around his daughter.

"We will buy you a very smart alarm clock. In fact, we'll each have a very smart alarm clock. We'll both learn to wake up alone. And we'll find a nice, kind, homely old lady to cook for us."

And that was that. Nick Graham did not mention Barbara's name for many years and he never married again. Instead, a succession of middle-aged housekeepers came and went until, at last, he found Mrs. Jenson—and she stayed.

Now, in bustling LAX, Nicola searched the faces of the waiting crowd, trying to calm herself. Barbara was blonde, she was tall and slender. She would dress well.

A graying woman in an elegant navy suit returned her gaze, half smiled, then turned away. No, not Barbara. Nicola put down her suitcase and stood very still. She will have to find me, she told herself. If she is here. And if she isn't . . . then I will get a taxi to her Bel-Air address. It is very simple. There is nothing to be nervous about. A slender blonde with a golden tan pushed past her. Nicola took a breath, then stopped. Too young. A little like Barbara many years ago. But her stepmother would be in her late forties now. Nicola felt very close to tears.

A tap on her shoulder. She turned quickly. A young man stood there, wearing a worn denim suit and, ludicrously, a chauffeur's cap. She had never seen him before. He did not speak at once, just stared at her unsmiling, chewing gum with one side of his mouth. Nicola held his gaze, absurdly frightened.

"Miss Graham? I'm from Mrs. Hampton-Norde."

Nicola, flooded with relief, realized that tiredness and strange surroundings had made her edgy. She smiled.

"Is she here?" she asked.

He did not smile back. He did not reply to her. He picked up her suitcase and began walking away, leaving Nicola to follow.

"How did you know me?" she asked. "Did Barbara . . ."

The man turned and glanced at her but did not slow his step.

"She showed me a picture," he said.

"What picture?"

The man sighed, put down her suitcase and pulled a crumpled newspaper clipping out of his pocket and handed it to Nicola. She studied it for a moment. A press photo of her father and herself attending the opening of a Ben Nicholson exhibition in London three years ago. One edge of the clipping was bordered with green paper, suggesting a clippings service detail that had been torn off. Nicola puzzled over why Barbara would have a clippings service on her father. Why, after all these years, she would still be interested in his activities. Still in love with him, perhaps.

"Thanks," said the man, holding out his hand for the clipping. He took it and turned away quickly.

Nicola, following him, was unnerved by his abruptness but felt unable to formulate the right questions, the right approach. Was he Barbara's chauffeur? He was young, no more than thirty, and untidy in those ragged jeans. He stowed the suitcase in the trunk of a large black Cadillac and, this done, opened the back door of the car and motioned her to get in.

The soft leather seat was comfortable and Nicola curled into a corner of it, watching through the window as the big car purred through the traffic. It was getting dark and the lights of deserted office buildings, small shops, used-car lots, flickered through the car windows. Apart from the fast-moving vehicles, three-deep on the wide street, it could have been an illuminated ghost town. No pedestrians, no strolling couples. Nobody to be seen, except half-visible drivers, safely ensconced in their cars.

"Where are all the people?"

Her question echoed around the car and was ignored. The driver, his eyes on the road, gave the slightest of shrugs.

"Doesn't anyone walk here?" Nicola continued doggedly.

She watched the back of his head, waiting for a response. He glanced once through the driving mirror at her, but said nothing. Nicola looked again at the empty sidewalks.

"Not a soul," she said to herself quietly.

She began looking for signs that would indicate Bel-Air but eventually the car pulled up outside an art gallery in what Nicola guessed was Beverly Hills, for that was where the exhibition was to be held. Beverly Hills of high fashion and discreet restaurants. She glanced around her quickly. No neon lights. The shops, discreetly lit, hiding behind subtle windows and thick wooden beams. A few strollers here and there, some leading small dogs.

The gallery lights shone brightly in the dusk. The windows were bare except for a poster in the right-hand corner. Her father's best-known painting of a young, brunette woman at her mirror, preparing, perhaps, for a party. Bright-eyed. He had painted it when Nicola was an infant. His name was imprinted in large gold letters across the poster.

Through the window, Nicola could see a number of people in the center of the room. She swallowed and walked in.

There must have been a dozen people there, in two distinct groups. All were talking loudly. Nicola searched the faces. Which of the women was Barbara? Helplessly, she turned to the driver for guidance.

"Where . . ."

He pointed to the larger group of chatting people.

"She's there," he said. Then he turned on his heel and left.

A number of faces turned to look at her then. In the larger group of people, three ultra-smart, blonde women stood together. They were almost identical in type: the flash of gold jewelry, hairstyles that indicated regular visits to a stylist, faces impeccably painted. They had been talking loudly but now stopped and, as if breaking step in a ritual dance, the blondest, smartest, loudest of the women moved out of the circle towards Nicola, arms outstretched. Barbara.

"Nicola, darling!" she said.

The face, though a few spidery lines were visible, was the same: fine bones, clear cornflower blue eyes, an over-wide mouth. But Barbara was heavier, the slender girlish figure Nicola remembered was lost under a layer of flesh that even her couture linen suit could not disguise. Her hair, once long and naturally fair, was brighter, brassier than it had been, and was arranged in a fluffy, cotton-candy style.

"You have grown up a *beauty*," she said, hugging Nicola.

"Nonsense," said Nicola laughing. "You look the same . . ."

But Barbara had turned back to the room, her arm still around Nicola.

"O.K., folks. She's here," she shouted to everyone. "Isn't she just gorgeous? Now, get your asses out of here."

There was some general laughter, some movement as people gathered up belongings.

"Oh, please don't let me interrupt," said Nicola, embarrassed.

"You're not interrupting anything, sweetheart. They were allowed a quick peep preview because . . ." she lowered her voice a little . . . "these are friends that just might be buying the stuff. But they've had their peep. And that's it. They'll be back for the opening."

As she was talking she waved her arm around the room. Nicola looked to see her father's paintings lined up against the white walls of the gallery. Not yet hung, they seemed smaller somehow, diminished, as they rested on the carpeted floor.

There seemed to be quite a few. Nicola recognized an oil that had once hung in their Brighton home.

"I haven't seen some of these for years," she said to Barbara. "Can I just take a quick . . ."

"Later, honey. Let's see these folks out."

Nicola stood at the door with Barbara. She felt like a bride in a reception line as Barbara introduced her to everyone as he or she left, showing her off to the others as one would a mascot, with a strange pride.

Barbara snapped off the gallery lights immediately after the last friend had left.

"Home," she said. "And a big drink. You could probably use one, too."

Nicola, beginning to feel deadened with tiredness, followed her to the Cadillac. She would look at her father's pictures when she was awake enough to see them.

"Step on it, sunshine," Barbara said to the young driver. "You have two thirsty people here."

He started the car. Nicola looked out the window at the high fashion shops—names she had only read about: Gucci, Pucci, Magnin's, Bonwit Teller. A whirlwind window-shopping trip. After a few minutes Barbara turned to Nicola and patted her hand.

"It's been a tough time for you, baby."

"Yes."

"A shock," said Barbara. "A shock. So, you're an art critic now?"

"A *junior* art critic."

"Nick must have just loved that."

"He jumped up and down a bit."

"I bet he did," Barbara chuckled to herself. "Remember when he invited the *Statesman* critic down to the cottage on the Downs?"

Nicola did.

"With the pump?"

"Sure. No goddamn water except for the well, and he had that guy running out there Sunday morning to pump water for his *coffee*." She shook her head. "He sure knew how to screw people up. He sure did."

Nicola was quiet for a moment.

"He loved that place," she said at last.

"Of course he loved it—it was cheap!" said Barbara. "Couple of quid a week? Dear God. Rustic, he used to call

28

it. Rustic, my ass. It was downright primitive. No heating, no water. Nothing."

She shivered at the thought.

Nicola was finding these memories painful.

"Where are we?" she asked to change the subject.

"Just turning into Bel-Air, baby," said Barbara.

They turned to go through the East Bel-Air Gate and drove uphill along what, to Nicola, looked like a wider but winding country road, lined with trees.

"Looks pretty," she said to Barbara.

"You could call it that."

Barbara sat back in her seat, closing her eyes.

"Dear God, I am *wiped out*. And I'm thirsty," she said.

Nicola looked out of the car window. After a few minutes they stopped at a set of electronic gates and then moved slowly up a long driveway to the place that was to be her home for a month.

The house was an enormous Regency structure, painted cream with green woodwork. A green and white Regency striped canopy hung over the front door. Wrought iron coach lamps on each side of the door were lit, giving the house an inviting appearance. The garages were alongside, as stables might have been in the genuine article, and Jeff, the driver, stopped just outside them.

Nicola climbed out of the car and looked around her. The grounds stretched downwards—a lilting hill with coral trees, cedars, and junipers—to a fruit orchard beyond. At the side of the house was a flower garden, wild roses climbing the trellis protecting it.

"What a super garden!"

"About an acre and a half," said Barbara.

Nicola followed her stepmother through the front door into a square hallway with parquet flooring and a number of Chinese scatter rugs. The walls held a collection of art work and one picture caught her eye immediately. An oil of Barbara, fingers trailing in a stream, a picnic basket beside her. The stream ran through a wood on the Downs, near Brighton. Nicola remembered it well. She had played there so many times as a child.

She swallowed.

"That was a lovely, lovely place," she said very softly, half to herself.

But her stepmother was not listening in any case.

"Ice, Maria. Ice, for Christ's sake!"

Nicola jumped, startled.

Barbara's cry ricocheted through the house, her voice aimed at a door Nicola imagined held the kitchen. Barbara had swept into a large lounge, with green-carpeting and chandeliers. Nicola followed, as the impassive driver carried her bags upstairs.

"What do you drink, honey?"

"Oh, well," Nicola stood uncertainly in the enormous room. "Do you have gin?"

"Sure I have gin."

"With tonic, please," Nicola said, hoping she could drink it when it arrived. A jet-lag headache gnawed behind her eyes.

"Coming up."

The voice was edgy and Nicola stared, surprised.

"That is when we get the fucking . . ."

A slender dark-skinned maid hurried through the door carrying an ice-bucket.

"Ice," concluded Barbara, softly.

Nicola tried to return Barbara's satisfied smile as the nervous maid put down the ice-bucket and left. Barbara took a long swallow from her own drink before bringing over Nicola's gin.

"I frighten the shit out of that broad," she said. "Christ knows why. I never say two words to her."

"She looks foreign," said Nicola, tentatively.

"They all are."

Barbara's irritation visibly changed her face. The smooth cosmetic lines altered, the flesh pulled downwards. Acutely uncomfortable, Nicola looked into her drink. She had sipped the gin once and it was so strong it had made her throat burn. If I weren't such a coward, she thought, I would ask for more tonic. Barbara poured another drink for herself then crossed the room to join Nicola on the leather-covered sofa.

"We've a lot to say honey, but I guess you're tired."

Nicola nodded.

"Just a bit," she admitted.

"That trip is a killer. I remember."

Her stepmother had sunk back onto the sofa and was sipping at her drink jerkily, like a marionette. She turned suddenly to look at Nicola.

"You're not like him," she said. "Not one bit. Though I never thought you would be. You look like your mother."

Though she knew the words were true, Nicola felt obscurely hurt. And she did not know how to reply. She ought to explain, she knew, how difficult it was for her to talk about her father. She ought to tell Barbara of the terrible enertia she felt and how jet lag and lack of sleep made her an uncommunicative companion this evening.

"Can we talk about him tomorrow?" she asked lamely.

To her surprise, Barbara laughed.

"Yes," she said. "Of course."

Nicola, ignoring her exhaustion, pulled herself together, sipped her drink with superficial relish.

"You haven't changed Barbara." It was a lie and she felt it must be obvious in her voice. Barbara laughed, loudly.

"Sweet child, *you* haven't changed. I look fifty years older, right? God, I feel fifty years older."

Nicola shook her head, smiling, then watched with growing unease as Barbara's expression changed. The smile totally faded.

Nicola struggled desperately to think of something to say but instead could only witness the older woman's sinking into a morose silence. Nicola might as well not have been there. Barbara was staring at the carpet, fixed on some depressing thought. Her breathing was heavy, the second large drink was almost finished.

"Are you all right, Barbara?"

"What? Sure."

Nicola knew it was time for bed and said so as brightly as she could. With a bellow from Barbara the maid was summoned and Nicola leaned down to kiss her oncestepmother good night. Barbara, diverted by her instructions to the maid and oblivious now to Nicola, ignored the shy cheek kiss, touched Nicola's arm abstractedly. Nicola left her sitting on the long brown sofa, sipping at an ice cube.

Barbara remembered a carpet of bluebells, a clear spring sky and the white cloth laid out on a mossy bank. It had been a cool day for their picnic in Epping Forest, the trees around them had swayed in the breeze. Nick Graham had mixed himself a flask of scotch and water and sipped from it as he rested on one elbow and watched his child slowly easing her tiny body up the gnarled trunk of an old oak. Barbara, setting out the food, glanced up and caught sight of a pair of dungareed legs disappearing into the lower branches.

"Nicola!" she screamed, frightened. "Come down at once. You'll fall."

Nick turned on her, he was furious.

"Never do that!" he hissed. "Never scream at a child like that. If she has confidence she won't fall. An hysteric yelping at her will make her fall. Use your *head*, woman."

Nicola's tiny face peered out from between budding branches.

"Have I got to come down, daddy?"

"If you want anything to eat you should. We're about to wolf it down. Every bit."

A rustling sound, a slither of blue denim and the soft thud of tiny feet hitting earth followed this advice; Nicola was over to the picnic immediately.

Barbara piled the chicken and salad onto paper plates and kept her face down. She did not want him, nor the child, to see how his harsh words had hurt her. Tears welled in her eyes. She opened a half bottle of wine for herself and gulped it quickly from a plastic cup.

Nicola had collected a small bunch of bluebells and with chubby, clumsy fingers was trying to make them into a chain. She was unable to pierce the slippery stalks and her face tightened with the effort. Barbara ruffled the soft, blonde hair.

"I'll be the hole maker, you be the threader," she said. "I've got good hole-making nails."

Barbara pierced the damp stems easily and the child enthusiastically threaded her flowers until she had a wilting coronet.

"Crown for me," she cried, putting the circle of blue onto her head. Too big, it slipped over her eyes but she was unperturbed.

"Not for me. For Barbara."

The child, holding her treasure with both hands, solemnly carried it to Barbara and ceremoniously placed it on her stepmother's head.

"Fits perfectly," said Nick Graham, approvingly.

Barbara, recovered now, jumped to her feet and threw out her arms gracefully.

"For I shall be Queen of the May, Mother," she sang to the trees. "I shall be Queen of the May."

Nicola laughed with delight and her father laughed with her. Barbara pirouetted around the picnic cloth, her face uplifted and for a minute or two danced for them, barefoot on the grass. When she stopped, giving a small curtsy, her audience applauded.

"More, Barbara. Do it some more," cried Nicola.

"Your turn," said her father. "Let Barbara take a break. She hasn't eaten yet."

He held out his hand and pulled Barbara down beside him. Together they watched the child as, self-conscious at first and then with oblivious enjoyment, she danced among the flowers.

"Don't think she's going to be a graceful woman," said Nick Graham, chuckling. He was softly stroking Barbara's hand.

"She'll be beautiful," said Barbara. She had forgiven him.

"Let's hope so," he said. "It helps."

Later Barbara and Nicola picked bluebells to take home. Nick stayed on the mossy bank, his sketchpad on his knee. When they returned to him, his crayon was still flying over the page. Barbara glanced over his shoulder. She saw a young woman, her hair lifted by the breeze and her arms full of flowers; near to her, the child, body bent, an arm reaching for a flower almost out of reach, intent absorbtion on the small face. He had depicted their day exactly.

It was the only sketch he ever kept of Nicola. He never had her pose for him:

"I'm not Augustus John. I don't want my child to suffer aching bones sitting like a robot in a studio. She mustn't feel that everytime I look at her I'm going to freeze her into a corner just to freeze her onto canvas."

Consequently, the only sketches he made of his child were made when she was not aware that he was drawing her. Once in awhile when she was engrossed in a game or running wild in the garden he would reach for his crayon, but he would invariably tear those sketches to pieces, unsatisfied.

The Epping Forest sketch survived, hung now in the large Bel-Air lounge, somewhat dwarfed by a full oil of Barbara. His sympathy for child models did not extend to adults and Barbara had posed for hours in the drafty studio while he painted relentlessly.

Barbara looked around at the pictures of herself in the room. They were hazy. The alcohol had clouded her eyes.

"That bastard," she said aloud, swallowing the last of her drink. "That fucking bastard."

Then she heard the sharp click of the front door.

"That you honey?" she called.

SIX

In the enormous, antique-furnished bedroom, Nicola looked around for her suitcase and found it had already been unpacked. That shy maid? She sat on the edge of the large bed and tried to organize her thoughts. She wished Felix were with her to help her make sense of the confusion she felt: a confusion she suspected, mostly caused by tiredness and, maybe, residual grief. But what was she doing here, in this claustrophobic, sumptuous house with a woman she could only see as a stranger? She sighed, then out of habit and a love for such silly luxuries, she inspected the bathroom. It was truly luxurious: a sunken bath, a wealth of soft towels.

She was fumbling through a drawer for her nightgown when she heard the slamming of a door. Barbara's voice sliced through the house.

"That you, honey?" she called.

Nicola strained to hear but caught only a mumble in reply.

"You're early," Barbara's voice vibrated clearly.

"Early for what?"

A male voice. A quiet but clear male voice. Nicola heard the lounge door close, a muffle of voices. She shrugged and got ready for bed.

A gnomic character, leaning at a crazy angle, was serving drinks while the plane plunged downwards. He was laughing maniacally. Then, a scream of engine noise exacerbated by the shrill screams of hysterical passengers. Terror. Nicola woke with a start, drenched in sweat. Unsure of where she was, she sat up in the large bed and remembered only as the golden, antique lamp on the bedside table became dimly visible through the gloom. She guessed it was an hour or so after midnight and she knew instantly why she had woken—downstairs some sort of violently noisy party was in progress. She could hear Barbara's high laugh, uncontrolled; a male voice too, quiet but carrying; and over the voices, the strong beat of music. She imagined they must be dancing, the house seemed to tremble.

At first Nicola lay still, watching the bedroom curtains billow in the light breeze. Gradually, the room became clearer as her eyes grew accustomed to the darkness: ornate splendor plus rock music. She wished they would turn the damn music off. There was a crash and the splintering of glass, followed by Barbara's screech and then more laughter. The record changed. Barbra Streisand's voice screamed through the house. Nicola, who normally found this singer's voice grating, pulled the pillow over her ears, trying to block it all out.

But the insistent beat continued, the voices became more hysterical and finally Nicola sat up in bed, turned on the bedside light and reached for her cigarettes. Curiosity had given way to a depressed anger. She felt like crying from tiredness and irritation. It would be around ten in the morning in England—almost twenty-eight hours since she had slept, since she had gotten up from her own comfortable bed in her own little apartment in Highgate. It seemed so very far away. She would, she decided, read for awhile; and if they were not quiet soon, she would shout down and ask them to . . . what? How could she complain about noise, her first night in someone else's house?

Huddled miserably against the pillows, Nicola stubbed out her half-finished cigarette and tried to concentrate on her novel. Her throat was tight with tears of self-pity. She should not have come, she told herself. She would leave immediately after the exhibition. If it was all too unbearable, she would leave before.

She woke with the bedside light still on and her novel open on the pillow. She was stiff, her neck aching from the

36

uncomfortable position in which she had finally slept. The house was quiet, the early morning chorus of birds the only sound. A shaft of sunlight picked out the gold edgings of the furnishings and the frames of pictures. From her window, the garden looked inviting, shrouded in a light mist as the sun tried to push through. A soft lawn stretched to the palm trees yards away.

In dressing gown and slippers, Nicola crept downstairs. No one was around it seemed, everyone in the house was still sleeping. The door to the lounge was ajar and she glanced inside then stopped abruptly. It looked like a disaster area. Barbara's clothes were strewn on the floor, though a cream satin bra lay across a bottle in the icebucket, rather as a waiter would arrange a napkin over champagne. A pair of men's denims were collapsed, concertina-style, by the sofa and circled by shoes and socks. A broken glass, the puddle of melted ice still around it, lay in the fireplace. There were other glasses around, gingerly balanced on chairs and tables. Bottles and overflowing ashtrays littered the room like confetti. Nicola whistled once softly and closed the door.

From the garden, the city was obscured by mist. Only shadowy forms were visible in the far distance. Nicola followed a cobbled path around the house, refreshed by the cool, slightly damp air. At the side of the house she discovered a large swimming pool, terraced by a paved area complete with chaise, deck chairs and umbrellas which seemed to her, then, a perfect place to sit down for awhile and try to put her fears into perspective.

She was nervous, unsure of exactly what she had to fear, but uneasy in this opulent house with the woman who had once cared for her. Had Barbara changed? Or was it that the child Nicola had not really known her? There had been noisy scenes then, of course, but Nick Graham could not live without occasional scenes and Nicola had never felt threatened by the raised voices of her father and stepmother on those occasions when, late at night, she had been woken by them.

There had been empty bottles too, for her father had always drunk heavily.

"Are you drunk, daddy?" the ten year old Nicola had asked once when she found her father steadily mounting the stairs on his hands and knees.

"Good grief, child, I hope so," he had said over his shoulder. "If not, I shall demand my money back. I have been drinking at that farcical club *all day*. Now come on, be a pet, give me a little shove."

Nicola smiled at the memory. Her father had never been aggressive with drink, at least not with her. He became a clown, an orator, occasionally a rather off-key tenor, but rarely a fighter.

She walked around to the front of the house and down to the edge of the lawn, taking off her slippers to enjoy the dewy, damp grass. A sudden, sharp slam of a door and Barbara's voice cracked the silence and Nicola turned to see Barbara and a dark-haired young man walking towards a Mercedes sports car.

Barbara, spotting her at the far edge of the lawn, waved.

"Morning, honey," she shouted.

Her voice carried easily. Nicola's reply seemed to get lost, deadened by the mist. She walked towards the two quickly.

"Get the maid to fix you breakfast," Barbara called as she climbed into the car. "Anything you like."

Nicola hesitated, realizing that Barbara was not going to wait to speak to her. The young man had hesitated too, he smiled a good morning and joined Barbara in the car. Nicola stopped, waved self-consciously as the car sped down the drive. She turned back to the house, feeling small and childish. The little girl who is ignored at the birthday party. Yet grateful in a way that she would have some time to herself. She wondered when they would be back.

A man was leaning against the garage, smoking a cigarette and Nicola stopped short like a startled deer. The young driver. She nodded and he gave a barely perceptible movement of his head, then lazily stretched out his arm to push open the garage door. Nicola froze with shock. He had a gun. Strapped tightly to the inside of his body was a shoulder holster and poking out of it, the butt of a revolver.

It was then that the man smiled, a slow, mocking smile that chilled her. She hurried past him to the house. She was grateful to find the young maid inside, clearing up the chaos in the lounge.

"Hello. I'm Nicola. Barbara said something about breakfast."

The girl jumped up quickly.

"Yes, of course. You would like eggs? Sausage? Big breakfast?"

Relief at the normality of all this made Nicola smile.

"Do you know I think I probably would. You're Maria aren't you?"

The girl looked down shyly, "Yes, I am Maria."

"Well, whenever you're ready Maria, a big breakfast would be lovely."

"I do it now," said the girl, smiling.

"Who is the young driver?" Nicola asked Maria over breakfast.

"That is Jeff."

"And is he the chauffeur only?"

Maria, refilling Nicola's coffee cup, shrugged.

"He does many things," she said. "You would like an English muffin?"

Nicola wanted to ask why he carried a gun but found that she could not. Instead, she said that yes, she would like an English muffin.

Barbara returned alone in the late afternoon. In a flurry of bags and packages she burst into the lounge where Nicola sat reading.

"Honey, I didn't mean to be so long. Have you been bored out of your mind?"

Nicola put down her book, watched as Barbara tore open bags impatiently.

"Not at all. I've been reading, resting."

"Rest you need. Ah, here it is."

Barbara drew a black, crepe garment from its elegant box.

"I've gotten this dress for you. Saw it, knew it was for you. Size though?"

39

She studied Nicola's figure critically.

"You're a bit thin, aren't you? Still, it should fit. It's sort of loose and easy."

"Barbara!" cried Nicola, embarrassed. "I've got plenty of clothes."

"Not like this little number, you haven't. An exclusive. Come on—look at it. Made for you."

Nicola took the dress reluctantly, felt the material then held it against herself. It was a beautiful gown but she was not used to accepting gifts. And from Barbara? She was unsure what it meant.

"Try it on, try it on," said Barbara, going over to pour herself a drink. She peered into the ice-bucket, her face creasing with annoyance just as Maria came hurrying into the room carrying ice. Barbara looked at the ice then Nicola and laughed loudly.

"Well, shit—would you believe that," she exclaimed, delighted. Nicola looked at the floor, embarrassed, as Maria scuttled from the room.

"Come on, get into it," said Barbara motioning with her drink.

Nicola, carrying the dress towards the door, was stopped by Barbara's loud laugh.

"Put it on here, sweetie. Who the hell is going to see you?"

Shyly, Nicola slipped out of her jeans and shirt and stepped into the garment. It was slippery against her warm skin, cool and light, falling in a graceful line to mid-calf. It felt like an expensive dress and she swirled the skirt with half-guilty pleasure.

"Could be a bit lower," said Barbara thoughtfully. "But, yep, suits you fine. You'll be the belle of tomorrow night's little ball, sweetheart."

Nicola, realizing now why Barbara had bought the dress, felt apprehensive. Art exhibitions, in her experience, were not overly sophisticated affairs; not in London, at least, except for the big charity ones.

"Isn't it a bit . . . dressy?" she asked.

"It's a dressy opening, darling."

"I didn't really want to look, well, conspicuous."

She looked pleadingly at Barbara and caught, for just a moment, a look on the older woman's face which baffled her: a hard, calculating look, almost triumphant.

"Are you kidding?" asked Barbara, sharply. "Of course you've got to look conspicuous. You're the Great Man's daughter. The Departed Great Man's only daughter."

Nicola, given courage through the stirrings of anger, stared hard at her stepmother.

"Don't talk about him like that, please."

"Darling, I adored him," said Barbara lightly, going to pour herself another drink. "So he ignored me? I still adored him." Barbara also poured a drink for Nicola and she brought it over, placing it on a side table.

"You'll look fabulous. And it's black isn't it. Quite proper, my dear."

This last was said with a fake British accent and Nicola began to take the dress off immediately.

"I'm not one of the exhibits, Barbara," she said, as she climbed back into her old clothes.

Barbara rasied an eyebrow.

"Darling, I never thought for a moment that you were."

"Good."

There was a silence in the room, heavy and uncomfortable, while Nicola buttoned her shirt then stood, sipping her drink. Barbara, settled on the sofa, was watching her, an expression of amusement on her face that caused Nicola a sudden flash of nostalgia. Barbara had always been amused when Nicola, normally a well-behaved child, had been naughty.

"Little girl sulking now?" asked Barbara, teasingly, then became serious, disarming Nicola immediately.

"Shit, there I go," she said. "Come sit down and talk to me, honey. I've had a tough morning and there's more to do but, God, I want to find time to talk with you. Hear all your news. Come on, sit down."

Nicola did so. Sipping her drink she told Barbara of her job, her friends, her London life. Barbara seemed to be only half-listening, though she nodded and smiled occasionally.

41

"Why did he do it, darling?" she burst out eventually, interrupting Nicola. "Why did he?"

Nicola said nothing for a moment.

"I don't know," she admitted with difficulty.

"Hell, he could be depressive. But suicidal?" asked Barbara. "No. I wouldn't have thought so."

"No one believed it," said Nicola. "I was in Florence when they phoned . . ."

"In Florence?"

Barbara's tone had changed and Nicola looked at her surprised.

"Yes."

"And how is that lovely city these days?"

An airy voice, a careless one, a flippant question spoken as easily as a casual inquiry about an acquaintance. For a few moments Nicola did not reply, but held her stepmother's gaze, ignoring the contrived twinkle in the eyes, trying to see deeper. Was it pain or disinterest that caused her stepmother to change the subject so abruptly? Barbara's expression gave nothing away.

"Florence is beautiful, as always," Nicola replied levelly.

Barbara looked away, gave a small smile. Nicola stood quickly, picked up the dress saying she would hang it up. She would nap and be down for dinner. Barbara called her back as she reached the door.

"You prefer to eat in or out, Nicola?"

"Whichever is easier."

"Well, we'll eat in."

Nicola hesitated for a moment.

"Will there be just the two of us?"

"You want me to invite some people?"

"No," said Nicola. "I just thought perhaps you had a . . . well, a boyfriend, I suppose. Last night I heard . . ."

Barbara laughed.

"David? He lives here. Honey, you know these little boy painters. No bread. Ever. He couldn't afford a pigpen."

She stopped and pointed to the dress.

"You will wear that, won't you?"

"Yes. I'll wear it."

SEVEN

Jerry Womberg had cut out from the conversation around him. He was sipping his fourth glass of champagne and watching the girl. Nicola. She stood in the far corner of the gallery talking to a young man. Or maybe he was a middle-aged man, thought Jerry with some disgust. Jerry, a New Yorker, considered all Californians ridiculously youthful for their years. It irritated him that they did not seem to succumb so early to the balding, bloating, wrinkling, and other ills that aging flesh is heir to. I've succumbed all right, he thought ruefully. I have indeed.

The gallery was crowded and Nicola, while speaking to the man at her side, was anxiously studying the faces of those few people who were actually looking at the paintings. If she's guessing their reactions she looks a little nervous, thought Jerry, which is not surprising. He felt that someone should tell her that the majority of people presently in the gallery wouldn't know a decent painting from a hole in the wall. Wouldn't know what to do with one. Put a painting on their breakfast table and they'd eat it with their eggs. Jerry was not much interested in women but he had a strong aesthetic sense and he liked the picture she made. A shy fawn among lions, he reflected, and out of place too with that pale skin, whiter still against the black of her dress, among all the bronzed bodies. The California sun worshipers, thought Jerry, looking around at the expensively-dressed, laughing crowd now heavily into the champagne. The followers of mindless rituals.

Voices in the room were getting louder as the cham-

43

pagne worked its devious magic. Barbara was, as usual, gossiping. Jerry suspected that she could be heard clearly in every corner of the gallery, which meant that the little story she was now relating would be all over town tomorrow.

"He never did divorce her," said Barbara. "The mean jack-off said he couldn't afford alimony payments. So he had her stay with him and Melanie. Three of 'em together."

Angie raised an eyebrow, her eyes were sparkling with pleasure.

"You mean a *ménage à* whatsit?"

"Why not?" asked Barbara. "Gets a few more pretty rocks coming her way. New car, nice home. Hell, Angie, you've done most things."

"Not quite as many, darling," said Angie sweetly, "as you have."

The group around the two women laughed. Jerry began to smile then spotted Nicola, easing her way shyly through the crowd towards them.

"Here's your stepdaughter," he said quietly to Barbara. She turned to look.

"Wow," she said laughing, "he said that like here comes the Dope Squad."

"Or Vice Squad," added a young man on the periphery of the group. There was more laughter and Jerry turned, concerned, to smile at Nicola as she reached them. Barbara put an arm around the girl.

"She's a big girl now, Jerry. Honey, meet Jerry Womberg, my attorney and worst critic."

"Pleased to meet you, Nicola," said Jerry. "But don't believe that because I don't criticize. Not as a rule."

"You don't speak it, Jerry, because you don't need to. You just stand there and *ooze* disapproval," said Barbara, merrily.

Jerry, aware that everyone around was listening with animated interest, spoke quietly.

"Sometimes, maybe, you deserve it."

"When you can get it up again, Jerry, if ever, you can *show* me what I deserve."

44

The crowd loved it. Jerry, used to taunts of this type from Barbara, said nothing out of courtesy to Nicola. Whatever insulting reply he made, and he could think of plenty, would only encourage Barbara to come back with a more cutting slur. And she'd be delighted at the opportunity. Verbal gymnastics, he thought, is her favorite game and she always wins. He smiled gently at Nicola who was frowning. Relief flooded her face as she smiled back.

"How do you think it's going?" she asked Barbara.

"Fine. Just fine."

"They don't seem very interested in the paintings," said Nicola, looking around at the partying groups.

"Honey, they don't come for the paintings," said Barbara, with amusement. "They come for the liquor and the gossip. Then they go home."

"Opening night's just an excuse for a party, Nicola," Jerry added. She smiled at him.

"Yes. I can see that."

The young man on the edge of the group had moved in more closely and was admiring Nicola openly. Jerry, who vaguely recognized his face, thought he was some kind of actor, television maybe.

"I think the paintings are terrific," said the actor in a solemn voice to Nicola.

Barbara gave him a disgusted look.

"What the hell do you know?" she said. "Ah—here comes America's Great White Hope."

Jerry knew who she meant even before he turned to see. Her protégé, youthful lover and, from the conversations Jerry has occasionally overheard, her verbal sparring partner, David Leyton. Jerry thought him an attractive young man. He certainly had the sort of lean, dark looks that attracted women and, had David's leanings been in the other direction, men too. Unfortunately, thought Jerry as he admired the tall figure weaving through the crowd, he's sexually straight it seems. Though God knows what he's doing with Barbara—that's surely a perversion of sorts. David was talented enough, in Jerry's opinion, not to need her patronage. To make it on his own.

"Right on the button," said Barbara sarcastically. "Punctual to the last. Sartorially perfect as usual. Doesn't the denim suit him? So smart. So—where the hell have you been?"

David smiled at everyone, picked up two drinks from the tray of a passing waiter and quickly downed the first and started the second before replying.

"Met a guy doing some plastic work. Had a look at it. Good stuff."

David smiled at Nicola.

"You're Nicola aren't you? Welcome to America."

Barbara waved an arm dramatically.

"And this," she said to the girl, "is David Leyton. Genius-to-be. He thinks."

Nicola, looking more at ease now, smiled hello.

"I've had no chance to look at these pictures properly," said David. "You can explain them to me."

He had taken her arm and began to lead her away from the group. Barbara turned away, exasperated, and went in search of a waiter. Nicola stopped, a little unsure.

"I can't explain my father's work to myself, let alone . . ."

"Why not?" asked David, firmly moving her towards the paintings.

"Really, you should ask Barbara," said Nicola. "She was with him when he painted the great ones. The early good ones, anyway."

"What Barbara knows about painting could be printed on a stamp," said David pleasantly. "She thinks she knows, but she knows shit. Forget it. Let's just look."

Jerry chuckled. Pity Barbara had not heard that little exchange. The young couple disappeared into the crowd. The noise in the gallery had increased tenfold since the early, rather respectful opening and the room was getting unbearably hot. Jerry took a stroll outside for a breath of cool fresh air.

When he returned he found Nicola and David near the entrance to the gallery. They were studying the first painting in the exhibition: Graham's girl at her mirror.

Nicola smiled as Jerry joined them.

"He really didn't follow a trend, did he?" David was saying. "No particular movement, no school. His own man."

"No." Nicola bit her lip. "He admired Nicholson, Sutherland, Klee . . . even Pollock up to a point." She smiled. "The 'Dripping Genius' he would call him. And, really, he did care what was happening. But he could be brutal about the camp-followers. Used to call them 'Schools of Fools.' And as for the younger abstract expressionists . . ."

She paused, hearing her father's voice in her head:

"If you can be so preposterous as to label a couple of parallel lines Birth-Death-Love-Hate . . . if you have to explain a painting with a title, or insist on this response or that, you are communicating *nothing*. Artistic masturbation. Nonsense!"

"No," Nicola continued. "He hated labels."

David was watching her closely.

"I think we all do," he said, unexpectedly.

"He reminds me a little of Edward Hopper," put in Jerry, studying the painting.

"Hopper's 'Hotel Room'?" asked David.

"Yes."

"Doesn't have the loneliness."

"No. But there's something."

"I think this one's more Fraginard," said David firmly.

Jerry turned from the painting and saw Barbara on the other side of the room watching them. With a determined stride she came towards them and put an arm round Nicola's shoulder. She did not speak to any of the three but instead shouted into the room.

"Ladies and gentlemen!"

Though some voices died, a few chatterers, unhearing, carried on.

"Ladies and gentlemen!"

There was silence finally as curious faces turned towards them.

Barbara was beaming.

"Let me formally introduce . . . Nicola Graham. Our guest of honor here tonight. And, as most of you know, Nick Graham's only daughter."

47

She turned to Nicola, her smile still wide.

"Thank you for coming so very far to be with us Nicola. And welcome. We are proud to have you here. We are especially proud to be able to view, in this one gallery, some of the greatest pictures painted in our lifetime. And painted by one great man. Thank you."

There was scattered applause, a few cries of "speech" directed at Nicola but the girl blushed, murmured a soft thank you, and bowed her head. Jerry gave her shoulder a reassuring squeeze.

"O.K., folks, on with the party," shouted Barbara.

She took Nicola's arm and led her over to a group of people nearby. Jerry watched as Nicola shook hands with the art editor of the *Los Angeles Times*.

"Sweet kid," he said to David.

"Very. I'm for food. Want something?"

"No thanks. You go ahead."

David moved away and Jerry wandered around the room scrutinizing the paintings. Many he knew, some he hadn't seen before. There *was* a loneliness in the Graham portraits, he decided. Like Hopper's work, it came through the gritty realism, was emphasized by it. And the women invariably had a wistful quality.

Jerry went in search of more cold champagne and ran straight into Barbara who was standing alone. This was so unusual that it shocked Jerry. She was sipping her drink thoughtfully. He followed her gaze and saw that she was watching Nicola.

"Pretty girl, Nicola," said Jerry.

"Sure she is."

Barbara glanced at him suddenly.

"Watch what you say to her," she said. "Don't go discussing my investments with her."

"I'm your goddamn attorney," he said angrily. "I don't discuss my client's business with anyone."

"Good," she said. "I don't want her knowing about my collection."

"I'm not surprised," said Jerry, feeling malicious. "Nobody likes to be ripped off."

"I haven't ripped her off," said Barbara, her eyes flashing at him. "You throw that crap at me again, Womberg, and you find yourself a new client."

"You don't say?" he said, raising an eyebrow. But Barbara had turned away. For the first time over the many years that Jerry had helped Barbara increase the number of her paintings, he felt uneasy. It wasn't illegal. In the art world it wasn't even unusual. But standing next to Barbara, looking over to the young Nicola, he felt like a conspirator. He didn't like the feeling.

Barbara had turned and was looking restlessly around the room.

"May as well ask a few of these frogs back to the house," she said.

Generally, Jerry hated Barbara's after-openings, after-hours parties, but he found himself back at her house along with twenty or so other people. Jerry suspected that some of them, like himself, hadn't been able to think of an excuse quickly enough. Inertia or cowardice, he wondered. Which was it that made combating Barbara's cheerfully insistent bullying so difficult for him? It wasn't simply that he needed her as a client. God knows, he had enough clients as rich as Barbara and a hell of a lot nicer. He was fascinated by her, he supposed, fascinated by the toughness he almost envied, still curious as to whether she had an undetected softer side. David must have found something in her that attracted him. Maybe she was good in bed. Jerry hadn't been able to tell, wouldn't want to know now, about that.

At this moment, she was giggling as she unsteadily danced alone in the middle of the room. The guests danced around her, most of them high on the booze and the home-made cigarettes David had rolled and passed around earlier. David was high too, but differently. He lay back in his chair and smiled to himself. A strange mood removed him from the others and the craziness around him.

Jerry thought Nicola had disappeared but now she came back into the room, looked around at the dancers, and appeared to be amused. He had thought she might be horrified. Jerry crossed the room to talk to her. The English

49

accent delighted him and he questioned her about her work, her home, London, just to listen to the soft voice answering.

"Gonna dance a little, Nicola?" Barbara's voice, thickened by the evening's alcohol, was behind them. Nicola turned with Jerry to see Barbara undulating wildly.

"No, thank you," Nicola said firmly.

Barbara threw herself into a chair with a sigh.

"This is a hell of a boring party," she said. "My openings are usually raves. Shit, all the fun people stayed away. All the beauties."

"All the beauties probably never heard of Nicholas Graham," said Jerry. "Most of them have never heard of Picasso."

"Christ, this clever beauty had heard of both of 'em."

Barbara kicked David lightly and still smiling blissfully he sat up, looking around at the crowd, his gaze fixing on the dancers. One young girl, bra-less in a low-necked gown, had let her shoulderstraps slip during the gyrations of her wild dance and her full breasts hung loose.

"Beautiful," muttered David, shaking his head. "Beautiful."

Jerry wondered what he had been smoking, sniffing, or swallowing.

"Come on fellow artist," said Barbara, giving David another light kick. "Let's have the verdict on Nick Graham. We need a little intellect around here."

"Christ, what do I know?"

"What's your opinion, dummy. What did you think of the pictures there tonight? Entertain us a little."

"The pictures were . . . very interesting," said David slowly, still watching the bare breasts of the dancing girl.

"Interesting? Vague isn't it? Ah—I see." Barbara's light laugh alerted Jerry. He knew what it meant. "You'd prefer to give an opinion when Nicola's in bed, eh? Or better yet, when we're in bed. The truth."

"I *meant* very . . ."

Nicola, her voice steady, interrupted him.

"You won't have to wait long. I'm going to bed now."

David sat up.

"Bullshit," he said. "Have another drink."

Jerry noticed Nicola's hands were trembling slightly as she placed her glass on the small table. Poor little thing, he thought, surprised at his own sharp sympathy.

"I guess you're tired," he said. "Jet lag can last for days."

"No, it's just that I have to write my piece tomorrow, early," said Nicola, gathering her cigarettes and purse.

"What piece?" asked Barbara.

"I have to write about the exhibition for the *Chronicle*."

"Now *that* should be fun."

Nicola touched Jerry's arm lightly and whispered good night. As she reached his chair David suddenly jumped to his feet, lifted his glass, bowed, and then slowly and ceremoniously lifted the glass to Nicola's lips. She looked steadily at David for what seemed to Jerry a long time then sipped from the glass. Afterwards she turned, called a soft good night over her shoulder to no one in particular and walked out.

EIGHT

Nicola had slept badly. The party downstairs had continued until just before dawn and had become progressively louder and out of control. In the small hours, screams and splashes from the swimming pool indicated that the party had moved outdoors and the music was turned up so that it would reach the swimmers. Now the house was quiet but Nicola still could not sleep. She got out of bed quickly, wanting to get out of the house for awhile, needing a walk in the fresh air, a look at the shops, any quietly normal activity.

Barbara's bedroom door was closed and Nicola, dressed and ready to go out, stood outside it uncertainly. She would have preferred to have left a note but could think of nowhere to leave it to be sure Barbara would find it: the house was in such a chaotic state. There was no sign of the maid, Maria. Nicola took a breath and tapped quietly, waited, then tapped again, calling Barbara's name. No response. She opened the bedroom door.

David was lying on his back in the rumpled bed, half covered by a sheet. His bronzed arms were outstretched, his bare chest, thickly covered with dark hair, rose and fell in sleep. Barbara, curled up beside him, was snoring softly. Nicola rapped hard on the open door and called Barbara's name until she stirred and opened her eyes. She sat up abruptly when she saw Nicola, pulling up the sheet as if to hide her breasts out of modesty. Nicola knew that vanity was closer to the truth: years ago Barbara had been proud

53

of her body, would often stroll around the house naked. The once firm breasts now sagged.

"I thought I'd do some shopping," Nicola whispered. "Is that all right with you or do you have plans or something?"

"That's fine," said Barbara. "Do what you like. But look . . ."

She reached over and tapped a button on the bedroom phone.

"Get Jeff to drive you."

"I can get a cab. Really, Barbara . . ."

Barbara, already speaking into the phone, ordered the car to be ready in fifteen minutes. Her voice roused David who smiled a good-morning to Nicola then stretched, yawning widely.

"O.K., baby, the Cad's all yours," said Barbara, snuggling back into the bed, cuddling up to David. As Nicola closed the door she heard their soft laughter and the creak of the bed as their weight shifted.

Jeff, as coldly impassive as before, stopped the car outside the Beverly Wilshire and pointed sourly in the direction of the larger shops.

"I'll pick you up here," he said. "It's easy enough to find."

Nicola thought he sounded angry.

"I'll be around two hours," she said. "Thank you."

The shops were lighter, airier, less crowded than the stores in England. Middle-aged women strolled aimlessly around the counters as if killing time; attractive girls, mostly blonde, long-haired, bra-less under T-shirts, wearing tight denim jeans, hurried through racks of clothes collecting garments in their arms carelessly like women collecting washing.

Nicola wandered out onto the main street, enjoying the feel of the sun on her face after the icy air conditioning of the stores. The sidewalks were crowded with window-shoppers, hurrying young men in summer suits and ladies with blue-rinsed hair walking small dogs. Nicola had never seen so many small dogs.

She'd had enough after an hour but the coffee shops looked exclusive and forbidding. She bought some perfume then entered Brentanos' to look at books until it was time to meet her driver.

He was there, waiting, and opened the back door of the Cad for her without saying a word. Damn you, she thought, determined not to waste her breath speaking to him. The Cadillac pulled out into traffic and Nicola, aware of gnawing hunger pains, realized that she'd had nothing to eat for over twenty-four hours. There had been a buffet at the opening but she had left too nervous, too uncomfortable, to eat. The sight of so many of her father's pictures, some of which she remembered him painting, had caused a sharp sense of loss—missing him again, wishing with a hard anguish that he could have been there to hear those loud people discussing his work.

"What a waste of time," he would have boomed so that all could hear. "Let's get out, kiddie. Fast."

His judgements on people on such occasions were widely quoted afterwards by his friends, mainly because Nick Graham always ensured that his victim was within earshot.

"He talks," he had said of a prominent but aging art critic, "as if he has a pebble on his tongue and an ice-block in his head."

And of a particularly pretentious socialite:

"She listens so attentively, so admiringly, to every word she says that in her company, even one-to-one, I feel, as if I'm intruding."

The lady in question had been furious, Nicola remembered. She smiled at the memory.

Nicola's stomach rumbled. The Cadillac had stopped outside a small printing shop and Jeff jumped out of the car and went inside. She looked around: a busy village of a place, lots of shops. A sign over a theatre indicated that this was Westwood and Nicola resolved to return. Could be a more comfortable place to shop than Beverly Hills.

When Jeff returned carrying a large package she leaned forward in her seat.

"Is there somewhere I can get a sandwich?" she asked.

He gave a slight nod of his head as the car started to move forward. They passed a hot dog stand, a hamburger restaurant, then a coffee shop. Nicola, about to repeat her request, sat forward in her seat but with a swift turn of the wheel that unbalanced her slightly Jeff pulled into the driveway of a Jack in the Box restaurant and came abruptly to a halt. He pressed a button so that her window wound down and Nicola, taking this as a hint, prepared to get out of the car. A deep male voice startled her and she stared in confusion at a plastic replica of a little fat man in a three cornered hat.

"May I take your order, please?" said a voice, seemingly coming from the depths of the dummy.

Nicola, astonished, stared at the thing, wondering if the crazy chauffeur was enjoying some private joke. The deep male voice began again and Nicola, looking around, saw that two cars had lined up behind them.

"Hello!" said the plastic man, loudly now.

"Sorry." Nicola whispered.

"May I take your order, please?"

"What on earth?" she asked Jeff, frantically. "What do I do?"

He turned very slowly to look at her.

"Order," he said.

Nicola forced herself to look at the bright red and yellow dummy and to speak loudly.

"A sandwich, please," she said.

The transmitted voice had become weary. It informed her that they had six different kinds of sandwiches. Which did she want? Finally, her face hot and red with embarrassment, Nicola ordered a hamburger and coffee, then stared at the floor. She did not dare look at Jeff. She wondered fleetingly if the packaged hamburger and coffee would appear magically out of the dummy's hat but Jeff, his face blank, drove to a window where the food was collected and handed to her.

"You pay him," he said, pointing to a young man leaning out of the window. He turned back to the wheel. As they drove away Nicola turned once to look out of the car window. The dummy stood rigid in the sunlight, waiting for the next order.

NINE

David had switched off the air conditioning and had opened the windows wide, a simple pleasure not allowed him when Barbara was around: she distrusted the Los Angeles air, had a neurotic hatred of flies, wasps, all flying creatures. A few buzzed around the room now, but the warm air, heavy with the scent of the newly mown grass outside, was a delight in that musty room, so often dense with cigarette smoke.

He was bent over an old notepad, sketching in miniature with an intensity that caused sweat to prickle on the back of his neck. Once done, the drawings would be expanded into the sketchpad next to him. Then, onto canvas. He loved this stage, always—the ideas still forming, the ideal still possible before the paintbrush was touched. He enjoyed having the house to himself—perfect quiet to work in. Barbara was out most of the time, most days. He hoped the presence of her sweet stepdaughter wouldn't change that. If so, he might have to move out, just to get some work done. And he didn't want to do that.

He felt no guilt at living with Barbara. The conventional view of ownership/sharing/earning one's place in society had long been dismissed by David. His parents with their rotarian ideas had seen to that—by default. And if he moved out he'd have to get a job. He couldn't live off his painting—yet. So it would mean nine-to-five or ten-to-six or whatever in some schlep job, five days a week. Every week. The idea was abhorrent to him. I haven't, he told himself savagely, got the fucking *time* to get a job. He followed his own version of the Puritan Work Ethic. When it came to his painting, he was aware that he worked harder than anyone he knew. It was, he would admit, the only thing that really mattered to him.

The sound of a car distracted him and he looked out of the window to see the Cad easing towards the garage. He had slipped the notebook into his pocket and assumed a relaxed pose by the time Nicola came quietly into the lounge.

"Enjoy yourself?" he asked.

Nicola put down her purse and a small package.

"Mmm, most of the time," she said. "Met a rather strange plastic man, though."

"Everyone is plastic in this town," said David, laughing.

"No. A real plastic man. Made of plastic."

David, puzzled and amused, studied her.

"Outside a cafe place," she said. "Jack in the Box."

David grinned.

"Don't you have take-out restaurants in England?"

"Of course. But not like that! Nothing like that, in fact. He nearly frightened the life out of me. Couldn't understand where the voice was coming from."

"The fun of being a stranger in a strange land," said David.

He watched her tentatively pick up her purse, as if about to leave. Maybe she felt she was disturbing him? He stood up quickly and offered her some cold white wine. She seemed unsure for a moment, then nodded and smiled again. It would be worth taking a comedy course, thought David as he collected wine and glasses, just to see that smile. When he returned to the lounge, Nicola was resting in an armchair, her head back, her eyes closed. He was tired himself and realized suddenly that she must be exhausted from all the craziness and confusion of these last few days—and, her father's death. He stood very still for a few moments, studying the pale face: fine skin, good bone structure; she must have inherited her mother's looks. David had seen pictures of Nick Graham: a broad, strong-boned man, large head, square jaw. A lion. Nicola opened her eyes, rubbed them with the back of her hands.

"Sorry," she said.

David began to open the wine.

"You look quite different when you relax," he said. "Lose that tense look."

"Tense?"

"Yes."

Nicola said nothing, took her glass of wine and sipped it slowly. She did everything, he thought, with a particular gravity. So seriously sipping her wine! A stillness about her. What did that hide? He watched her, fascinated, until, as she shifted a little, stared down at the floor, he understood that he was making her uncomfortable. He looked away.

"Have you been working today?" she asked.

"If you mean, have I been painting . . . no."

"You have your sketchpad."

"Unopened."

For some reason he felt defensive. There was no criticism in her steady look but David felt the need to explain, or to try to explain. But he knew it would be impossible.

"You think I'm a parasite, don't you?" he began.

She smiled, shaking her head.

"You think I'm deliberately living the easy life. Doing nothing. That's not usually the case, I promise you. I do work. I work very hard. Today's lethargy is mostly a hangover from last night's little celebration."

He saw her flinch at this and cursed himself.

"No, I didn't mean celebration. Excess alcohol and other unhealthy chemicals."

She looked at him levelly but there was an amused light in her eyes.

"You're thinking—'serves him right,'" he continued. "I'm thinking—serves him right."

She leaned back in her chair. He saw her stifle a yawn.

"Sorry," she said. "I'm ridiculously tired. Can barely keep my eyes open."

"It's been a pretty exhausting time for you."

"Yes."

"And grief, too, can be exhausting," he offered gently. She looked over at him for a moment, then looked away.

"That's so true. I've felt tired all the time since . . . it

59

happened. I sleep all right. After the first week I managed to sleep all right. But . . ." she was talking very softly, almost to herself. "I dream a lot. Strange dreams. Not quite nightmares . . ."

"About your father?"

"Not specifically. But of . . . loss. Losing things. Searching for things. Frantically."

"I would think that's pretty common when you lose someone you love," said David.

"Yes. But there's the . . ." unexpectedly she looked straight into his eyes. Her expression was almost pleading. "There's the suicide, too. Looking for reasons. Why would a man like my father do that? Was he so unhappy? And if he was, why hadn't I guessed. Why didn't he tell me how depressed he was?"

"You would be the last person to tell, Nicola. Loving you as he must have he wouldn't want to worry you. Involve you."

"I wish he had. I might have been able to help." She paused, thought for a while. "And I wonder if the very fact of being an artist is involved. The temperament needed to paint. I mean, so many artists have killed themselves. Didn't Jackson Pollock . . . ?"

"No one knows," said David. "His car hit a tree, but that could have been an accident. He drank a great deal."

"So did Dad. That's another thing that seems to . . ."

"Go with the paintbrush?" asked David. "Yes, it often does. But you see, there are so many pressures. Standards to reach. Standards that you impose on yourself which can create tension and problems. And beyond that, the matter of surviving as a painter, being recognized as a painter in the world outside. To most of us, that matters too. It isn't so much a question of fame and fortune, but of recognition."

"But he had those things. Recognition, anyway. The fortune somehow eluded him. He was very, very bad about money. He left enormous debts. And nothing new on his easel. No paintings finished. Nothing left to sell."

"Wouldn't that be reason enough? Debts? Money problems?"

"Not for a man as strong as my father."

"It's possible he felt that he hadn't gone far enough towards his own vision," said David. "In his work, I mean."

"Yes."

David took a breath, thought for a moment then plunged in.

"His later work is pretty static," he said, as gently as he could.

She looked at him, a small frown creased her forehead.

"Do you think so?"

"Yes. There was a point in his work—somewhere after the girl at the mirror painting—where he seemed to get stuck. He began repeating himself. He didn't move on very much." He stopped suddenly. "I'm sorry. I ought not to be saying this to you right now."

"No, please. Thank you for saying it. Because if it was something to do with his work, then I couldn't have helped with that."

"No. Not at all."

"Though I wonder if just the responsibility for us—my mother and myself and Barbara, later . . . if the need for earning a living for us might have made him . . ."

"Play safe?"

"Yes."

Her inquiring look held such pain that David shook his head vigorously.

"No way. That's usually the last concern for a painter. The work itself is the driving force. New directions present themselves and just have to be followed. It's not a matter of choosing . . ."

To his horror he saw that she was biting her lip hard, eyes down. He knew she was close to tears.

"Oh Christ," he said, coming towards her. "I am sorry. You obviously don't want to talk about it."

She looked up at him. There were tears in her eyes but she swallowed hard and when she spoke her voice was quiet but steady.

"I haven't been able, up to now, to talk about it really. And you have helped. Thank you."

He stood looking down at her and attempted a rueful smile.

"I am known for my crass ways and opinionated statements but I turn to jello when I see a woman cry. So, for now, change of subject?"

"Please."

"For a start," said David, reaching for the wine bottle. "Have some more wine."

He took the glass from her and as their hands touched, David felt a sudden jolt. A loss of place. Meeting her eyes he saw, in Nicola too, puzzlement. A confusion of feelings.

He noticed that her cheeks were burning as she bent her head.

Barbara, pulling into the driveway and catching her first glimpse of the green striped canopy, smiled a little, as always. Her house. And God Bless Jack Hampton—that dear departed dummy—for buying it for her. He hadn't wanted it. When it came to the crunch he didn't have much choice. Barbara wanted to live in Bel-Air. Not Beverly Hills or Malibu or Palm Springs but Bel-Air.

"We'll find ourselves a nice spread in the desert," Jack had said confidently just after they were married.

"A vacation place in the desert, sure," Barbara said gaily. "But our house . . . ," a smile, a fast correction, "our *home*, darling, will be in Bel-Air. I'll find something."

She knew the house might be coming up for sale long before the real estate agents heard a whisper, due to her ability to eavesdrop on any conversation while seeming to be involved in her own. She'd found this little gift very useful most of her life.

Barbara was lunching with Angie in the Bistro when she overheard an aged actress at the next table tell her girlfriend that the Delaneys were thinking of moving to Gstaad. Barbara knew the Delaney house. It was a beautiful Regency style structure with an acre and a half of ground. She'd attended a party there. Delaney, a one time great actor, now crippled with arthritis, used to invest heavily in art works. Since he'd married his third ingénue wife the spending had toned down a little. The house was not only large and elegant but it was close to the Beverly Hills Country Club—many of Barbara's art-buying clients were members—and only a few minutes away from the Hotel Bel-Air, an excellent place for brunch meetings. Barbara wanted that house.

She telephoned Tony Delaney that night and chatted politely for a minute or two.

"Well, Barbara," he said finally. "It's nice to hear from you but whatever painting you're selling I have to say no. Sorry."

"I'm not selling, sweetheart, I'm buying."

"Oh," his voice brightened. "If it's the Frank Stella—no. The others I'll consider if the price is right, And I mean *right*."

"Nope. Not even the Stella. It's the house."

"The house? Which one . . ." there was a stunned silence, and then . . . "You mean the *house*."

"Right."

He was astounded.

"Good grief, Barbara! We haven't decided to sell yet."

"You're thinking about it."

"Only loosely. Very loosely. How on earth did you know?"

"Psychic powers. How much?"

There was a long pause.

"Just a moment," he said at last. "I have to talk to Mirabel."

Barbara, hanging onto the telephone, could hear Mirabel's twenty-two year old squeak somewhere in the background. That two-bit player, Barbara thought angrily, will go for every little penny she can get her grubby, talentless paws on. Tony Delaney came back on the phone and named a price 20,000 dollars higher than Jack had stipulated he would pay for their home. Barbara figured that a few thousand more wouldn't hurt him.

"You've got yourself a deal," she told the dumbfounded actor. "I'll get Jack's attorney to contact you."

And that was that, save for a few angry words from Jack and a minor hassle over the price of a few pieces of Sheraton furniture the Delaneys wanted to leave behind.

The day they moved in was one of the happiest of Barbara's life. She inspected every inch of the mansion, padded contentedly around the grounds, making plans. There was a small pool and two tennis courts. All in good shape. Tony Delaney hadn't been on a court in years, the guy could barely walk, but Mirabel and a succession of Beverly Hills Country Club studs had used it well. Barbara couldn't play tennis, didn't want to go through the clumsy learning process as she hated to be amateur at *anything*. If she could pick it up in a day, be good in a week and learn totally unobserved, she would give it a shot. Since that was impossible she had no interest at all in tennis. Jack, however, enjoyed the game, slow and lumbering though he was. Barbara imagined some of the younger set popping over on weekends for a game. California gals with their sleek tanned limbs darting around in front of *her* French windows with *her* husband. No way, she decided.

When Jack was away on a business trip, Barbara had the tennis courts torn up and a larger pool built. Jack was, predictably, furious.

Now, as she pulled the Mercedes to a screeching halt in the driveway, she thought the house was worth every little minute she'd had to spend with old Jack Hampton. The blunt, impatient sound of the car door slamming brought Jeff from the garage. He walked around the car slowly.

"So what's the sneer for, sunshine?" asked Barbara.

"Maybe time for a new car? The new Mer—it is elegant."

"Sure, elegance I need," said Barbara, then paused, thought. "Check out the new model. But I don't want it delivered yet. Wait 'til this show's over and the birds have flown. Nick Graham can buy me a new car."

"I'm sure he would be just delighted," said Jeff solemnly.

Barbara chuckled.

"He'll do a complete somersault in his grave. So—*good*."

They laughed together. Barbara patted Jeff's shoulder affectionately, then walked briskly to the house.

* * *

He had given Nicola the sketchpad to glance through while he opened another bottle of wine, but David was beginning to regret having done so. She was examining them so seriously, looking long and hard at each one. He wasn't very proud of those sketches. He'd done better, could do much better. She had said nothing so far. He felt unusually nervous as to what she would say and it was with some relief that he heard Barbara's footsteps in the hall. Barbara stopped in the doorway, looking at them both.

"Ah, *another* party," she said sharply. "What fun."

Nicola looked up, smiled a greeting, offered to pour Barbara some wine. David knew what the reaction to that would be. Barbara gave a brief, disdainful smile and poured herself a large scotch, looking from one to the other as she sipped at it. It has been a tough day, thought David, another tough day. Barbara worked as hard as she played, hated to be idle; reveled in the battle and competition her work involved. He found that sort of robust determination attractive. Now, as she sat angry at finding herself on the outside, if only temporarily, he thought she had a splendid sort of grandeur. The chin was tilted high, the mouth, a firm straight line. And those eyes: bird bright, seeing everything. They met his and noting, perhaps, his admiration, she relaxed. He knew her fears and her jealousies. Often he could reassure her with a look. She was talking idly but there was a point she wanted to make and she was not long in making it. David sat back and listened to the two women chatting. With amusement, he heard Barbara twist and turn the conversation until she was saying to Nicola:

"And don't go falling for the sweet talk of any of the young painters you meet. Starving little boys in garrets you can live without. I did it. Remember?"

"My father was hardly living in a garret."

"We didn't eat that well, that often. Why go hungry . . ."

"When you can feast," finished David.

"Exactly. Genius."

Nicola looked puzzled.

"What exactly are you trying to . . ."

"Just don't do it kid. O.K.? Right. Shower for me. Dinner in an hour."

Class dismissed. Barbara got to her feet and passing David's chair rumpled his hair. But it was less a caress than an admonition. When Barbara had left Nicola looked at David, frowning a little.

"I don't even know any starving young artists," she said finally.

David laughed.

"You know me."

"Barbara wasn't talking about you." She paused. "Was she?"

"Probably," he said, coming over to her chair. "But don't worry about it."

Teasingly, he leaned forward as if to pat her cheek but she moved back and in a voice so cool and strong that it surprised him said:

"Don't play games with me, please. I'm not quite that young and stupid."

"I know that. But let's be friends. I could get to like you."

"I could probably get to like you, too."

"Probably?"

The ring of the housephone jarred the room. David knew instantly why it rang. He sighed. Was he playing games with Nicola? He had no idea. He knew, though, that for the moment he would prefer to sit and talk with her than answer that call from upstairs.

"Yes, of course I'm coming," he said into the phone.

Nicola slid past him, was out of the room before he replaced the receiver.

Barbara had the shower running when he entered the bedroom. Wearing a sheer wrap, she was tying her hair up in a plastic clasp and watching herself in the mirror.

"We can shower together," she said, as if simply being practical. "I need a back rub."

He grinned.

"That all you need?"

Through the ornate mirror her eyes met his and it was a moment before she smiled.

"Let's find out, shall we?" she said.

She has a lovely back, David thought, as he soaped it gently. Strong shoulders, golden soft flesh.

"Ah, Rubens lady," he whispered into her neck.

She turned and embraced him as the water cascaded around them, running her hands along his body, finding what she wanted then caressing it slowly, tantalizingly, so that David, the blood throbbing in his head, took both of her hands and led her out of the shower. Knowing what he wanted, she positioned herself over the bathtub so that he could penetrate her from behind and both could watch themselves and each other in the now steamy mirror over the tub. Two shadowy pulsating shapes. Her breasts hung down, swung slightly as the bodies moved. He waited until she was close to climax then stopped.

"Please, honey, please," she whispered.

"On the bed."

Their bodies were still wet, dampening the bedcover. The soothing nipple in his mouth had a soapy taste. He entered her fully, moving frantically until she cried out and he could take himself with her to the inevitable explosion.

"Nice shower," he said, as he settled his head against her shoulder. She was silent for a while.

"Rather be rapping with Nicola?" she asked at last.

Psychic female, he thought, but she was twenty minutes late with her mind reading.

"She's a child," he said. "I like women."

With his cheek against the soft cushion of her flesh, one warm breast full in his hand, he believed it.

He had first met her at a party given by a sculptress friend, Mickey. Barbara was the oldest woman there and her expensive, sophisticated clothes easily set her apart from the others. But that didn't seem to bother her: within thirty minutes of her arrival she was surrounded by a crowd of denim-clad guys all laughing at her ribald humor.

"I only invited her because I thought she might do me some good," Mickey confided to David as he helped her mix punch in the tiny kitchen. "And the bitch hasn't spoken to me once."

"Go speak to her."

"Fight through that crowd? Are you kidding?"

Mickey's flowing caftan was suddenly splattered with red as she stirred the punch too vigorously in her anger.

"Fuck it," she said, close to tears.

"Come on," said David, putting his arms round her. "It's a great party."

"It's shitty."

"How can it be? I'm here. Jo-Jo's here, isn't he?"

"He," she said with another spurt of anger, "is over there."

David looked through the kitchen hatch to where Barbara Hampton-Norde held court. The tall, lithe, black figure of Jo-Jo could be seen near the group. He was leaning against the wall, contemptuously studying the brash blonde. David laughed.

"Come on Mickey! He's giving her his 'Me black man. You white trash' look."

"That's what I mean," wailed Mickey. "That's when he's coming on strong. That's when he's most dangerous. He's after that bitch."

"No," said David, studying the finely planed face of his black friend, the hooded eyes, the curling lower lip. "She's the type he despises."

"That's why he'll ball her."

David turned back to Mickey and hugged her for a moment. He was fond of Mickey. A tiny, brittle-thin girl, given to frequent tears and bouts of crazily contagious giggles, she had been living with Jo-Jo for nearly two years and, unlike him, never played around. David had known her since their mutual incarceration at Chouinard Art College when Mickey had quietly been creating outrageously obscene figures with clay. Their shared unpopularity with teachers had drawn them together and, though they had never been lovers—too thin, too *neurotic* for him—they'd stayed friends.

"I'll go reclaim the black bastard," he said now to Mickey.

"You can try," she said tiredly, without much hope. He left her still stirring the punch.

He knew he was going to be too late before he got halfway across the room. Barbara Hampton-Norde had disentangled herself from her admirers and stood looking at Jo-Jo.

"Take me home, would you?" David heard her say as he reached them. Jo-Jo peeled himself from the wall very slowly.

"Sure," he said. "See you, honkey," he added as David was about to speak.

"How long you going to be?"

"As long as it takes," said Jo-Jo.

Just about everyone in the room watched as Jo-Jo loped casually after the woman. It took two days. Mickey, as usual, threw tantrums and threatened suicide but when he returned accepted him back.

The second time David and Barbara crossed paths was rather different. One of his father's friends was down from San Francisco and offered to buy him a drink in the Polo Lounge. David had accepted reluctantly: his father's business friends bored him and the endless polite talk about his parents wearied him. His parents wearied him, in fact. Their preoccupation with home, garden, the rotary club, the country club, and why-their-only-son-should-have-turned-into-a-bum-instead-of-an-upright-member - of - the - community-with-a-good-job-in-business etc., made him furious. He saw them as rarely as possible.

Now, sitting uncomfortably in the Polo Lounge in his only decent jacket—corduroy, too tight under the arms— he wished to hell he hadn't come. Sam Wishaw, bursting out of a charcoal suit and tie, his face red with the excitement of the husband-out-on-parole, was rubber-necking frantically, trying to spot someone he might have seen on television.

"So, how are the folks?" David asked dutifully.

"Gee whiz, they're just fine. Fine," said Sam, his eyes

roaming round the room. "Your Pa's threatening to resign this year, just like every year, so he can concentrate on his garden."

Sam turned back to David.

"You know him," he continued. "Every year he says he'll do it and every year he don't. And your Mom's as ever. Not a day older. Marvelous woman. Such energy she has. Always doin' . . . that's what Martha says."

"And how is Martha?" asked David, glad to dispense with one subject and get onto another.

Sam was waving for more drinks. He sighed.

"Well—the arthritis, you know. That holds her back a bit."

"Oh," said David. "I'm sorry."

"She don't complain. She's no complainin' woman."

"No," said David.

Fresh drinks were put in front of them and later, more fresh drinks. David had made one attempt to leave and had been battened down with another scotch. He was working out a final getaway line when to his relief Sam Wishaw spotted somebody he knew, an attorney from San Francisco.

"Old Jake!" said Sam, pleased as punch to know people in the right places. "Let's go say Hi."

Which is how David found himself sitting next to Barbara Hampton-Norde. She was with Jake and an L.A. attorney, Jerry Womberg. None of the three looked too happy at the interruption but Sam didn't notice, or didn't worry about, things like that. He pushed David into one seat at their table and himself into another and waved for the waiter.

David, after the introductions, said nothing. Nor did Barbara Hampton-Norde, but he was aware of her eyes on him as the three other men discussed some complicated business fraud.

"Well, excuse me folks but I have to leave," David said eventually. "Sam, good to see you."

Barbara Hampton-Norde also stood up, causing the three men to struggle to their feet politely.

"Me too, I'm afraid," she said. "I wonder . . ." She

turned to David and smiled charmingly: "I wonder if you could give me a lift home. I don't have my car with me today."

"Sorry," said David. "I haven't got a car."

Barbara looked crestfallen. Sam was horrified, his red face creasing at this rudeness.

"I'd better call for a cab, then," said Barbara, waving to a waiter. She made her request to the waiter while Sam furiously whispered in David's ear.

"Take her home in a cab, lad," he said. "She's a lady."

"Balls," said a crystal clear voice in David's head.

"No bread," he said to Sam.

He refused the twenty dollar bill Sam tried to press on him. But he took Barbara Hampton-Norde to her Bel-Air home in a taxi. She let him pay for it, too.

"Come in for a drink," she commanded, as they pulled into the driveway of her house.

"Thanks, but I'll need this cab to get home."

She looked at him hard.

"My chauffeur will drive you home," she said.

Her chauffeur did not drive him home that night, nor the next.

Once inside the house, they had two drinks then she kicked off her shoes.

"Let's go upstairs and ball around some," she said.

David, who up until then had been enjoying her venomous observations on L.A.'s most distinguished, stared at her.

"I'm not Jo-Jo," he said. "I'm not some stud."

"Who the hell is Jo-Jo?" she asked, angry.

"Black guy you picked up a few weeks ago."

She thought for a moment.

"Oh, him," she said dismissively. "Hostile prick."

"Somewhat," said David.

Barbara leaned back in her chair, sipped at her drink.

"What's wrong?" she asked. "Don't you fancy me?"

He looked at her for a while, dispassionately, from head to foot. Overweight, certainly, but a curving voluptuousness. Rubens-soft. A good face, the fine edges blurred now, but excellent bones. Eyes of a clear cornflower blue, amazingly untouched by her cynicism and the liquor she must put away. Tarty blonde hair, sculptured into a ridiculous spatial form.

"Could fancy you, I suppose," he said. "You're in pretty good shape."

To his surprise, she laughed. A real laugh that lifted the soft flesh of her face and brought a fresh shine to the blue eyes.

"I like you," she said. "You've got balls."

Because it is difficult to refuse a woman who smiles with admiration and who does not flatter but, instead, compliments, David followed Barbara upstairs.

He made love to her roughly for most of the afternoon until she lay exhausted across him and the sweat from their bodies had soaked the sheets.

"I'm betting you don't have to go without much," she said at one point. "They must come to you begging."

"True," said David.

She smiled into his shoulder.

Later, after a few more drinks and a little pot, he made love to her again, this time very gently with the beginnings of affection. She clung to him like a child.

"Come live here," she said the following afternoon. "You need space to paint and, shit, I've got plenty of it."

"No," he said. "I prefer my own place."

"I bet your place isn't big enough to swing a cat."

"So? How often do I swing cats?"

Two weeks later he moved in with her.

TEN

If Mayfair is discreet then Bel-Air is invisible, Nicola thought as she took her first exploratory stroll around the neighborhood the following afternoon. On Bellagio Road all she could see were high sculpted hedges, iron gates, and jagged topped fences. Signs warned of electric gates and suggested elaborate burglar alarms, and each home, it seemed, was protected by the Bel-Air Patrol. Once in a while she caught a glimpse of tennis courts or the blue glimmer of a pool, but the houses, shrouded by trees, were far back, well hidden.

She stared in disbelief at those dwellings closer to the road. They reminded her of the ancestral homes in England she had visited as a schoolgirl. On Copa de Ora she stood outside a gray stone Victorian mansion and counted the upper windows. Eighteen, ignoring the smaller ones that could be bathrooms. Eighteen bedrooms! Did anyone, anywhere, need eighteen bedrooms? The house looked deserted until an old man, wearing a blue shirt and dungarees, came out of a side door and set up a garden hose. He turned to stare suspiciously at Nicola. She smiled.

"Who lives here?"

"Why you want to know?" Spanish accented. The gardener.

"Just curious."

"No business of yours."

"True. How many people then?"

"Him and wife. O.K.? I have work to do." He turned his back.

Nicola, doggedly curious, could not resist:

"Are they in?"

"No. Traveling."

"I expect they travel a lot."

"Yes. Good-bye."

He turned on the hose at full force, sending a whoosh of water a little too close to Nicola. She walked on.

Around a sharp bend she discovered a modern wood-frame home perched on the edge of a canyon and stopped to admire it. The large windows of smoked glass commanded a superb view. A simple rock garden graded downwards from the house to where she stood. A modest house by Bel-Air standards but the effect, understated, with colors merging into the hillside as if the house belonged there, was tasteful. A maid in a starched apron was lazily polishing a chrome doorknocker, her face up to the sun.

Can't be bad, thought Nicola, being a little old domestic in these circumstances: live in opulent splendor, boss away most of the year, sneak a swim in the pool, and sunbathe on the terrace so long as you give the doorknocker a rub every now and then. Caretakers for the rich—a long way from "Upstairs, Downstairs."

At a fork in the road she stopped, breathing in the scented air: fuchsia, lemon, eucalyptus . . . how lovely this area must have been before it was inhabited. A garden behind her held banana palms with miniature sprouting fruit and a graceful avocado tree. She would have liked to have walked further but was unsure which road to take. It would not do, she chuckled to herself, to get lost in Bel-Air. She was about to turn back when a puffing jogger, wearing blue striped shorts and sweatshirt, ran past her.

"Excuse me."

The man turned, wiping the sweat from his eyes, looking grateful for the chance to take a breather.

"Please, can you tell me where that road leads?"

He took a deep breath and smiled.

"Bel-Air Hotel."

The voice, though hoarse, was familiar and Nicola looked again at the pink, sweating face. Adam Jamesson, middle-aged actor once known offscreen for his heavy drinking and roustabout ways. He was now doing a television series and had well publicized his new sobriety. Nicola, studying him, thought he looked in pretty good shape.

"That where you wanted?" he asked, tolerant of her scrutiny.

Nicola smiled back.

"It would be if I were dressed for it," she said, indicating her old jeans and sandals.

"You wouldn't be the only one dressed like that," he said. "Nor would I for that matter. I'd offer to buy you a drink there but as it is I've got to finish this idiotic run in ten minutes. Doctor's orders. You're English aren't you?" he added.

"Yes."

"Staying with Barbara Hampton-Norde?"

Nicola blinked.

"Yes. How on earth did you know that . . . ?"

"Word gets 'round. I liked your father's work."

"Oh . . . I see. You were at the opening?"

"Nope. Can't stand those damn things. Not since I jumped on the wagon anyway. But I took a look yesterday at the exhibition. Some good pictures. A shame he . . ." Jamesson stopped. "Good pictures," he repeated.

"Thank you," said Nicola. She stood embarrassed for a moment, then coughed.

"Well, I'd better walk back this way."

"See you again," he said, and with a cheery wave of his hand began jogging down the hill.

"Good luck," said Nicola impulsively. The hand waved again then he disappeared around a bend.

The sun was hot on her head as she turned finally into the driveway of Barbara's house. She could feel a trickle of sweat between her breasts, her face burned. She felt that she had walked for miles and the long driveway seemed endless.

A window high up at the top of the house was wide-open. Shielding the sun from her eyes Nicola paused: David's studio she guessed. The window was bare of drapes and the outline of an easel was just visible. As she watched, a figure appeared at the window. David, looking out towards her, brushing one hand through his hair. Nicola shyly turned away, pretending not to see him, and hurried into the cool house.

Downstairs was deserted. A vacuum cleaner hummed upstairs: Maria cleaning. No sign of Barbara. Nicola, her throat dry, made for the kitchen and searched in vain for a bottle of orange soda. Eventually, she settled for a bottle of Perrier and sat down at the scrubbed wooden worktable to sip it. It was icy and refreshing, bubbles danced in the glass. Nicola slipped off her sandals, enjoying the cold tile of the kitchen floor on her feet, feeling in this unpretentious room more at home.

She stiffened when she heard footsteps on the stairs and a low whistling. David. The lounge door opened, then closed again. The whistling stopped. David went back upstairs. Nicola stayed where she was until all was quiet. She was just placing her empty glass in the sink when Maria hurried in. The maid stopped, surprised.

"Can I get you something?"

"No, just skulking in the scullery," said Nicola lightly, knowing she would not be understood. "Thank you, Maria, but I helped myself to a drink."

The maid nodded, smiled. Nicola stepped quickly upstairs, decided she would spend the time before dinner writing to Felix.

Wish you were here. Truly. You'd make it amusing. My sense of humor could really use that. I can only find it strange. "A stranger in a strange land." Perhaps it's all this sunshine. I'm ill at ease in bright places. I like things dark and forbidding once in awhile. (What does that say about the state of my soul?)

Dad's pictures created a small stir, but nothing earth-shattering. We had a write-up in the local daily. An impressive exhibition though—Barbara must have worked very hard at it. She had just about every painting he'd done that was really worthwhile. Must have done a lot of research, spent a lot of time tracing them. God knows why she did it. And how she did it. We used to try, now and then, to get a few together for small shows but could never quite manage it. I must ask her . . . though it's difficult to ask her anything. What do I mean by that? I don't know. She's changed a great deal. She's rather unapproachable. She's bawdy (very!), alcoholic, perhaps. Certainly drinks as much as Dad did—and that *is* saying something. Very snappy and quick with the bitchy comments.

I suspect she doesn't like me, or rather resents me for some reason. She's awfully possessive about her young boyfriend—nice enough fellow, a painter—but she acts as if I might snatch him away. As if I could or would want to!

Bel-Air is incredible, as indeed is Beverly Hills. Come the revolution—poof! Seriously, there is just too much of everything here. It's all too big and brassy. Janey was right—it is vulgar. But not deliciously so. Exclusively so.

Really must find interesting things to do with the rest of my time here. There are a couple of exhibitions in L.A. that I can cover for the *Chronicle* and I might take a trip to San Francisco to see what's happening in the art world up there . . .

I thought Barbara might have made a plan or two like that (I would for a visitor to England) but it doesn't seem to have occurred to her. So—on my own, perhaps.

This is a boring letter, isn't it? Little shafts of self-pity. I'll close it, pronto. I wonder how you are, think of you a lot. It's strange how far away you seem. It really is a different world here. Not so much laid-back as virtually laid out . . . mostly at the side of a swimming pool with a glass of something cold and throat-clutching strong at hand. Write soon and take care.

She scrawled "much love," then pondered a moment. Would Felix misunderstand that in a letter that said she was missing him? It would look ridiculous to knock it out. She added a balancing P.S.: "How goes the redhead hunt? Good luck!"

Nicola read the letter again and was thoroughly dissatisfied with it. It sounds like a mawkish, adolescent letter to an uncle, she told herself. She added a little more:

Remember thar car mechanic in Hampstead we thought had been put together by a computer? Barbara's chauffeur is just like him. Doesn't move his face muscles at all—not sure if he even blinks. He's virtually mute. Really weird. And he carries a gun! I suppose lots of people here do but I'd never seen a *real* one before and I nearly fell to the floor shouting don't shoot, don't shoot! I'm innocent! (Of course I am.)

She folded the letter quickly and sealed it in an envelope. She could hear Barbara and David talking as they went downstairs. Almost time for dinner. As she dressed she wondered what plans had been made for the evening: the tinkling of ice against glass told her that whatever else was in store, the evening would begin with some pretty serious drinking. It did. And at midnight a slightly tipsy Nicola found herself sitting with David and Barbara in a booth in a discoteque. It was a tiny, dark place crammed with people. Barbara had told her it was "very exclusive." Nicola wished the management had excluded a few more people to allow more breathing space.

"Gin and tonic, Nicola?" asked Barbara.

"Just the tonic, please," said Nicola.

Barbara laughed.

"Come *on*."

"No. Really."

Barbara, exhibiting a noticeable liquor glow, said she wanted to dance and David led her onto the floor. They were gone for three dances and Nicola, feeling uncomfortably conspicuous by herself, watched the dancers covertly. Certainly enough vaguely familiar faces to justify the "exclusive" tag, though Nicola could only put a name to one or two of them. Nicola wished she could curl up on the leather seat and go to sleep.

A little later she danced with David—one dance only. As the music stopped she glanced over at Barbara. The older woman was watching them intently.

"Let's sit down now," Nicola said to David.

"After the next one."

"I'd prefer now, please. I feel a bit dizzy. All that booze."

"Nicola's woozy with booze," said David to Barbara when they returned to the table.

"Right," said Barbara. "Let's go."

When they returned to the house Nicola yawned and said she was going straight to bed.

"Have a nightcap," said David.

"She doesn't want a nightcap if she's had too much already," said Barbara sharply, pouring herself a drink.

Nicola said good night.

ELEVEN

During the next few days Nicola sat in the sun by the pool, read a great deal, walked around Bel-Air for exercise. She combed through the "Guide to Galleries" in the Sunday *Times* but the only two exhibitions that might interest London readers—a Rodin sculpture exhibition at the L.A. County Museum of Art and a Retrospective on Clyfford Still in Beverly Hills—did not open until the following week.

Barbara was out most of the day, David was at the top of the house working. Nicola found that she avoided him when Barbara was not there; she was nervous that her stepmother would misunderstand if she found them chatting together.

"I'm frightened of her," she admitted to herself with surprise.

At last the weather changed. Nicola woke to a nostalgically gray sky, the bright sun temporarily extinguished. Weather forecasts warned of storms out over the ocean and a ninety percent chance of rain hitting the area by evening. Nicola thought it a good day to get away from the pool and explore a little.

She walked to the main Bel-Air gate and picked up a bus going east. She had heard of the Sunset Strip and when she heard a slow Southern voice behind her inform his companion that this was where they were, she jumped off the bus. She was rather disappointed. The famous Strip looked like any other street. Very few people strolled, the dark skies having put off the wanderers and tourists. The few people she saw on foot were either leaving or entering restaurants or clambering into cars. When she was outside Cyrano's restaurant it began to sprinkle and Nicola paused as a group of horrified Californians rushed from the building, almost trampling over her in their rush to get to the dry safety of their cars. Nicola held up her face for a moment, enjoying the cool dampness, homesick for England, then realizing that her T-shirt was getting soaked, her jeans uncomfortable against her thighs, she waved down a taxi to take her to Bel-Air.

The house was silent, no sign of Maria or Jeff. Barbara and David were obviously out. Barbara's desk was littered with papers, suggesting a hasty exit. Nicola glanced down at a list of paintings then, ashamed, turned away. None of her business. Her clothes still felt uncomfortably damp and she decided to shower and change.

At the top of the stairs, she paused: the heavy wooden door that led upstairs to the loft was slightly open. David's studio, she guessed. She had never seen it, wondered what it was like, what his paintings were like. A good opportunity now to take just a tiny peek. She hesitated—it *was* sneaky. But Nicola could not resist. Quietly she slipped through the door and climbed the last few stairs.

The stairs ended at a wide corridor and at the very end an archway showed a white, bright room. David stood there, motionless, staring at his easel. He was unaware of her, unaware, she knew, of anything except that blank sheet in front of him. That same intensity she had witnessed in her father. She did not make the mistake, as others might, of thinking that he was simply dreaming. The tension in his body, the complete absorption, she could recognize that.

He picked up a crayon and slowly, almost nervously, he began to draw. Within a minute the crayon began to move swiftly across the paper. She could sense the growing confidence, the excitement in him. He is *serious* then, she thought. Nicola began to tiptoe away.

At the top of the stairs, trying hard to be quiet, she misjudged the first step and stumbled. She did not dare turn around.

"Don't creep away," said David's voice behind her.

She turned. He was walking along the corridor, crayon still in hand. She blushed.

"I'm so sorry. I didn't mean to pry. Or interrupt," she added.

David watched her discomfort with amusement.

"Quite natural for you to be curious," he said kindly. "With your background. If you want to take a look—please do."

He waved an arm towards the stacked sketches and paintings. Nicola was tempted but remembering his previous concentration backed down a step or two.

"I'd like to very much at some point. But . . . I'm disturbing you now. I know I am."

"You're a very disturbing girl," said David with a smile.

Nicola looked away.

"Perhaps tomorrow," she said, turning and beginning to descend the stairs. "Thank you."

She knew that he was watching her as she stepped quickly downstairs. When she reached the landing she heard his fast footsteps along the corridor to the studio. Back to work.

Nicola was typing in her room when Barbara returned from the gallery. Her stepmother came straight into the room without knocking.

"You should get out more, honey," she said with disapproval. "Have to find you a date. Maybe make up a foursome for tonight. Seen anybody you like?"

Nicola did not know how to react to that.

"Well, perhaps Jerry," she suggested tentatively.

"Jerry's a fag," said Barbara.

"That doesn't matter."

Barbara threw back her head and laughed loudly.

"Doesn't matter! It might not matter for lunch at Chasens, honey, but it sure as hell matters in the sack."

Still chuckling, Barbara went back downstairs.

Nicola was relieved that no date was made for her and in fact all three of them stayed at home that evening. Barbara, a bottle of scotch at her elbow, pored over accounts,

David sketched for awhile then played some music. Nicola, engrossed in Lillian Hellman's *Pentimento*, felt comfortable and at east for the first time. It was a cool, quiet night, the rain still pattering lightly outside; Maria had cooked a superb veal piccata meal and David had uncorked a bottle of cold white wine for Nicola to sip as she read.

It was when Barbara closed her books, locked them away in her desk, then idly flicked through David's sketchpad that the atmosphere changed.

"These are crap," she said harshly.

David looked up.

"They're just quick sketches," he said surprised.

Barbara looked at the sketches then over at Nicola. Her look was poisonous.

"They're crap," she repeated.

Nicola bent over her book and pretended to read. She had not known he was sketching her, though she had felt his eyes on her once or twice during the evening. She could not ask to see lest she incense Barbara. Besides, she did not like seeing herself portrayed and was unsure of what David might see in her face. And if they were "crap"? She suspected they might be flattering.

There was a heavy, uncomfortable silence in the room after that. The mood of the early evening shattered. Nicola waited half an hour then went to bed.

TWELVE

She was avoiding them both, she knew. She deliberately rose late the following day so as to miss Barbara at breakfast but her stepmother had left a note for her. "Get Jeff to take you anywhere you want." Nicola asked the driver to drop her in Malibu and spent the whole day sunning and swimming. Jeff arrived to take her back in the late afternoon. Nicola stayed in her room until the preprandial cocktails had been swallowed and Barbara yelled up the stairs to say that the meal was on the table.

There were four courses at dinner and most of the food went back to the kitchen untouched. Barbara ate hardly anything though she was drinking steadily. Nicola, uncomfortable and tense, picked at the food. Only David seemed to be enjoying the meal and he was having difficulty getting at it because Barbara, visibly drunk, was constantly touching him: ruffling his hair, stroking his face, kissing him.

Nicola sat rigidly, toying with the sticky chocolate dessert, as Barbara nibbled at David's ear. She was acutely embarrassed by this display and knew that, if it was a show, a play, as she suspected, it was solely for her benefit. Barbara was claiming territorial rights to her lover.

"You are the cocksman of my life," Barbara sang softly into David's neck. "And you will always be a-round . . ."

Nicola wished she could feel amused by such childishness, but she was beginning to feel angry. Her attempts at conversation fell flat, and her inquiry about a newly-opened gallery was ignored. David had begun a reply to her but Barbara wrapped both arms around him and kissed him full on the mouth. Nicola pushed away the dessert and stood, wanting to leave the room quickly, unconcerned, for once in her life, that such a gesture would normally be considered rude.

David disentangled himself and looked up.

"It's the Tempo, Nicola."

"Pardon?"

"The gallery you want is the Tempo. Isn't it, Barbara?"

Maria came in with coffee. Nicola sat down again.

"*Isn't it,* Barbara?"

His voice was hard and Barbara, who was sleepily nuzzling her face against his shoulder, sat up. She looked at Nicola and smiled.

"Oh you'll love the Tempo, darling," she said softly. "You will, if you're lucky, meet lots of sweet little artists 'round there. Lots of 'em. Some a little sexually inadequate, shall we say. A little perverse. But . . ."

Nicola sat stunned at the hostility behind her words. David had intervened and told Barbara sharply to "cut it out." Barbara, stung, swung around at him.

"For Christ's sake, I'm only warning her. And hell, she should know enough."

"Cut it," he said.

"She damn well ought to know then. I went through that scene. Hell, her own mother *died* because of it. The whole fucking . . ."

As Nicola registered the words, she felt as though her body were turning to ice.

"I beg your pardon," she said, clearly.

"The goddamn ego trip of the artist . . ." Barbara continued.

"*What* did you say!" Nicola's voice was loud in her ears.

Barbara looked at her for a moment, then stretched her hand across the table as if to touch Nicola's arm. Nicola, stiff as a puppet, moved away.

"What did you say about my mother?"

Barbara sighed.

"She died because of him. The truth."

"She died of pneumonia."

"*Neglected* pneumonia, sweetheart." Barbara's speech had cleared now, the slurred drunkenness gone. "He was so fucking busy, so self-obsessed . . . It was his first London exhibition. He didn't have time to get hold of doctors. She died while he was away. He felt . . ."

Nicola, staring at her stepmother with growing horror, interjected wildly:

"That's not true!"

Barbara looked steadily into her eyes.

"Honey, it is true," she said softly. "He told me. Often. He felt guilty about it always. He knew . . ."

"It's not true! It's all lies."

Nicola stood up, holding onto the table, feeling a terrible anger she'd never experienced before. She had a real desire to strike out, wound, damage this woman who was telling lies about her father. But why such lies? What buried hatred caused this?

"Darling, it is true," the liquid voice continued. "Your father lived his life for himself even when he had some piece of ass around the place to . . ."

Nicola stepped backwards, a glass clattered to the floor.

David had jumped to his feet and moved as if to put an arm around her. She shrugged him away. Her chest felt tight, breathing was difficult.

"You should sit down, Nicola," he said.

"Why is she lying like that?" Nicola whispered. "She's a cow to lie like that."

She stopped, the tears rivulets on her face. Barbara was staring at her sadly.

"Nicola, I am not lying," she said.

Nicola had to get out. She turned quickly, stumbling against the French windows, into the cool evening. She breathed deeply, trying to ease the pain in her chest. She walked slowly around the half-lit pool, her mind a turmoil of Barbara's words and half-formed plans. She would leave tonight. But could she? She would leave tomorrow. How could she stay here and why should she stay with a stepmother who was half-crazed? And David who was . . . what? Dangerous, in that he would disturb her, she knew. An easy man to care too much for and be hurt by.

On the dark side of the pool she stopped, watched the lights of the city below her. Just one more night to get through and she would be home. The security of Felix and her apartment and a life that had order. Not like this . . . lunacy. She turned and could see Barbara and David sitting at the dining table still—Barbara sipping from her glass mechanically, David leaning forward, talking. He looked angry. She hoped he was. Barbara stood suddenly and Nicola pressed back into the shadows.

Barbara's footsteps on the paving around the pool. Coming towards her. Nicola turned her back. The woman's arm was firm around her shoulders and Nicola stood rigidly. Stay calm, she told herself. Home tomorrow.

"I know you're badly hurt, honey. But give me a chance to explain." Barbara spoke very quietly. "I thought you knew.

"I thought he must have told you. He talked about it a lot when he drank."

"I didn't know."

"Then I'm sorry I told you." A gentle pressure on Nicola's shoulder. "Come on. Come back to the house."

In silence, Nicola allowed herself to be led towards the open French windows. She stopped then. Not wanting to go inside. As if sensing this, Barbara motioned to a garden sofa and, as Nicola sat down, lit a cigarette and handed it to her.

Nicola took the cigarette.

"Why do you hate him so much?" she whispered.

Barbara sighed and sat down next to her.

"I didn't hate him. I loved him. Remember? You were there. You saw how much I loved him."

"But you left him."

Barbara paused and drew heavily on her cigarette.

"I had to, honey," she said. "He was breaking my heart."

A distant memory nagged at Nicola and then with a click, the shutter of the camera in the mind's eyes, the picture she groped for: Barbara, in tears, standing in the kitchen in the old Hampstead house. Her father slamming out the front door. He had not come home that night. How many nights?

"And . . . my mother?" she asked, with difficulty.

"I know she loved him," said Barbara. "Desperately."

"And he loved *her*."

Barbara was silent for a few moments.

"Maybe," she said slowly. "Maybe he did. He had other women always. But that doesn't necessarily mean very much. But—I don't think he could love anyone. In those days his paintings, exhibitions, shows—that's what he loved. That was all that really mattered. He was ambitious. He didn't want to be good—he wanted to be great. He wanted to be known as great. In the art world that's not easy. But he really thought he could make it. I really thought he could make it."

"He did," said Nicola loyally, knowing it was a lie.

Barbara shrugged.

"Not soon enough. Not far enough."

Nicola turned for the first time and looked at Barbara. The older woman was staring into the distance, frowning slightly. In the shadowy light she looked her age, tired, and unhappy.

"Why are you doing this show, Barbara, feeling as you do?"

Barbara, recovering herself, smiled slightly.

"For the money, sweetheart. No. It's my job and he was a good painter. It was meant as a sort of—tribute."

"Tribute to a bastard?"

"To his art. Not to the man."

Nicola stubbed out her cigarette with her foot and wiped her still-damp face with her sleeve. Barbara took her hand.

"This is hateful for you. I wish—well, it's said now."

"Yes."

"Look, why don't you wash up and maybe change and we'll all go out somewhere. Somewhere nice."

"No," said Nicola. "Really."

"Please," she said softly.

Nicola shook her head, tired, not wanting to talk anymore, not wanting to hear anymore. She was unable to think clearly, one half of her mind, like an uninvolved observer was checking her reactions: not angry anymore, simply shocked.

"Think about it for a moment," said Barbara and with a pat to Nicola's shoulder disappeared into the house. Nicola sat for awhile, hunched over, watching the water in the pool. She turned at a sound inside the house and saw clearly through the French windows into the bright dining room. Barbara, smiling, was reaching down to stroke David's cheek. His face was serious, he looked very angry. Barbara, teasingly, ruffled his hair.

Nicola stood up and walked quickly and quietly past the pool, along the path towards the drive and out of the gates of the house.

Jeff, emerging from the shadows of the house, watched as she turned into the Bel-Air street. He could follow her on foot or in the Cadillac. He turned to the garage. He would take the car.

Nicola did not know where she was going. She knew only that she had to get away from the house. Let her head clear, get rid of the tight knot of pain in her chest. And the anger that had returned in a choking wave when she had seen Barbara smiling in the house.

The road was well-lit and Nicola felt like a character on a film set. She could hear her own footsteps and Barbara's words echoing in her head in rhythm:

"Hell, her own mother *died* because of it . . . she died because of him . . . felt guilty about it."

Felt guilty? She had never known her father to mention guilt about anything. He was a man who looked forward.

"Don't look back, Nicola," he had told her years ago. "Don't ponder over might-have-beens. Keep your eye on the horizon and concentrate your energies on the day ahead. Good grief, enjoy the damn day. Enjoy it."

Bitch Barbara. But what long-nurtured resentments caused her to say such things? He must have hurt her badly. But then he had hurt many women. She was right about that. Women had not mattered to him, not as much as his work. But my mother was different, Nicola told herself. He loved her. *Neglected* pneumonia?

The sound of a car behind her encouraged her to walk faster. The car slowed down—a long, open roadster, curb-crawling.

"Take you somewhere, honey?" asked a male voice.

"No, thank you," said Nicola, walking quickly.

"Hey, you British?"

Nicola ignored this, the car kept level with her.

"Hey, I just got back from Europe," said the driver. "Paris, Rome, London . . . took a trip to Stratford upon Avon. You know . . . Shakespeare."

Nicola glanced at him: a young face, fair hair.

"Yes, I know Shakespeare."

He laughed:

"Come on. I'll give you a lift. I'm not out to hurt anyone."

Nicola studied his face for a moment. A healthy, open face, a scrubbed youthfulness. She got into the car.

The roadster spun off into the night. Jeff, in the stationary Cadillac, switched on lights and engine again. The car purred forward to follow.

The bored female voice at the end of the phone exasperated David. He visualized her as having crimson, claw-like nails, false eyelashes, and a frequent, totally damning yawn.

"Just put a call out for her," he said, with contrived patience. "Page her, for Christ's sake."

Barbara, who was pacing the room, a drink in one hand, turned and raised an eyebrow.

"Yes, I *have* tried British Airways," he barked into the phone. "O.K., right. Thank you."

He slammed down the phone.

"Bitch," he said.

"What can she do?" asked Barbara, tiredly.

"Maybe I should go over to the airport."

"How can she be at the airport?" asked Barbara. "Her purse is here."

"Where else would she go?"

"How the hell would I know? I wish she would go back to England. Silly child."

91

"That's why you threw that shit at her. To get rid of her, right? You've finished with her now. Is that it?"

"That's about it," said Barbara. "In any case she's a bore. A bore with a daddy complex."

She had turned her back on him. He crossed the room, took her shoulders and turned her around.

"Aren't you capable of simple kindness," he said angrily. "Aren't you?"

Her eyes met his but there was an uneasiness in them. Just the faintest shadow of fear.

"With Nicola," she said, "I don't know."

He dropped his hands and turned away.

"Maybe we should call the police."

"Don't talk crazy," said Barbara, adding as David turned back to her: "Not yet anyway. Not yet."

Nicola remembered Cyrano's restaurant on the Strip and because it was the first place that came to mind she asked the driver of the roadster to drop her there, saying she had to meet someone. To her horror, he offered to escort her in.

"You don't want to walk in alone, honey. I'll see you settled then I gotta vanish. I got a date."

"Look, it's not necessary," said Nicola, as he pulled into a parking place. "My . . . friend will be there."

"Wouldn't mind a quick one myself," he said, smiling. "Come on."

Nicola reluctantly got out of the car. She had no money with her, she had not intended to go into bars. How could she pay for her drinks if this young man did not and how long would he wait with her for her "friend." She swallowed.

"Look, I'd rather you didn't. He's rather jealous and he might think . . ."

"Of course he won't." He took her arm. "I've got to vanish in ten minutes."

They sat at the bar. Nicola turned frequently to watch the door as if searching for someone. Her fresh-faced driver—he said his name was Don—glanced at his watch then looked at her worriedly.

"You sure this is where he said?"

"Positive," said Nicola.

"Well, I hate to leave you, honey, but I . . ."

"That's fine," said Nicola quickly. "Go ahead. I'll be all right here."

"You sure?"

Nicola nodded, and Don, looking relieved, waved for the check.

"And give the lady another drink, would you," he told the bartender.

Don pocketed his change and turned to Nicola.

"It's been great meeting you, honey," he said. "But if he's not here in ten minutes, I'd just get on back."

"Fine. I will."

He stood for a moment, uncomfortable, and Nicola, guessing what was coming next, looked away. But the ten dollar bill was pushed quickly under her glass.

"You might, well you could need a cab. I don't know how much . . . look, have it on me."

She felt as if every eye in the place was on her, embarrassment made her cheeks burn.

"No, really," she whispered. "I couldn't possibly."

"Please," he said. "I'd just worry. Anyway, honey, you can pay me back when next I come to the old country. How about that?"

Don patted Nicola's cheek and turned to leave.

"Just a minute," said Nicola. "Have you a pen?"

He produced one hurriedly and Nicola wrote down her London address on a napkin.

"I'll pay you back," she said. "Thanks."

Don smiled, tucked the napkin into his pocket.

"Take care," he said.

Alone, Nicola sipped her drink and kept her eyes on the bar counter. She was conscious of two young men behind her staring curiously. One of them slipped onto the empty stool at her side.

"Hi," he said.

Nicola ignored him, swallowed her drink quickly and weaved her way out of the bar.

After the air-conditioned bar, the air felt warm. Nicola

breathed in deeply to steady herself. There had been wine at dinner and she had drunk three—maybe four—glasses, and another two large glasses in less than twenty minutes. She was walking steadily enough, she thought, and walking quickly but the edges of her vision blurred. A drowsy numbness pains my sense, she quoted to herself.

Many people seemed to be walking, strolling players in groups and pairs. The nightly carnival of Sunset Boulevard. And she was part of it . . . a player. A few voices called to her. Once someone caught her arm and, tiring of the carnival, she turned off Sunset, walked unsteadily down Palm Avenue, a steep hill. She wanted to find somewhere dark and quiet where she could hide and think.

The coffee houses along Santa Monica Boulevard seemed to be full of young men. One, crowded to the door, displayed a crush of male bodies clad in tight denim jeans, shirts open to the waist, gold chains against the golden flesh or the macho matted chest hair. A couple of young men, blond, tall, as alike as brothers, glanced at her as she paused. Then they looked away with a pointed disinterest. Nicola walked on.

A middle-aged woman, a little overweight, cheaply but respectably dressed, turned into a small bar. The bar had a neon light, half-broken, flashing foolishly into the night. Nicola followed. The place was very dark so that, at first, shadows, not faces, could be seen. The shadows sat up on stools at the bar. A juke box quietly played a sentimental love song. A stool at the very end of the bar was empty. Nicola walked purposefully towards it, her eyes gradually able to register the patrons and the bar itself. It was tiny and narrow with no more than a dozen customers. Behind her stool it opened up to show a pool table with two black guys playing pool. There was a light over the table and it illuminated Nicola too, so that she felt like an actress spotlighted center-stage.

Nicola ordered a glass of white wine. She had to repeat the order and the bartender loudly repeated it after her. A woman to her left laughed. Nicola sipped the drink slowly, turned once to glance at the pool players just as one of them made a shot and looked up at her.

"Hi there, beautiful," he said.

Nicola quickly turned back to her drink. The woman on her left wheeled around on her chair.

"You talking to me, Big Sam?" she shouted. There was laughter from the players and Nicola glanced at the woman and smiled slightly. She was a busty blonde, wearing a short skirt—a type Nicola hadn't seen in years—her face was positioned by pancake make-up. At the end of the bar, two middle-aged men, drunk and disheveled, were eyeing her. Nicola stared hard at the top of the bar. What the hell was she doing here? She should simply have ignored Barbara and stayed in her room and packed to go home. To go home? There was something she had to think out. A cluster of memories that had to be put into order. Her mother dying . . . Nicola hadn't known she was seriously ill. One day she was sick in bed and the next day she had gone. Vanished and never returned. Her father had taken Nicola to stay with Aunt Helen, her mother's cousin. Had he been so busy then with his exhibitions? Was that why she stayed with Aunt Helen for what seemed like many weeks? And Aunt Helen had never liked him. Was that because . . . ?

Nicola sipped some more of her wine. And later, Barbara . . . Barbara crying in the kitchen. But more often singing in the kitchen. Inventing games. Dances. Was that the same Barbara?

"Wanna drink?"

The younger of the two drunks was behind her.

"No thanks," said Nicola.

The man jolted sideways a little, trying to see her face more clearly.

"I can give you twenty dollars for a trick, sugar."

Nicola glanced at him quickly, confused. What on earth was this?

"I don't do tricks, I'm afraid," she stammered.

The drunk bellowed with laughter, repeated her words, struggling to imitate her accent. A number of people in the bar laughed. Nicola bowed her head and fumbled for the ten dollars Don had given her so that she could pay and get out quickly.

"Knock it off, dummy," said the blonde woman. "Leave the girl alone to have her drink."

To Nicola's relief the man staggered away, still laughing. The blonde shifted along the stools until she was sitting next to Nicola.

"You ain't no professional, honey," she said, in a friendly way. "I can sure see that."

"Christ, it's impossible. I drove around Hollywood, around Beverly Hills. To the gallery. Nothing."

David threw the car keys on the table and looked angrily at Barbara. She was reading a magazine and as if suddenly aware of him, she put it down.

"The silly bitch," she said.

David, feeling stifled though the room was cool enough, opened the French windows and began pacing up and down the patio. Barbara stood. She was going to close the windows, he knew, in case some tiny moth or fly . . . At that moment the phone rang. Barbara reached it first and he stood close to her while she talked, unable at first to guess the identity of the person calling. Barbara's tone was flippant. Eventually, she laughed.

"Nice place," she said into the phone. "O.K., hang in there. Bring the child right back when she's had enough."

Barbara put down the receiver and took a long swallow of her scotch.

"What on earth . . . ?" began David impatiently.

"Jeff saw her going into some bar." Barbara was amused. "He thought he'd better just check it out. Jesus, that guy is *useful*."

"I'll go get her." David reached for the car keys.

"He'll bring her, idiot."

"Better if I go."

"He'll bring her," said Barbara. "We don't know the bar. Could be anywhere."

He looked at her angrily.

"You know the bar. I heard you say . . ."

"Let Jeff do it. You'll just embarrass her if you go rushing in there."

David doubted this was true but he sat down again.

96

"Drink?" Barbara was pouring another one for herself.

"No."

They sat in silence until Barbara's glass was empty again. She yawned:

"I gotta get up in the morning so—bed. Coming?"

David was astounded.

"Are you serious? You are seriously going to bed?"

"Of course. For God's sake you don't think we should sit here waiting up like old mom and pop."

"Yes, I do."

"Don't be an asshole."

"I'll wait then."

The blue eyes were narrow, tired, and he couldn't read them.

"She won't want to chat, I wouldn't think."

"No. But she'll realize we've been worried." He was annoyed with her and his voice rose. "We *have* been worried, haven't we?"

"Oh shit. O.K., we'll wait up."

She was doing it for him, he knew, not for Nicola, but it was a small victory. Barbara curled up on the sofa and promptly went to sleep. Despite himself, he smiled. How like a child she was—if she couldn't get her own way she nevertheless managed to make it *look* as if she had. He settled back to wait, listening for the sound of the Cadillac.

Nicola, to her own surprise, was almost enjoying herself. Maybe it was the wine. The blonde, whose name was Lindy, and she had been joined by two of the bar's regulars—a middle-aged man and a young black guy. She had been told their names which she had instantly forgotten. They stood behind her chair and studied her admiringly.

Lindy was explaining, in a voice that during the last three drinks had slurred noticeably, the intricacies of the California welfare system, and the need to supplement the amount given to applicants with a little freelance prostitution.

"You can get disability, honey. Or you can get the goddamn welfare. Either way, *either* way, you need a bit on the side."

97

Nicola smiled and the two men laughed. Lindy continued, encouraged by this.

"Especially now, *especially* if you like your liquor. But that don't apply to you none," she said to Nicola. "That wine you drinking there? You some wino?"

"Not really," said Nicola, amused.

"You want something else, Nicola?" the young black butted in quickly.

"No thanks. I'm fine."

"You oughta try Johnny's Tequila Sunrise," he said, his head nodding rapidly, nervously. "It sure blows the top of your head right off."

"She don't want her head blowed off," said the older man.

"No," said the black, chastened.

Nicola thought wryly that the wine was doing a pretty good job on her head. It was spinning pleasantly. She was also having difficulty focusing. She turned back to Lindy.

"But what about those girls you said about—with babies. How do they manage?"

"Well, honey, they ain't got no choice." Lindy lowered her voice. "Now her. See her?"

Nicola looked at the end of the bar where a young, olive-skinned girl sat alone, toying desultorily with her glass.

"She gotta do tricks understand, because her old man left her and she's got three kids."

"Couldn't she . . ." Nicola hesitated. "Well, couldn't she get a job?"

Lindy looked at Nicola indulgently, forgiving the foreign girl's ignorance of what Lindy considered obvious.

"She's a Chicano, see. She's illegal. She ain't got no papers. What's she to do?"

"Lindy, for the fuck's sake." The older man turned to Nicola and said a polite "excuse me" for his obscenity.

"For the fuck's sake," he continued, "watch what you're saying here."

"What?"

Lindy looked from him to Nicola and laughed.

"Shit, she ain't no immigration. She's British."

"Nicola's O.K.," said the young black with conviction. "She's got an honest face."

"Thanks very much."

Nicola began to lose track of time. She had no idea how long she had been sitting in the bar. She had also lost track of how many drinks she had had. The group around Lindy and herself had grown. They were all men, about six of them. They listened to Lindy but they looked at Nicola. I am an orphan, she told herself in that abrupt switch to the maudlin mood that alcohol often creates. I'm sitting in a bar surrounded by strangers and unlike Blanche duBois I cannot depend on their kindness. I've no husband, no lover that counts, and all my friends are six thousand miles away. And I have learned, though I choose not to believe it, that my father killed my mother. Not deliberately. By omission, rather than intention, but she died nevertheless.

Nicola struggled to recall the exact timbre of her father's voice but couldn't. She did recall, though, his words at her twenty-first birthday party. She had been wearing a long dress, new, made of turquoise raw silk.

"Jesus, but you look beautiful," he had said, hugging her. "You're as lovely as your mother was and twice as mischievous."

He had stood back and studied her:

"God, if she could only have lived to see you like this."

If she could have lived! He had given the party for Nicola, and his latest mistress had been hostess. A bright, attractive woman, she had served drinks and food, introduced people and encouraged them all to dance. She had helped the party go with a swing. And she had left early, in tears. Another one.

Someone tugged Nicola's arm. She turned on her barstool to see a middle-aged man, smartly dressed and clearly drunk. He had a soft leer on his face.

"Come on, limey," he said, grabbing her arm clumsily. "You deserve to have a good time."

"Pardon?"

"I said—come on."

He had a tight grip on her arm and Nicola suddenly felt

99

afraid. But the young black had stepped forward and roughly removed the man's arm.

"Vanish," he said.

The man swayed on his feet for a moment.

"You talking to me, Sambo?" he hissed.

With lightning speed the black produced a knife and the group instinctively moved back. Nicola, trembling slightly, turned back to the bar. Lindy patted her hand consolingly.

"I said—vanish," said the voice behind them. Nicola watched through the bar mirror as the drunk backed away and walked carefully towards the door. He halted just before he left and shouted into the room:

"You're welcome to her, Sambo. Limey girls screw like boa constrictors."

Lindy clucked with annoyance.

"Take no notice," she whispered, as if there could be a danger of Nicola believing his words. Nicola felt sick.

"Where's the ladies room?" she asked Lindy.

" 'Round the back there, honey. Got a dancer on the door."

In the dark corridor leading to the toilets was a pay phone. Nicola stared at it for a full minute, fighting her nausea. She had a bedroom and a bathroom in Bel-Air waiting for her. She wanted nothing more at that moment than to lie down on that bed. Barbara or not. Regardless of the hostility, the chaos, and craziness in that house, there was a small space in it that was hers. To borrow. Until tomorrow. A shout of raucous laughter from the group she had been with convinced her. She fumbled for a dime.

To her relief, David answered the phone. He said they had been worried sick about her. He said come back quickly.

"I don't think I've got enough money for a cab," she said. "Will you stay up to pay for it?"

"A cab?" He sounded perplexed. "Isn't Jeff with you?"

"Jeff?"

Nicola stared stupidly into the phone.

"Hi," said a voice behind her and she turned and stared unbelievingly at Jeff.

She turned back to the phone, her mind whirling with alcohol and confusion.

"Yes," she said. "Yes, he's here."

"This way," Jeff said, as she hung up the phone.

She followed him down the corridor to a rear door and looked back once. There was a clear view of the bar (was this where Jeff had been?). Her previous companions still stood, talking less now, drinking steadily. Jeff said nothing to her as he drove efficiently to Bel-Air, but he did one small thing for, which Nicola was grateful. He pressed a button so that her window wound down slightly. Nicola breathed in the cool night air hungrily, praying that she would not vomit.

David opened the door of the house. Barbara stood a little behind him.

"I don't want to talk," said Nicola, making straight for the stairs. "I want to go straight to bed."

David stood back, his face concerned, but Barbara came over to her quickly and took her shoulders.

"One thing, honey. Just one. We've been worried out of our minds about you but that doesn't matter. What does matter is that I want you to ignore what I said. Forget it. It was bullshit. All of it. I loved your father and he treated me badly. I made myself believe he treated every woman badly. I *convinced myself* of all that stuff I told you. Forget it. Please."

Nicola looked into the pleading blue eyes. Like a window thrown open, a draft of icy air, the words had sobered her. Her head cleared. She believed Barbara—not now—but she believed that what Barbara had told her, all those hours ago, was the truth.

THIRTEEN

Nicola did not leave the next day because there seemed as little point in leaving as in staying. And staying was easier. She felt deeply depressed: a stultifying inertia left her unable to make a positive decision. She stayed in her room for most of the day, staring out the window, lying on the bed in an attempt to just sleep away the time, and finally smoking cigarette after cigarette.

She tried to read; attempted to note the women artists she should study at the Tempo exhibition; then threw down her pen and picked up the novel again.

In the late afternoon Barbara popped her head around the door. Nicola picked up her novel at once.

"Ah, you're reading," Barbara said brightly.

"Yes."

A silence. She could hear her stepmother's steady breathing.

"Have you eaten anything?"

"Not yet. Not hungry."

"Back in a moment."

Barbara disappeared and returned only a minute or two later with a plate of cheese sandwiches and a glass of milk. These, obviously, had already been prepared. Nicola looked at them without appetite.

"Thanks."

She wanted Barbara to leave but the older woman came into the room and stood looking at her.

"You feeling better, honey? After last night?"

"Yes, thank you."

Barbara stood unsurely, considering.

"Sweetheart, why don't you take a nap, get washed up later and come along to this party tonight?" she asked at last.

"Don't want to go to a party."

"You'll feel better."

"I won't."

"It won't do any good to sit here brooding."

"I am not brooding, for Christ's sake!"

Nicola picked up her novel deliberately and turned away. Barbara sighed loudly as she left the room. The moment the door closed Nicola put down the book and walked again to the window. The coral tree cast a weird, twisted shadow on the lawn in the late afternoon light. It was very still and close, and there seemed to be no sound at all outside. Unreal. She shook her head quickly then turned from the window.

"Feel like a zombie," she muttered.

There was a light tap on the door. Nicola ignored it.

"Nicola?" David's voice.

"What?"

The door opened and he came into the room, stood looking at her for awhile. She turned away so that he could not see her face.

"Are you talking to yourself?"

"Almost."

"Come on, come to this party. You can't sit here *almost* talking to yourself."

"Yes I can."

David came up behind her and gently stroked her hair.

"Look, you don't understand," Nicola began, wanting to explain how she felt but uncertain of how to do it. "I've lost my father."

"I understand that."

"No, you don't. Not lost him just because he's dead. Lost him altogether. All I thought he was."

"You mustn't believe that shit Barbara told you," said David angrily.

"But I do believe it. And I feel so horribly confused."

The words sounded pathetic even to her and she lapsed

104

into silence, staring out of the window. Should it matter this much, so many years later, why or how her mother had died? But it did matter. Because if her father hadn't cared that much about her mother, perhaps he had not really cared for his daughter. And, perhaps, he had not been the man she thought he was. Duped. Nicola shuddered and David put his hands on her shoulders.

"Come on. Let's go to a party," he said.

"What's the point?"

Nicola had never before seen a party quite like it. The Bel-Air house where it was held was enormous, pseudo-Georgian in style, and painted an unbelievable pink. She stared at it in amazement. The house had a large swimming pool, brightly lit with a canopy hung with paper streamers. Colored lights flashed in the trees, illuminating the faces of the guests.

There seemed to be hundreds of people there—some were inside the house dancing, some fully-dressed, half-dressed, or completely naked were in or around the pool.

Nicola was wearing a long cotton dress, very simple in style, and she felt immediately out of place. Most of the women were wearing denim jeans, bikinis, or exotic feather and fur creations. She paused to watch this array of color and contrast.

"How do you like the waiters?" asked David.

She looked. The dozen or so waiters, most of them bearing trays laden with drinks, were dressed as penguins. Black and white stumpy creatures, the outfits mysteriously affected the way they moved—they *walked* like penguins.

"Good grief," said Nicola.

"Let's find us a drink," Barbara suggested.

Nicola had a number of drinks before the numbing affect of alcohol, tiredness, and tedious conversation caught up with her, and the visual shocks caused by the extravaganza wore off. She looked for Barbara, couldn't find her, and flopped down onto a chaise lounge by the pool. Within minutes she was joined by two bronzed young men who, without saying a word, passed a hand-rolled cigarette between themselves and then to Nicola. She puffed it lazily, recognizing the distinctive, pungent aroma even before she put the cigarette to her lips.

"This is going to send me to sleep," she said to the surprised young men and determinedly got to her feet. The pool seemed to be swaying slightly. Eventually, she found Barbara.

Her stepmother was flanked by two graying men and involved in a long, laughter-interrupted story. Nicola waited until the laughter had subsided before touching Barbara's arm lightly.

"Barbara is that driver chap around? I want to go home."

Barbara narrowed her eyes and looked around the room.

"He should be . . . somewhere. Yes, there he is."

Jeff was standing on the periphery of the party, near some bushes, smoking and watching, as apart from the party as he could be without distance. Looking at him Nicola was half glad when Barbara insisted she stay—and backed up her insistence by selecting a dance partner for Nicola.

"Alan!" she shouted across the room, after a cursory glance around at all the available men. Alan bowed and came over.

"Meet Nicola. Nick Graham's daughter. Fresh from the old country."

Alan smiled hello.

"She feels like dancing," said Barbara. "I know you think you're good at it."

"Me? I was the understudy for Fred Astaire."

Nicola smiled, allowed him to lead her to the dancing area and, watching his dance movements carefully, began to copy them. Easy. Just shimmering and shaking. She looked across the room and caught David watching her. He had an arm around a tall brunette wearing a low-cut, diaphanous gown. His fingers traced the neckline of the scarlet dress. Nicola looked away quickly.

Margie was an old friend David had bedded briefly at a time when she was in hot pursuit of one of the richest movie men in town. She'd gotten him eventually but he hadn't left his wife and Margie's way of getting back at him, when her lover was attending the same parties with his wife, was to flirt outrageously with all her old flames. It was David's turn and he was quite enjoying it. Even Barbara, knowing the facts, treated Margie with the friendliness awarded to a woman who was no serious threat.

He watched Nicola involving herself in the dancing while he enjoyed the texture of the soft upper-breast under his fingertips.

"Why don't we just split," said Margie, softly. "We're doing nothing."

"Told you sweetheart. I can't."

"Come on. My place."

David removed his hand and kissed her lips lightly.

"Another time."

"Now," said Margie, but without force.

"Sweetheart, you're beautiful. But I have commitments."

"You got a feathered nest, dummy," said Margie lightly. "That what you mean?"

David caught her look and grinned.

"So what's yours, honey? What's old Lenny doing for you?"

"Not enough," said Margie.

They laughed together.

"I'm betting his wife says that too," said David, catching sight of the man in question dancing with his wife.

"What does she care?" said Margie, suddenly miserable. "She wouldn't recognize his cock if she saw it again."

"He says."

"O.K. He says. Let's dance then."

"In awhile," said David. Nicola was now dancing with a measure of expertise and extroversion. David guessed that she'd had a lot to drink. "Let's just stand here and watch the people awhile."

"What's there to see in these dummies," said Margie.

There is Nicola to watch, thought David. In the flashing strobe lights she looked ephemeral, as if she could simply vanish at any moment. She is beautiful, he considered, in a way quite unlike any woman I've ever seen. No California sparkle. A soft, dreamy quality. And intelligence in the wide eyes. And, last night such pain in them. Vindictive

Barbara. He had come very close to hitting her for causing such pain. David knew little about Barbara's life with Nicholas Graham. He had sensed though, many times, that it had not been a happy one. He hoped he could convince Nicola that *anything* that Barbara said about her father should be ignored.

Nicola was smiling now at the antics of her dancing partner, and David with an effort looked away. You don't have the time nor the need for bird-watching, Leyton, he told himself sternly. You've enough on your plate as it is.

He sighed and removed his hand from Margie's shoulder.

"On a list of priorities, people have to come last," he said.

Maggie raised an eyebrow.

"Leyton's Law," he explained.

"Doesn't sound like Leyton's Law to me," said Margie. "Sounds like Bullshit."

He laughed.

"Could be."

Nicola woke suddenly, full of dread. Her head was pounding. The strong sunlight behind the billowing drapes indicated that it was late, midday perhaps. But the house was quiet. A sound disturbed her, a soft snoring and she looked instinctively, uneasily, to the other side of the large bed. The top of a dark, male head was visible, the face turned away from her. Christ. The party. Who was he?

She searched back through half-remembered incidents. She certainly couldn't remember coming home. Couldn't remember leaving the party. But . . . she had been dancing with Alan. Yes. Someone had told her fortune. A crazy man dressed like an Indian seer with a fake accent.

"You are strong. You are hurt. But you will be strong again. You, too, can destroy."

"Just like my father."

Had she said that? Yes, that she remembered. But Barbara had appeared then, staring down at the Indian with contempt.

"Still churning out the crap, Sinbad."

"Fuck you, Barbara," he had said, in clear Californian. Some fortuneteller.

The body in the bed stirred slightly. Who the devil was he? After Sinbad—more dancing? Or had the dancing been earlier? David had been dancing with a tarty brunette. Blank. She remembered looking for her handbag. Was that to come home? Or for a cigarette? And smoking someone's pipe. God. She lay very still in the bed, afraid to disturb whoever it was who slept next to her. After some minutes he turned to face her and smiled.

"Morning, Nicola."

Was he Alan? Alan had been dark-haired, surely. Yes. Must be.

"Morning . . . Alan?" He frowned. "You're not Alan are you?"

"No. I am not."

He sounded angry. She couldn't blame him.

"I was dancing with Alan."

"You were. You came home with me."

Nicola, rigid at her end of the bed, struggled for words.

"I'm afraid I was pretty smashed," she said. An apology of sorts. Or an excuse.

"Weren't we all," he said, and reached for her.

Nicola stiffened. She moved away, her heart thumping. He sat up in the bed, looking affronted. A dark, attractive young man, brown hair and eyes, a broad chest with thick curling hair. Familiar but unknown.

"Freeze out, eh?"

There was just a touch of humor in his voice that lightened the words.

"Didn't have little scruples like that last night."

She swallowed. She had to know for sure.

"Did I . . . Did we . . ." she began.

"Fuck? Certainly did. You were great. You give good head."

"What?"

She had never heard the expression. Her cheeks flushed as she guessed what it meant.

"Forget it," he said, looking at his watch.

He climbed out of bed quickly and began to dress.

109

"I've got to split," he said.

Nicola watched him for a moment or two then slid down under the bedcovers, pulling the sheet over her face. She felt that she should be ashamed, but she was mostly embarrassed.

"You hiding?"

His voice was friendly enough. Nicola emerged and, looking at him, caught a flash of sympathy in his eyes.

"You passed out, baby. Last night." he said.

Nicola nodded, relieved.

"I thought that maybe this morning you might feel different," he looked at her questioningly, then shook his head. "But I guess not."

"No," said Nicola. "Sorry."

"See you," he said and was gone.

Nicola pulled back the sheet and stared at the ceiling. I have certainly never done that before, she thought. Attempted to sleep with a total stranger. And if I hadn't passed out . . . who knows? But does it matter? *Should* it matter? Men did it, and many women did it, and no one much cared. A way, perhaps, to hold back the dark, help us all make it through the night. To be comforted. She had never needed that sort of comfort before.

But what the hell, she thought wryly, was his name?

She heard voices downstairs just before the door slammed and her mystery lover left. The voices continued. David and Barbara were obviously up, had seen her visitor leave. But then they must have known last night. What the hell had happened? She lay for a while, frantically trying to put the pieces of the night together. A tap on the door and Barbara, holding a cup of coffee, jokingly made a tiptoe entrance

"Hi, sweetheart. How's the head?"

"Fussy," said Nicola and groaned. "Fuzzy, rather."

"Aspirin?"

"Later."

Nicola tried to sit up and with a soft moan sank back onto the pillows.

"Christ," she said.

"No big consolation," said Barbara. "But David thinks

he's got five minutes to live. I think I died in the night. This vision you see is my spirit."

Nicola smiled weakly. Barbara was trying to be nice again. As she had been yesterday. Nicola had no idea why her attitude had changed since those terrible revelations at the dinner table. Perhaps Barbara felt genuine sympathy, or sorrow for the pain she had caused, deliberate or not. But Nicola felt intuitively that the explanation for her stepmother's sudden kindness had something to do with David. Nicola had to force herself to respond with equal friendliness: her feelings towards her stepmother were still ambivalent.

"Drink some coffee and have a long shower," said Barbara now. "Then we're all going to check out the Tempo gallery for your little article. How's that sound?"

"Sounds great," said Nicola. "But can I make it?"

"Sure, you'll make it."

The Tempo gallery was small, brightly-lit, but empty and echoing. Nicola studied the pictures and catalogue carefully, taking notes as she did so. David wandered around the small room looking at pictures while Barbara chatted to the owner.

"His daughter," Nicola heard her say. "So like him. Talented, too."

David glanced at Nicola. He had been rather reserved all day (disapproval of her behavior last night? Was that possible with a man like David?) but now, he smiled. Nicola smiled back.

The three had an early dinner in a smart Beverly Hills restaurant that seemed to Nicola more like a social club than a place to eat. Barbara seemed to know everyone in the room and table-hopped continuously; bringing people back to meet Nicola, ushering David towards gallery owners and those who were, or knew, art critics. She's like some frenzied social secretary, thought Nicola during a short hiatus, but how she enjoys it. To her own surprise she found, as she sipped her champagne, that in a remote way she was almost enjoying it, too.

FOURTEEN

A few days later David swan in the pool while Nicola, her typewriter on a small table she had dragged out from the lounge, sat in the sun on the patio finishing her gallery piece.

He had put in a full morning's work—some sketches, some crucial work on a major oil—and he was feeling satisfied with himself and deserving of the break he was now enjoying. The water was warm, the sun, though it was late afternoon, was still hot in the sky. He dived underwater and emerged to the staccato sound of Nicola still typing. Her hair was loose, flowing below her shoulders and a strand fell over her face. She pushed it away impatiently. David floated on his back.

"Come on. You don't know what you're missing," he shouted.

"I haven't got *time*," said Nicola, without looking up.

"Screw time—come try the water."

Nicola shook her head and the clatter of the typewriter continued. David watched her bowed head as he floated on the water. Then, on impulse, he quietly swam to the side of the pool, crept out, and sneaked up behind her. She shrieked when he first touched her, and struggled frantically as he lifted her in his arms. With a tarzan cry he jumped, still holding her, into the pool.

"Bastard!" Nicola screamed, splashing furiously.

David dived underwater out of her range, then when he saw she was swimming swiftly and strongly to the side of the pool, came up under her and grabbed her legs. She

113

fought him and he quickly let go and turned away. Somehow she jumped on his back. He swam, panting hard, carrying his slender cargo to the side. He helped her up onto the steps and she sat, breathing heavily, pulling her hair away from her eyes.

"You monster," she said, smiling despite herself.

David was watching her admiringly. The wet T-shirt clung to her firm breasts, the nipples clearly visible; the normally tight jeans, another layer of skin. He took a deep breath then whistled softly.

"Wow," he said. "Just like a cigar ad."

Nicola looked into his eyes, amused, and as he found himself reaching for her she put one slender foot into his chest and knocked him back into the water. He cursed out of habit rather than anger as he bobbed back to the surface, spewing water into the air. Nicola was back at her chair, fumbling for the towel. He stepped out of the pool and approached her menacingly.

"You'll suffer for this, missy," he said in his best Boris Karloff voice. Nicola cringed, smiling, holding the towel against herself.

"Don't you dare . . ."

"Dare?" said David, softly. "Dare what?"

As he reached her, she backed away giggling. With a flourish he pulled the towel away from her and at the same time pulled her towards him. She felt soft and damp in his arms. Tiny, as if should he hug her too hard her body would melt into his. She had lifted her face and was watching him seriously—that solemn look! She was so unsure of him. Maybe she had reason. He kissed her gently. She did not pull away but the kiss was too soon over and when he released her she stood very still, her eyes holding his. David was disconcerted. He had kissed many women lightly, a few seriously, and here he could not tell the difference and she wasn't going to help him. He led her by the hand back to her chair and, as a distraction, held up the typed sheets she had been working on.

"Work?" he asked her.

She looked at him doubtfully.

"Why are you doing it?" he asked her. "Is it important? To your job, I mean."

She thought for a moment.

"Not really. It's an extra, I suppose."

"You should be enjoying the sun. Relaxing. Enjoying yourself."

There was silence for a moment.

"Oh, what the hell," she said finally. "Screw it."

He held up the notes for a few seconds watching her face, then he held them over the pool. When she smiled, giving the slightest of nods, he dropped the notes and the typed sheets into the water. Nicola moved to watch the paper floating, gradually disintegrating. She said nothing. He put a hand on her shoulder watching with her when, startling them both, Barbara's voice boomed behind them.

"Been balling around some?" she asked.

David felt Nicola stiffen and he kept his arm deliberately around her shoulders, turning her around slightly to face Barbara.

"Hi, toots," he said casually.

"What's going on?" The voice was light but her eyes were bright and hard.

"Poor Nicola fell into the pool—notes and all."

"I did not fall into the pool," said Nicola harshly, moving away from his arm. "I was pushed."

Nicola sat back down at her typewriter. Barbara smiled then at Nicola's anger. Her eyes meeting David's were amused.

"Notes too. Sad," she said, patting David's cheek affectionately. "Naughty boy."

Barbara stood next to him and looked down at the disintegrated paper in the pool.

"When work is done—or drowned in this case—it's time to boogie. Why don't you children change your clothes?"

The disco was one which David particularly disliked and Barbara loved. He saw it as the gathering place for the most pretentious of the Beverly Hills/Bell-Air monied and careless. Barbara enjoyed it because she knew just about

115

everyone there and because the clientele, unlike that of the other discos, was made up of all age groups.

"It's the only goddamn disco that doesn't make me feel like a freaky geriatric," she'd said once.

She also secretly enjoyed, he suspected, the proximity to those involved in the film world—a few directors, producers, and actors were members—though the entertainment industry was one she affected to despise. She was having a ball tonight, he thought. She had danced with a few old flames, greeted just about everyone in the room and was now having a rest period in order, he guessed, to catch up on the many drinks littering the table. She was chatting to Nicola.

David stretched back in his chair and yawned, enduring a boredom that even watching the dancing super-chicks couldn't dispell. He caught fragments of the conversations going on at tables nearby:

"He's a Leo, honey. It's obvious."

"Annie? A head full of sheepdip, but wow, those boobs."

"I told him. Talk to my friggin' agent will ya. I don't have time to play around with *breakfast* meetings."

David sighed inwardly, sipped his drink and turned back to the two women.

"You like him, honey?" Barbara was asking Nicola.

"Who?"

"Jason—that guy you were dancing with."

"Seemed nice enough."

"Because I'll tell you something, honey," said Barbara leaning forward. "That guy has the biggest dong you ever saw in your life. It's this long . . ." she made a graphic "big fish" gesture. "And this thick!"

David grinned. Christ, she was incorrigible. Nicola was laughing.

"Bring him back," she said.

David had danced only once with Nicola and then in virtual silence. She seemed shy of him since the play-acting at the pool. But was it play-acting? He didn't know himself. He knew that he found her attractive. Intriguing. But his feelings were controllable. He hoped. He had all he needed for the moment with Barbara, and Nicola was too sweet to play games with. Nevertheless . . .

"Dance?" he said to both women, casually.

"Sure," said Barbara standing up. Nicola smiled, her eyes following them to the dance floor. He watched her covertly over Barbara's shoulder. Some guy with a health-and-wealth golden tan and a mouthful of expensive teeth had sat next to her. She was laughing. Flirting? As a strobe light picked out some of the audience David recognized the young man—Don Elliott. That prick, thought David contemptuously. Nicola, now smiling sweetly, was looking into Don Elliott's eyes. She *is* flirting, thought David with a jolt.

By the time David and Barbara returned to the table Don had his arm around Nicola's shoulder. Barbara, noting this, smiled.

"I suppose you've introduced yourselves," she said cheekily.

"Sure we have, Barbara," said Don.

David nodded to him and sat down. It could be a long, long evening. Barbara had turned her full attention and high voltage charm on Don. Temporarily, David knew, just to welcome him to the family. The silly bitch. He was relieved when a neatly dressed, graying woman came shyly to the table to claim her attention.

"Barbara, how are you?" said the woman, softly.

"Well, hi to you," said Barbara. "How are you, hon?"

"I'm just fine."

"Nice to see you around again. It's been a long time."

"Yes," the woman smiled nervously. "Thank you."

"And looking so well."

There was a note in Barbara's voice David didn't like. He turned, frowning.

"You look just marvelous, honey. Marvelous. Well, nice to see you." Barbara had dismissed her. The woman hesitated, then turned away.

"That is the most boring woman in the world," said Barbara loudly to Nicola. "Like being in a fucking morgue talking to her."

The woman had turned quickly, colored, and began to hurry away. Obviously she had heard. Barbara continued regardless:

"She went crazy last year. Completely flipped her lid. They've just let her out of the funny farm. And that don't please her husband none. He'd rather they kept her. He likes little girls. Young 'uns."

"Barbara!" said Nicola, horrified. "She heard you."

David turned away. He had seen this act too many times to be embarrassed by it. It still made him angry.

"Shit, so she heard me," said Barbara. "So what? Come on, Nicola. You turn into a boring bitch and they'll be taking *you* away to the funny farm."

Nicola smiled very slightly and turned back to Don. Barbara glanced at David.

"You're quiet," she said accusingly.

"That's because I'm not saying much," said David, yawning.

"Poor little boy bored, is he?"

"Out of my mind."

Barbara, obviously annoyed, was about to speak when Nicola and Don stood and said good night. They were going somewhere for supper. Barbara smiled, kissed them both elaborately as if giving a necessary blessing. David stood, shook hands with Don quickly, then turned to Nicola. She held out her hand. He took it, held it gently, thought what the hell, and kissed it. Her eyes, amused, met his for just a moment then she turned away. Barbara and David watched the couple as they eased through the crowd towards the door. Don was leading Nicola by the hand.

"She learns *fast*," said Barbara admiringly.

"Maybe too fast." David tried to keep his voice light, knew he had failed.

"Are you kidding?" Barbara was incredulous. "That guy's worth a couple of million."

"He's a jackass."

"So what the hell difference does that make?"

FIFTEEN

Nicola was restless for days after that night with Don. Sex with a stranger, she discovered, need not be a painful experience nor an embarrassing one. It passes time, it leaves little space for too much introspection. The body can be involved while the mind stays numb.

But Don—he was such a boring stranger; his conversation was hip and empty, and his vanity, though at first amusing, quickly became tiresome. He had carefully brushed his hair with her hairbrush before getting into bed, had admired himself for a long time in her mirror then asked her what she thought of his body. She had said she thought it a very attractive body. Later, he had asked what she thought of his performance. Nicola thought it had been professionally proficient. But she said it had been marvelous. Later, she realized that he had said not one word, complimentary or otherwise, about her body, nor commented, favorably or unfavorably, about her "performance."—which no doubt lacked the expertise he was used to in this promiscuous city.

There was a certain life-style to be enjoyed here, she realized. An escapist, hedonistic life which possibly, just possibly, she could grow to like. A life-style to get lost in. But she needed more amusing people. She resolved to find them.

She had two weeks left and had done little work except her father's exhibition and the piece on women artists. She remembered the Clyfford Still notes floating on the pool and smiled wryly. The stifling sense of responsibility to her

119

job, so strong in London, seemed irrelevant here. She felt that she need not feel responsible to anyone. Not even to that self she had thought was herself. There were dimensions of herself she had never explored. She wondered why she had never taken chances before.

At quiet moments it occurred to her that mostly she did not want to go back to London. London was where her father had lived. London was where she had grieved for a man she had loved deeply and possibly never known.

Nicola began a social campaign. For the first time she attended a party alone. David and Barbara, surprisingly, felt like an evening at home. The party, given by a respected insurance broker, was in Beverly Hills and was well attended. After her rather nervous entrance and the first uncomfortable five minutes, Nicola relaxed. It was not difficult. People introduced themselves to her casually. If her glass was empty someone invariably would ask to get her a drink. She stayed only a short time with any particular group, moving around the room, exploring, talking.

At the end of the evening four fairly successful men had her telephone number and she had met Pete Fletcher.

He was very, very drunk and caught her as she tried to move past him on the stairs.

"You," he said accusingly, "are wearing pantyhose."

"So what?" asked Nicola, coldly.

"California gals don't wear those anymore."

"I'm not a California gal, I'm afraid. Now, please excuse me."

"Hey, don't be *afraid*. I love 'em. Love to take 'em off. Not as nice as stockings, of course. In the old pics . . ."

"Excuse *me*," said Nicola, crossly, pushing past him.

He held her tightly. He was grinning.

"What's your number, tiger? I'd like to take you out."

"None of your business. Now, if you don't mind . . ."

He held her, studying her angry face, then seeming to sober up a little, stood back. He took a card from his pocket and held it out.

"Then you call me, baby."

When she made no move to take the card he unsnapped her purse quickly and slid it inside.

120

"See you," he said, moving back into the party.

As Nicola took her wrap from the bed upstairs she caught an older woman watching her with an amused smile.

"I see you got entangled by young Pete," said the woman.

"Lout," said Nicola.

"He can be. Indeed he can. Strange, considering his family . . ."

Nicola looked up.

"His family?"

The woman smiled at her.

"His father's Alvin Fletcher. You know? The studio . . ."

Nicola had heard of Alvin Fletcher. The president of one of the biggest studios in town and a very rich man.

"They should have taught him manners," said Nicola.

"I think they tried," said the woman, as she left the bedroom.

Nicola, alone, opened her handbag and found the card Fletcher had given her. A Westwood address and telephone number. No mention of profession or occupation. Very carefully she slid the card inside her address book.

Then she picked up her coat and left the party.

Studying herself in the mirror the next morning she wondered whether a few more hours sleep might have been more sensible. She had shadows under her eyes and though she had a little color now and her hair had been bleached by the sun she looked, she decided, English. Primly English. She would have to do something about that.

She took a taxi to the gallery, knowing she was late to meet Barbara for lunch. Ten precious minutes had been spent looking for Jeff who had taken the Cadillac somewhere. The gallery was almost empty; a few viewers gazing at paintings with the usual hushed reverence. Nicola walked briskly through, ignoring the paintings. There was no sign of Barbara. Nicola made for the desk at the end of the gallery where a young girl sat, writing into a ledger.

The girl smiled brightly: "Hello. How are you today?"

"Fine. Is Mrs. Hampton-Norde in?"

"She's at lunch," said the girl. "Can I help you?"

"Do you know where she's eating? I promised to come in earlier but I overslept."

The girl's bright smile returned.

"I guess you're Nicola, right?"

At a nod from Nicola the girl produced a note, written in Barbara's large, sprawling handwriting. It was cryptic and to the point.

"Lazy bitch. We're at Joe's. Two blocks."

Nicola grinned and thanked the girl.

"You're welcome," said the Smile.

Near the door Nicola noticed a large painting she had never seen before. A woman in a long, cotton nightgown, brushing her hair before a mirror. A fair, pale young woman with a wistful beauty. Nicola stopped. Her mother. Unmistakably. She had never seen a painting of her mother but she had seen photographs. That shy yearning, almost a central sadness, came through in photographs too. But not as powerfully as this. A picture painted with love? Hell, it couldn't have been.

"Incredible sensitivity," said a woman's voice beside her.

"Yes," said Nicola, still gazing at the picture.

"A great man."

Nicola said nothing and felt the woman turn to look at her.

"Oh, excuse me," said the woman. "But aren't you his daughter."

"No." The word came easily.

"I thought you were. At the opening I saw . . ."

"I'm not her," said Nicola sharply, surprised at her own anger.

"Well you *look* like her."

It was almost an accusation. Nicola turned to leave hurriedly but not before she caught a glimpse of the face of the girl at the desk. The smile had turned to a puzzled frown. And if I am her, Nicola thought on the sunlit street, I won't *look* like her much longer.

Barbara and David were sitting in a booth at the restaurant.

"At last . . ." began Barbara.

"Sorry, sorry. And I can't stay even now. I've got this appointment and they said they could only do it right away."

Nicola enjoyed the curious expressions on both their faces.

"Do what right away?" asked Barbara.

"Just a little whim I had. Impulse. Anyway, I could be back in around two hours."

"Honey, we could still be here. We plan on having a quiet afternoon, seeing a few friends and drinking tea."

Barbara lifted her glass of scotch delicately.

"Tea for you?"

"Wish I could, but no time."

David handed her his glass.

"Have this one."

Nicola smiled at him, took a long swallow, then handed the glass back.

"I'll check just in case when I come out."

"Have fun," said David.

"Well, it might be fun. Then again it might not," she said as she prepared to hurry away. Barbara and David exchanged a puzzled look and Barbara gave a how-should-I-know shrug as he raised an eyebrow. Nicola smiled and hurried out.

The hairdressing salon was one of the most prestigious in Beverly Hills and Nicola sat uncomfortably under a vast potted palm waiting her turn and debating in her mind what sort of style, or cut, she wanted. In any event, she had little choice; the slender-hipped young man had his own ideas. He asked her simply what sort of image she wanted. Nicola thought for awhile.

"Christ, I'm not really sure. Up-to-date, I suppose. Sophisticated. No—casual-sophisticated. Wild-sophisticated," she finished helplessly.

He nodded as if she had made perfect sense and began working. Two hours later Nicola studied herself in the mirror. He had given her hair a light perm, cut it into a halo round her head and given it a weak, henna dye. She loved it.

Her head felt lighter as she swung down Rodeo Drive. When she caught sight of her own image in a shop window she started, then felt immediately pleased with herself. Nice change. A very nice change.

In the restaurant, David sat alone, sipping his drink. She hoped he wouldn't recognize her until she actually reached the table but he glanced up at her, looked away, and then looked back—double-taking the new Nicola. She smiled.

"Wow, what can I say?" asked David when she reached the table.

"Like it?"

"Love it. Just right for you."

"Should be at the price they charged. Still. Where's Barbara?"

"Had one of those impressive phone calls and swept out looking important. A gallery."

"Is she coming back?" asked Nicola.

"Maybe. But we won't be here."

Nicola settling back in her chair paused for a moment. "We won't?"

David left her waiting for an answer while he beckoned the waiter and ordered drinks.

"No," he said finally. "Because we're going home."

Nicola studied him, feeling a little out of her depth and not wanting to appear so.

"Barbara might be at home."

"So," said David cheerfully. "We can all play together." Nicola, unsure of what to say, looked at him nervously. He laughed at her expression.

"I promised to teach you backgammon. Today's a good day."

Nicola smiled with relief. He leaned forward.

"So what did you think I meant?" he asked, and gently kissed her on the mouth. A casual kiss, but it left her lips feeling slightly bruised. Nicola looked away and caught a woman across the restaurant looking at David with that thoughtful, measuring look that all women recognize. Unaware of this admiring appraisal, David strode out. Nicola followed.

* * *

124

They played backgammon with a childish competitiveness, each crowing and groaning at every toss of the dice. Nicola, after a shaky start, won two games in a row and swept the counters off the board with a flourish.

"Gotchya!" she cried.

"You've played before."

"Of course I haven't."

"Well, you're good."

"Beginner's luck," said Nicola soothingly.

"Maybe. Another game?"

Nicola took a sip of the cold white wine he had poured for them both and looked at him over the rim of her glass.

"Is that what you want?" she asked, her eyes holding his. "I didn't really believe you. You know—backgammon."

He didn't reply at once.

"No, well I guess . . ." he stopped. "It wasn't what I really wanted."

"What did you really want?" she asked softly.

"You."

For a moment they were silent.

"So?" said Nicola. Her breath caught in her throat.

He glanced away for a second then looked back at her.

"So, I copped out. You seem . . . you seem more difficult. No, different now. As you are now."

"Try me," she said, after a moment. She sensed a struggle in him.

"I am scared," he admitted, at last. "Of caring too much for you."

"We're both much too sensible for *that*," stated Nicola.

She knew as soon as he touched her, such a gentle stroking warmth on her face, arms, shoulders, that she wanted him as much as he wanted her. Not, this time, sex with a stranger. The difference that affection makes.

David undressed her slowly, murmuring as he kissed her warm skin. She clung to him, her face hidden against his shoulder, until her clothes lay in a heap on the floor. He began to ease her towards the bed and she moved quickly out of his arms, and lay down on top of the sheets, waiting for him to remove his own clothes. He undressed quickly, his eyes never leaving her.

"You are very beautiful," he said softly, coming at last to lie beside her.

Then he froze. She heard it seconds after he did. The sound of a car coming up the driveway. Instinctively, Nicola rolled under the light sheet, pulling it up to her chin, a cold fear swamping her. David was at the window in moments.

"Barbara?" asked Nicola in a whisper.

"Jeff, in the Cad. Jesus. She has the Mer today."

Nicola sighed with relief and he returned to the bed but the previous loving warmth had gone, leaving only a sharp excitement. He stroked her body urgently, entered her too soon. Nicola hid her face against his arm but he turned her head slightly so that he could look at her. His eyes looking into hers as their bodies moved swiftly, compulsively together.

"Sweet Nicola," he said. So close like this his face looked younger. Softer. A beautiful face.

It was over too quickly for her but she moaned a little out of kindness and clung to him, burying her face in his soft dark hair.

They lay for a minute or two, still clasped tightly together, then he lifted his head, looked down into her face and smiled.

"Next time," he said, "it will be slower and fantastic. But Christ, I wanted you so badly. It wasn't too fast . . . ?"

She smiled, reassuring him.

"It wasn't too fast and it was fantastic."

He stroked her face.

"You're not sorry?"

"No. But . . ."

She could not finish the sentence. She had little idea of what she wanted to say. Not this? Not you? Not yet? A vague sense of mistakes being made. Of opportunities as yet unexplored.

"But? But . . . Barbara?"

His voice was gentle.

"Something like that," she said. "For you too."

"We can sort it out. I feel . . ."

She stopped him, horrified at herself, but feeling the words must be said.

"I don't want to know how you feel. I don't think we should sort it out . . . yet. If we ever have to sort it out. Let's . . . leave it for the moment," she concluded lamely.

David was frowning.

"O.K.," he said. "If that's what you want."

Nicola got out of bed quickly.

"Where are you going?" he asked.

"Shower."

He lit a cigarette and watched her sadly.

"You don't waste much time, do you?" he said, with a trace of bitterness.

Nicola wanted to go back to bed, to hold him tightly, and be held by him, but she stopped herself. He was angry at her flippancy, she knew. Hurt, perhaps, too. But David, like her father, was ambitious. He needed Barbara. As for me, she told herself miserably, I need . . . other things. More than he has. More than he'll ever have. She clenched her hands and tried to speak lightly.

"There's a party tonight, remember," she said. "And Barbara will be back soon. So—shower."

When she came back into the bedroom, he was gone.

In the aqua tiled bathroom attached to the master bedroom David turned on the shower taps as hard as they would go. Under a violent cascade of water he scrubbed away the traces of Nicola's perfume that still clung to his skin.

"Goddamnit," he shouted, aloud. "She is fucking up my *life*."

And his stomach contracted with so strong an emotion he did not know if it was pleasure or pain.

SIXTEEN

This party, thought Jerry, has all the desperation of Prohibition days—will the booze still be here tomorrow?—and none of the fun. He wondered, as he did at every one of Barbara's parties, why he had bothered to come. He didn't drink much, hated dope, couldn't dance, and had given up casual sexual encounters years ago—as soon as his law practice started flourishing, in fact. Must still be hoping though, he considered, some subliminal optimism propels me to gatherings such as these in the hope that . . . what? Some young man? Some experience that may change my life? Something that might give *meaning* to my life? He sighed and went in search of some food before the caterers cleared the lot away.

He caught sight of the henna-tinted hair on the other side of the room. What on earth had made her do it? Her blonde hair had been so pretty. And that freaky hairstyle. He had not had a chance to speak to Nicola so far and he promised himself he would do that as soon as he had gotten some food inside him. She was certainly putting some energy into that dance. She had been dancing with various young men most of the evening.

After half a lobster tail, some French bread, and a mouthful of fresh fruit salad, Jerry felt more party-minded. Nicola was still leaping around and Jerry, exhausted by the sight, settled down on the long sofa to watch her. After awhile he began to feel uneasy: there was something unsettling about the way she moved; a conscious abandon that was not—or was it?—natural to her. Once he heard her laugh—loudly. It depressed him. She must have been aware of his scrutiny for when the dance was over she came over immediately, flopping down onto the sofa.

"Jerry, what a crazy party!"

"Enjoying it?"

"It's fun."

He shrugged.

"Isn't it?"

There was a thickness in her voice he put down to the evening's alcohol, but something else, too—an insistence.

"God, I don't know," said Jerry.

She frowned, irritated, and his heart sank.

"If you're not enjoying it, Jerry, why not go home?"

She patted his cheek then. It was almost flirtatious as gestures go, but meaningless. She was playing the role for herself, not for him. Obscurely, he sensed a trace of something like panic in her.

"Why don't *you* go home?" he asked gently.

"Home? I don't have a home."

"You have a home and a life to lead in London. And what about your job?"

"The job can wait."

Jerry stared at her for a moment.

"I think I'd like a new life to lead in any case," she said with a grin.

"Like this? This nonsense? It's a sham."

"No, Jerry. Wrong. The old life was a sham. Now, come on, sourface. Let's dance."

Had this been anyone else Jerry would have refused, politely, of course. But Nicola had gotten to her feet and had a firm hold on his hand. She was laughing but for a second or two her eyes met his and he saw that same panic in them. He stood up, unsure of why he felt so profoundly uneasy.

Nicola danced with the same abandon as before. Jerry, who had no idea what he was supposed to do, jogged hopefully from one foot to the other and felt utterly foolish. After one number he groaned:

"No more, Nicola. No more."

"Jerry, you can't be tired. You've hardly moved. You just stood there and swayed a bit."

"No more, I insist. Let's sit it out and talk for awhile."

Nicola kissed his cheek lightly.

"You sit it out."

She whirled away. Minutes later she was dancing with a fair-haired actor. Jerry returned to his sofa. He watched Barbara and David smooching around the floor to the long, tedious record. Barbara had her eyes closed. Sleeping off a little of the scotch, thought Jerry maliciously. David stared over her shoulder. Looks worried, Jerry opined to himself and no wonder with that barracuda around his neck, but who or what is he staring at so sadly? Jerry turned to look. Nicola.

Of course. It looks as if we have a mild case of infatuation here, thought Jerry. A little later he realized that the case was not so mild. He saw David tap Nicola's shoulder in an invitation to dance. She turned, looked at David, then the party-girl smile faded. Her eyes quickly scanned the room. Why she did this was clear to Jerry: she was locating Barbara. Her stepmother was dancing, flamboyantly as usual, on the other side of the room. Nicola nodded, moved towards David, and at that moment the music stopped. The two looked at each other. The Beach Boys were replaced by Roberta Flack's "The First Time Ever I Saw Your Face." Nicola stopped dead, shrugged her shoulders oddly and turned away from David. Jerry, across the room, could feel his pain. The young man stood awkwardly, then turned and strode out towards the bar.

No one else seemed to have noticed anything, but to Jerry the situation was as clear as if the two of them had written their feelings in large red letters on the lounge wall.

They have made love already, he thought. There has been, there is still and even if she is running from it, something physical between them. Now that could mean trouble from the Grande Dame.

The Grande Dame, in fact, came over to Jerry just when he was planning to leave.

"Jerry, darling, I actually saw you dancing. I was overcome with admiration. Such grace! Such style! Who would have believed it."

"All right Barbara. Unlike you, I've never considered grace one of my attributes."

She grinned.

"I never thought I would see the day. Nicola must have used some pretty powerful persuasion."

"Brute force," said Jerry smiling.

"She can be forceful, can't she," mused Barbara. "Who would have thought it. Doesn't she look cute though, with that hair?"

"I think it looks awful," said Jerry.

"You would. The young guys like it, though. That's what matters."

"Is that what matters to Nicola?"

Barbara shrugged.

"At this point I couldn't say exactly. But it looks as if what matters to Nicola is gelt."

"Gelt?"

"Money. Cash. *Gelt*. She's not stupid. She's not going to waste her time with losers. She could get it all. And good for her."

Barbara watched her stepdaughter for a while.

"But the sooner the better," she added.

Jerry did not ask her what she meant by this. Barbara's expression had changed, the old hard look returned.

"I don't want her hanging around much longer," she said, and began to walk away.

This was a normal thing with Barbara. When a conversation bored her she would simply turn and go find somebody else to talk with. Never a good-bye or any of the usual parting excuses. This time, however, she stopped and came back to Jerry.

"Remember what I told you," she said. "Keep your mouth shut about my affairs."

Jerry was furious.

"Goddamn you," he said. "You know I don't discuss your fucking affairs."

"Good," said Barbara and turned on her heel. He was dismissed. Jerry fumed inwardly and poured himself a large drink. He took a couple of mouthfuls then put it down again. His own large, comfortable, quiet house, just ten minutes away, seemed like some haven he should never have left. He wanted to get back to it—fast.

He was unlocking the doors of his Cadillac when he saw Nicola silhouetted against the lighted doorway. She was with a young man Jerry knew vaguely. Yes, Blanche's son . . . Anthony. And Anthony, Jerry remembered, was married to Dick Starling's daughter. Jerry knew that for certain because he had attended the wedding—a large, ostentatious affair. Jerry watched Nicola drive off with Anthony, then sighed. He drove home feeling very tired and old. And sad.

SEVENTEEN

David had endured the party, felt lucky, in fact, to have survived it at all. The evening seemed endless. The afternoon with Nicola flashed constantly in his mind. He could recall the exact perfume of her hair and at one moment during the party, catching sight of her dancing, he felt again clearly, surely, the touch of her fingertips on his skin. It had been a nightmare of an evening. All he had wanted was for the guests to go home so that he might talk to her.

Then she had left too, with Anthony Peacock—for a Baskin Robbins ice cream, they had said. It was taking a hell of a long time to get an ice cream.

Now, he paced the lounge. The room had a musty, after-party smell. Stale cigarette smoke hung in the air, empty bottles littered the tables and the floor. David, deliberately ignoring the rubble around him, tried to stretch out on the sofa and concentrate on a magazine. His body felt as taut as a bow string.

He wanted to walk in the garden but he feared he might wake Barbara. It was unlikely—he had kept her glass well filled all evening—but he didn't want to risk it. He did not want to miss Nicola. He began to wonder if he had simply imagined making love to her . . . the afternoon seemed so far away.

He looked at his watch for the third time in ten minutes then reached for a glass somebody had abandoned. It was half full of golden liquid and he sipped it carefully. Southern Comfort. It soothed his stomach but he thought it would not help his pounding head. He put the glass down again. He stiffened as he heard the faraway sound of a car. He waited. It turned off somewhere. The silence flooded back.

Impatiently, David stood and looked out the French windows into the gray night. A few stars were visible through the slight mist and bulky blackness of trees. He heard another car. This time it pulled into the drive and David sat down quickly. He picked up the magazine and studied it as if reading intently.

He realized that his heart was pounding. A schoolboy, he told himself. I feel like a trembling schoolboy.

He could hear Nicola whispering good night, then her key in the lock. Her footsteps hesitated outside the half-open lounge door then moved towards the stairs. David sprang to his feet.

"Nicola," he called softly.

She turned, surprised.

"Everyone still up?" she asked, coming down the stairs slowly.

"I am," he said quietly. "Barbara passed out."

"*Not* surprising," said Nicola with a laugh. "Mr. Johnnie Walker must be . . ."

"Shush!" he interrupted. Her normally soft voice sounded loud in the quiet house. "I wanted to talk to you."

Nicola glanced at him quickly then she followed him into the lounge. He poured the Southern Comfort into two clean glasses and handed her one.

"I hoped you wouldn't bring that jackoff back," he said.

Nicola smiled and sipped her drink.

"He had to get back to his wife."

"Of course."

She sat down in the large armchair and stretched out her legs.

"Don't look so miserable," she said. "Cheer up, for God's sake."

He wanted to sit on the arm of her chair, instead he sat on the sofa.

"I need to talk . . ." He thought he sounded plaintive and hated himself for that. "Talk to you," he said, more strongly.

"Talk away," she said. "I'm a good listener. Everyone says so."

He paused for a moment, letting the warming golden liquid slide down his throat.

"I have to get out," he said finally.

"Barbara?"

"All of it."

"So get out," she said briskly.

"I think I want you to come with me."

Once said, the words hung in the air like the cigarette smoke in the room. Nicola did not reply at once.

"You think?" she asked eventually.

"Well, I'm pretty sure."

She looked at him searchingly then handed him her empty glass. He fumbled around the bottles until he found one that was half full and poured scotch into their glasses.

"David, are you kidding?"

"No."

The blue eyes looked troubled. He had not expected that.

"But what do you want?" she asked. "A roommate?"

He smiled—she had misunderstood him.

"No, not that."

"Good friend? Mistress? Wife?"

"Whichever you want," he said levelly.

Nicola was frowning, she looked away then looked back at him.

"David are you *proposing* to me?"

He didn't really know and he paused before answering.

"If you want that, it's possible. I only know that I want you."

Her face was very serious. He had anticipated a different reaction. He had thought that at the very least she would be flattered. He had hoped for joy.

"But where would we go?"

"We could live anywhere."

"On what?"

"I could get a part-time job."

"And your painting?"

"I'd do that too. I'd do it more."

Nicola was half smiling now.

"So, how do we pay the rent?"

"We'd cope. Maybe you could get a job."

She had turned away slightly and was looking out into the garden. Her voice was quiet in the large room.

"And keep you?" she asked.

"This afternoon was . . . more than special," he paused. There was no other way to say it. He had never said it before. "I love you."

She turned back to him. He could not read her expression.

"Ridiculous," she said. "You barely know me."

"I know then, that I *could* love you."

"Bullshit," said Nicola.

He had to smile—that so American word in that accent.

"How Californian," he said.

Nicola smiled back.

"Humor returns. Thank God."

He felt too far away from her and moved to sit on the arm of her chair.

"I'm very serious. Really," he said, stroking her hair.

Nicola had taken his hand and she held it to her mouth and kissed it gently.

"I like you, David. I really do. Perhaps I could love you. But I don't want to try. That's the point. I don't want to be tied to you in any final way."

"Why not?" he asked, watching the light playing on the crazy hennaed hair.

"Because I don't want that poverty scene. For what? Why do it? Barbara was right about that. It is crap. I don't want the sort of life my mother had. I don't want to replay that. Not with you, not with anyone. To quote my dear stepmother—or was it you?—I want to feast, not fast."

She said this so sensibly that David became suddenly and blindly angry.

"You'd rather replay Barbara's life?" he asked as he got to his feet and walked restlessly round the room. "This bullshit?"

"Why not?"

David felt like kicking hard at the windows.

"Shit," he said. "Shit."

138

"Look, sit down. Behave reasonably." Her voice was low but firm. She seemed entirely in control of herself. "You couldn't live my father's stupid life. Have you any idea what it was like? He lived from hand to mouth. Sold every painting he ever did as he painted it—for the money to survive. He worked like a demon all his life and gained nothing. An obituary in *The Times*. Big deal. And a lot of people suffered because of him."

"It doesn't have to be like that," David said. He was deeply disappointed in her. He had miscalculated.

"You don't want to try it really, do you?" Nicola's voice was sharp now. "You won't try it alone. You won't leave Barbara by *yourself*. You'll stay."

He turned angrily from the window, pain swamping him.

"How the hell do you know I'll stay!"

"Because it's cushy for you. Don't lie to yourself."

"I said I am getting out and I am getting out."

He was still angry but the blinding fire had gone.

"We'll see," said Nicola. Like a governess, he thought. He put down his glass and moved to the door.

"Good night Nicola."

"Good night."

He was almost out the door when her voice called him back.

"David . . . ?" He turned. "I'm sorry," she said.

He came back into the room and kissed her mouth gently. He looked at her face for awhile, stroking her soft cheek with one finger. There was something he wanted to say but the clear blue eyes inhibited him.

"Perhaps I should add something," He said finally.

"What's that?"

"If you change your mind. If you feel differently—tell me."

Her face was sad now.

"I will. I promise," she said. "Thank you."

There was tension in the room as David walked to the door. He imagined that if he left things as they were, there would be a noticeable strain between them tomorrow. He snapped out of the mood quickly.

"Good luck with your treasure hunt," he said mischievously, as he got to the door.

To his relief, Nicola laughed.

"Bastard," she said.

David climbed the stairs slowly, feeling as if his body were heavily weighted. He had seriously miscalculated her. He had called her quest a "treasure hunt." In the old days in Hollywood, she would have been called a gold-digger. Nicola? It seemed incredible. What did she want? More than a rich husband, a sugar daddy, a benefactor? He had thought it was a game she was playing—all the studs, the California super-pricks with fat bank accounts. If she was playing a game, she was playing it seriously—to win. Vengefully? To kick back at her dead father?

He remembered the melting body under his, her fragrant hair against his face, her soft mouth, the small firm breasts. He had wanted that body, that girl. Now, he did not know who she was.

He paused outside the bedroom door. Barbara's heavy snoring must be audible all over the house. He checked an impulse to go back downstairs—hold Nicola, shake her, bully her into admitting what she was really thinking, what she really wanted. If she knew. Unexpectedly, he felt a moment's sympathy. A lovely, thinking girl—how could she not know the emptyness of what she pursued? He opened the bedroom door quietly, undressed in the darkness so as not to disturb Barbara.

In her room, Nicola stared for a long time at her reflection in the mirror. Attractive enough, she told herself. Then, suddenly, she began to cry. Tight, harsh sobs that hurt her chest. She wished she had not made love with him. She remembered too well the strong, brown body against hers, and its sun and air smell. That quick grin, creasing his eyes. David.

She cried hard for long minutes then rinsed her face in cold water.

"And now," she said aloud, as she reached for a towel, "that is *over*."

EIGHTEEN

The gold Ferrari was parked outside the house. David watched from his studio window as Nicola climbed into it. She was wearing tight white pants, a blue silk shirt that tucked in smoothly at the waist, and the sun glinted on her hair. Fletcher said something to her and she laughed, a soft sound that was cancelled out a moment later as the car engine revved and they were gone.

David turned from the window and, summoning concentration, went back to his canvas. He studied it frowning, knowing something was wrong but unable to see quite what. He should begin again—the lines were wrong to start with. He groaned once out loud: the image of a girl climbing into an expensive car. So simple a thing. It shouldn't disturb a whole afternoon's work. But he knew it had.

The door slammed downstairs and even from this distance he could hear Barbara calling for something from the kitchen. He didn't want to go down and talk with her but neither could he stay a moment longer in the studio. He felt imprisoned. He lifted the canvas from the easel and threw it deliberately onto the discard pile. He felt better after that. Better no work at all than bad work. He grabbed his jacket, picked up the keys to the Mercedes from the hallway and left the house without saying a word to anyone.

He drove west along Sunset, uncertain of where he was going or where he wanted to go until he arrived in Santa Monica. He turned left along the ocean, a shimmering mirror this windless day, and decided to carry on to Venice

141

and see Dan, an old friend he hadn't spent time with in months.

Daniel Matthews was a sculptor and at only thirty-one had achieved a measure of success. He sculpted the heads of the famous for money and of the poor for pleasure. He gave a lot of excellent stuff away. David began to cheer up the moment he pulled into Dan's small yard and saw that the studio door was open. A tuneless whistling coming from it meant that Dan was home and working.

To David's surprise, Dan was sitting on a small stepladder chipping at a marble figure that was at least five feet tall—a female, arms raised to her head.

"Wow. Baby. A full figure. Into the big stuff these days?"

Dan grinned at him.

"Hey, hey, buddy. What you doing, slumming?"

"Not slumming. Just visiting. Are you too busy? Say so, and I'll split."

"Nope. About enough for today. Could you go for a beer?"

"Sure could."

He followed Dan out of the studio and through the back door of the small woodframe house Dan shared with his long-time girlfriend Annette McLaughlin. Nettie, assistant to the top agent of one of Hollywood's largest theatrical agencies, was ambitious and determined to have her own agency one day—"have a little muscle in this damn town" as she put it. She was obviously at work. David was glad about that. He enjoyed her sharp wit and her keen insights but he was in no mood for smart female repartee just then. He was in no mood for females period, he told himself. He'd had enough of them for awhile.

Dan gestured David to an overstuffed chair in the dining alcove attached to the cool, neat kitchen and pulled a couple of cans of beer from the refrigerator. David took a long swallow, sighed and looked up to see his friend scrutinizing him.

"Thirsty?"

"Somewhat."

"So what's the problem, sunshine?"

"Problem? No problem."

"You have, old buddy, a definite lack of your usual bounce and brimming confidence. A pissed-off look, some would say. However . . . how goes the work?"

"It goes. But slowly."

"Did you talk to Harry about hanging a few?"

Harry owned a coffee bar in Venice and was willing to hang paintings for sale, exhibit sculptures, even display handcrafted silverware on his breakfast counter. He took no cut from the proceeds, was simply pleased to decorate the place.

"No point. Whoever goes there? The kids that hang out there can barely afford to buy their damn coffee let alone . . ." David sighed again. "It has to be a gallery. Somehow."

"That," said Dan, throwing himself into the opposite chair, "could take forever."

"I'll wait."

They sipped their beers. After a minute or so David waved an arm in the vague direction of the studio.

"So, what turned you on to the big stuff?"

Dan chuckled.

"Nettie. Not her idea or anything. She was just standing in the bathroom one morning, looking at herself in the mirror, stark naked, drying her hair, and I looked at her and thought, sweet Jesus, I have to catch that. Preserve the . . . hmm . . . the *innocence* of that. You know?"

David nodded.

"Just couldn't wait to get going. Heads are fine. They sell. But for years I've wanted to try a full figure. Kept putting it off. Just needed a push. And that was the push—her standing there, completely absorbed, dreaming a bit." He coughed, a little embarrassed. "Sounds stupid."

"Far from it. Sounds beautiful."

"Dear God, but it's been tough. She hates posing. Can't stand still for ten seconds, cusses and threatens," he chuckled again. "Makes that peaceful innocent quality I was after somewhat difficult."

"Looks good so far," David offered. "I'll take another look before I leave."

"Please do, sunshine."

Another silence. David drained his beer. Dan glanced at him and brought another one from the refrigerator.

"O.K. Out with it. What's bugging you?"

David began to shake his head, stopped, looked at his friend and, groaning, leaned back in his chair.

"It's this damn chick. Can't get her out of my head."

"Barbara?"

"Christ, no. Barbara's . . . well, something else. No, this English girl. Stepdaughter. She's . . . Jesus, Dan . . . she's really got to me. I can't think straight. Can't work, damn it."

"You're in love with her," stated Dan calmly.

David looked up sharply.

"Good grief," laughed Dan, "you look as if I'm accusing you of having a very unsociable disease."

"Feels like a damn disease. Never wanted this sort of shit."

"What does she feel?"

"Nothing. She's busy chasing rainbows. Rainbows like Pete Fletcher," he added darkly.

"That jack-off? What does she see in him?"

"He's rich."

"Hey, ho. *That* kind of gal."

"No. No, she's not like that. Not really," said David, angrily defensive.

Dan studied him for a moment.

"You told her how you feel?"

"Yep."

"And?"

"She said 'Thank you and good night'."

"Hmm," said Dan, going to get another beer for himself. "Tough. Very. Stay away then. Get on with . . ."

"How can I stay away. She lives in the same goddamn house."

Dan paused, pulling at the tab on his beer can.

"Mrs. Hampton-Norde must be *very* happy about that situation."

"She doesn't know shit about it."

"Just as well, or she'd be having toasted English gal for

144

breakfast." He smiled sympathetically. "It might wear off buddy. Sometimes it does. Just stay calm and friendly with her and it might go away."

David said nothing.

"The alternative, of course, is that you move out. Leave the ladies to their own devices."

Dan raised an eyebrow as David shook his head.

"Dan, listen. I'm doing the best work I can—well, I was before. I've no hassles there. I've got space. I've got time. Barbara? O.K., she makes a few demands. But not many, considering. She leaves me alone to paint. She's encouraging. So, I'm living cheap. But so what? If it comes together, my stuff, and dear god it must one day, I'll pay her back. I intend to do that," his voice had risen angrily.

"I'm sure you will," soothed Dan. "But that's not the problem is it?"

"No," said David, deflated. "No, it's not."

Dan glanced at his watch.

"Stay to dinner. Nettie will be home soon, it's my turn to cook and I am planning my world famous, unique version of that delicious, gourmet speciality . . ." he paused dramatically . . . "spaghetti Bolognese!"

David pondered for a moment.

"You can't resist it," prodded Dan. "Come on, admit it."

David grinned finally.

"No, you're right. I can't. Thanks."

"You can help me chop onions, then, you bum. Can't stand people lying around drinking beer while I work."

The Bolognese sauce was simmering and the table set for three when Nettie came noisily through the front door. She stopped when she saw David, let out a loud whoop and came forward to hug him.

"Sweetheart! It's been months!"

"Too long," said David, kissing her cheek. "You look terrific."

Nettie, since she started what she called her "upward mobility campaign," had lost ten pounds, had her dark hair cut into a short and sassy style, and decked herself out in fashionable, if casual, clothes. She looked what indeed she was—an intelligent, attractive woman on her way up.

"You'll see the real me in two minutes when I take the fancy gear off. Hello, darling . . ." she said to Dan. He came forward to kiss her.

"I see the McLaughlin image is emerging in the studio," David smiled.

"Did you see that? I suggested he do an impressionistic thing—you know, a Henry Moore lump with a hole in it and just call it Nettie. But no, has to be lifelike. Has me standing there stark naked for hours and hours, shivering . . ."

"Bullshit," shouted Dan, with a laugh.

"*Shivering* and miserable. I've told him, realism is one thing but just one hint, the merest hint, of my lumpy thighs and I'm out the door. *Improve* on nature. But he'll do it his way," she added grumpily, "just you wait and see those lumpy thighs emerge."

"Honey, you haven't got lumpy thighs," said Dan mildly.

Nettie gave him a disbelieving scowl then turned towards the bedroom.

"One of you gentlemen pour me a large red wine—very large—while I change?"

David poured the wine while Dan carefully eased spaghetti into boiling water.

"So, what's been happening, David?" Nettie asked when she returned wearing old denims and a red T-shirt.

"Not much. Just more of the same."

"Painting and partying?"

"More of the former than the latter."

"Good for you."

Nettie took a mouthful of red wine.

"Hmm. Needed that. Did you ever finish that lily series?"

He looked at her, surprised that she remembered.

"Yes. There were four finally. They're at Womberg's place. Did you like them?"

"Loved the first three. Best thing you've done that I've seen."

David smiled, pleased. He liked the water lily set himself. He had been almost satisfied, as close as a painter ever gets anyway to satisfaction with a finished picture.

"Bless you, Nettie. You are a tonic."

"Me? I'm just a thing that once was a woman after the day I've had. Our new guy couldn't package a chocolate chip cookie let alone a suspense thriller . . ." she sighed. "However, I won't spoil this deliciously aromatic dinner with rantings and ravings."

"Good," said Dan from the kitchen. "Take your places, please."

The spaghetti sauce was hot and spicy; Dan was strong on the red wine and garlic. He'd also made garlic bread and put together a large mixed salad. David ate hungrily.

"God, I wish I had a wife like yours, Nettie," he said towards the end. "Cooks like an angel, looks like a million dollars. Where did you find him?"

"Up yours, buddy," said Dan pleasantly.

"He is good, isn't he?" said Nettie. "Though I confess I'm better."

"You're just more varied," said Dan "Experimental. I'm consistent."

"Consistent with the hamburger anyway." Nettie looked, smiling, at David. "If it doesn't have hamburger in it, he can't cook it."

"Ungrateful witch," said Dan.

Nettie leaned across to ruffle his hair, laughing, and Dan took her hand and kissed it. At that, a looked passed between the two of them that caused David to sit back in his chair, swamped again by a strange sadness. These two had been together for five years, fought often he knew, and loudly, but that they loved each other equally and deeply was clear.

Dan, looking up, must have seen something in David's face for he smiled wryly.

"Tell Nettie about it."

"Christ, no. Why . . . ?"

"She's a woman," Dan explained.

Nettie looked from one to the other.

"Sounds like a good reason. Tell me what?"

David stared at his plate, uncomfortable. Nicola, Nicola, he thought, I am turning into a bleating idiot, a stammering schoolboy and it is your fault. Goddamn you.

"What?" repeated Nettie.

"David's in love," said Dan.

"Hey, at last! God, good, good! Old iron heart himself . . ."

"Not so good, Nettie," said David, and as she sat back, staring at him, he began to tell her a little about Nicola. He kept it short, sketchy. He felt foolish. But Nettie listened intently.

"So . . ." he concluded. "It's really no go. I just can't seem to get her out of my hair."

"Are you *sure* it's no go?"

"Yes. She wants . . . God knows. Some big million-dollar scene. It's more than just the usual gold-digging thing. It's almost defiant. As if she's trying to get at Barbara, her father, me, everybody."

"*Was* her father such a bastard?"

"Christ, I don't know. She obviously never thought so before."

Nettie traced the edge of her wineglass with her finger.

"She could just be flipping temporarily. You could sort of hang around and . . ."

"Before long," said David in a harsh voice, "she will have hooked someone like Fletcher and that will be that."

Nettie and Dan exchanged glances. Nettie moved to pat David's hand.

"Let her go. Be a friend to her because . . ." she paused, ". . . it sounds to me as if she's unhappy and needs a friend. But let the romantic hopes go. Work hard. Get back to yourself."

He stared at her for a long moment. The green eyes were gentle.

"I'll try," he said. He took a long gulp of his wine. "All right. Romeo will now shut his stupid mouth about this. Who wants to lose their shirt at poker?"

Nettie jumped up quickly. She loved cards.

"Me, me, me," she said, hurrying over to get the deck. "Don't pull a face, Dan. You know you enjoy it."

"Whoever enjoys losing?" asked Dan, who did, invariably, lose.

"Your luck could change sweetheart."

They each put five dollars in the pot and after an hour Dan was cleaned out. Nettie and David went on to black-jack and David had the deal. Thirty minutes later David scooped the money off the table and put it in his pocket.

"Proves it," he said. "Lucky at cards, unlucky at love."

He smiled at them.

"You two are probably ready for the sack. Look—thanks for tonight."

"Great to see you buddy," said Dan.

Nettie stepped forward to kiss David's cheek.

"Get some good work done," she said, then stopped. "Which reminds me. Remember when you were doing that lily set, you did a small oil of butterflies and . . . daffodils, I think. Tiny one . . ."

"Sure. It's in my studio."

"When I get my bonus, could we sort of talk about . . ."

"It's yours," said David, hugging her. "Gift."

"No, no," said Nettie crossly. "I didn't mean . . ."

"Please," said David. "Please. I'll drop it off."

Nettie and Dan were looking at each other. At last Nettie smiled, put her arms round David tightly.

"Thanks, love," she said. "Take care."

David drove the Mercedes too fast along Sunset, taking the wide bends easily, enjoying the drive, letting his mind drift. At the East Bel-Air Gate he slowed, pulled through the wrought iron porticoed gates reluctantly and began the ascent up Bel-Air Road. Elaina Jansan's white Rolls passed him on the hill and a slender, gloved hand waved from the back window. Elaina returning from yet another Beverly Hills charity function. Elaina once again certain of seeing her name in Jody Jacobs' column—the only thing that really mattered to her since her industrial tycoon husband died.

David slammed on the brakes suddenly and stopped the car.

"What the fuck am I doing here?" he asked aloud.

A breeze rustled a nearby oleander bush. He could smell juniper. The car had stopped underneath an overgrown avocado tree, lurching over someone's stone wall to overhang the road. He could glimpse the sky, a clear sky, through a lacework of branches.

He lit a cigarette and sat for five full minutes watching those branches and when he finally ground the cigarette into the ashtray he had decided. He turned the car around and drove back to Sunset.

When he returned thirty minutes later to the Bel-Air gate he had two newspapers on the seat beside him: the *Los Angeles Times* and the *Santa Monica Evening Outlook*. He had decided. He was getting out.

He heard Dan's voice in his head as he drove along the dips and turns of Bellagio Road.

"The alternative, of course, is that you move out. Leave the ladies to their own devices."

He'd argued against that. He'd said his work was more important, the opportunity he had to work. And that was true. But he wasn't working, damnit. He was fussing around like an old lady. He was wasting time. He was, he told himself with a half-smile, turning into a basket case.

The decision made, he felt more relaxed. He tried to work out ways and means. He had a few hundred dollars of his own, he had a couple of paintings he might be able to sell. He had turned down offers previously as being too small but he would take them now. Might mean getting a part-time job—bartender, bellhop, gas attendant. He tossed the idea of teaching right out of his head. Some goofy job would be less draining and leave his head clear.

But now, he had to tell Barbara. Immediately. Get the damn fight over with.

All the lights were on downstairs but there was no sign of Barbara. Her empty glass was on the floor by the sofa, an ashtray overflowed with cigarette butts. He climbed the stairs. Barbara was fast asleep in bed, snoring softly. David glanced at the clock: twenty minutes after midnight. He sighed. Too late for confrontations. He went back downstairs to turn out the lights and on his way back to the bedroom stopped for just a moment outside Nicola's room. The door was a little open, the room dark and silent. She was still out, probably for the night. At Fletcher's pad, in

150

Fletcher's bed and . . . He shook his head quickly. Forget it, dummy. Forget her.

He lay down next to Barbara on the king-size bed and slept immediately.

When he woke, Barbara, fully dressed and made-up, was combing her hair at the dresser.

"So, the sleeping beauty awakes," she said, turning to face him. "What happened to you last night?"

"Saw Dan. Had dinner there."

"You didn't think to make one phone call to say you'd be late getting back?"

"No. I didn't think."

"*Rude,* young man," she said. She seemed unbothered.

David climbed out of bed and stretched.

"Give me five minutes to shower and I'll have breakfast with you," he said. "We've got things to talk about."

But Barbara had thrown a coat over her shoulders and was heading for the door.

"I have to split," she said. "See you later."

With a clatter of heels she was gone. David shrugged. So he'd find a place first and tell her later. Present her with a *fait accompli.* And tell Nicola, too.

He drank coffee at the writing desk in the lounge, ticking off likely apartments in the rentals section of the papers. The ones in Santa Monica were expensive and he didn't want to live in the periphery areas of Palms and Culver City. He turned instead to the *L.A. Times* and found a few in West Hollywood that might do.

He was in the hallway, ready to leave, when Nicola came through the front door. She smiled weakly. She looked tired and pale.

"And a very good time was had by all," he said, "by the look of things."

She yawned.

"You could say that. God, I am *exhausted.*"

"You need coffee."

"No, sir. I've had dozens of cups of coffee. What I need is a nice cup of tea and sleep. Hours and hours of sleep. All day, probably."

"Go do it," said David, touching her cheek lightly. "See you later."

Driving the Mercedes towards West Hollywood David wondered how on earth he would get around, once free, without a car in a city that ran on wheels. He had managed before, he told himself. He would manage again. He didn't intend to go out much in any case. He intended to stay home and *work*. He began to whistle.

An apartment complex on Palm had a pool, a rooftop patio, and a number of singles and one bedrooms to rent. David knew he needed at least one bedroom. He needed one room for a studio.

The manager was a gangly, graying woman with a lantern jaw. David thought that Modigliani would have enjoyed painting her. Sullenly, she showed him a one bedroom apartment. The rooms were tiny. The living room had a kitchen attached and a small balcony facing east, but it was dark. Too dark to work in. The bedroom was worse, barely any light at all. He shook his head.

"This the only one?"

"Got a single. $425."

David stared.

"For a single? You've got to be kidding."

"That's the rent."

"And do you need security?"

"Of course. First, last, and two hundred security. Plus seventy cleaning."

David tried to work that out, gave up.

"How much is that in all?" he asked.

"One thousand, one hundred twenty dollars."

"Good-bye, and thank you, ma'am," said David.

The others in West Hollywood were asking for similar amounts of front money.

"You gotta go east of La Brea for anything cheaper," said a sympathetic manager on Larrabee.

David studied the paper again, crossing off places in Hollywood itself. Then he drove along Franklin to Argyle Avenue where just about every apartment building was advertising something to rent.

Argyle wound into the Hollywood Hills. At one time it

152

may have been a pretty street, the older buildings elegant, the new ones designed with pools and patios to perpetuate the California dream and the worship of the sun-god. But now there was an air of decay, transiency, an atmosphere of menace in the street activity. Groups of unshaven young men lounged against cars. Smoking. Watching. A few brown-skinned kids skipped up and down the steps of a crumbling manor house that had blankets hanging in front of broken windows, improvised drapes. Dogs barked.

On the bend, just before the road wound into the hills, David stopped the car outside one of the newer buildings. He locked the Mercedes carefully. The building had a central pool and the number of small children and dogs chasing round it indicated that the Adults/No Pets sign out front was not taken seriously. The manager, a smooth-skinned black, showed David a one-bedroom apartment.

The living room was long with a wide window overlooking the pool and a long window in the dining area. The carpeting was old, worn, and stained; the drapes, dirty and wrinkled. David ignored the kitchen, a greasy miniature addition, and studied the large room from all angles. The light was good. It was spacious.

"Bath here. Bedroom there," said the black, lazily.

David looked at both perfunctorily. Adequate, though dirty. He returned to the large room.

"How much?"

"Three hundred."

"How much up front?"

"Two hundred security. Five hundred in all."

"Can you make that one hundred security?"

"No way."

"O.K. I'll take it," David sighed. "But not 'til next weekend. I've got to get the bread together."

"You betta put down somethin', sweetie," said the black. "Because it might just be gone by next weekend."

David pulled out his wallet and handed over twenty dollars.

"That do?"

"Sure. Just a good faith gesture."

"Fine. Now I'd like a good faith receipt."

The manager scribbled one for him, smiling a little.

Driving back west, David did sums in his head. He could move in next weekend but that would leave him absolutely nothing to live on. He could sell two sketches for the price already offered by Barbara's real estate friends, Art and Angie. Jerry might buy something, if asked. He could hang a few at Harry's—just in case. He stopped for a coffee at the Old World on Sunset and realized that it wasn't going to be possible without some major compromise. He headed for a phone.

Ted Andrews ran a small public relations agency in Beverly Hills. Once in awhile he needed illustrations for brochures, posters, and mailers.

"To the point, Ted. I need bread, urgently. I need some work. What've you got that has to be done, like now?"

Ted laughed.

"Shit man, I've been begging you for months."

"I know, I know. What've you got?"

"Hold your horses. Let me look."

David hung onto the phone.

"There's the park presentation thing still hanging. I told you about it."

David thought back.

"The La Brea Tar Pits job?"

"That's the one."

"That was months ago!"

"Still have it. Getting close to the wire. Smithy was going to take a shot at it, but he pissed off to San Francisco. God know's why."

"I'll do it. I'll have the first sketches to you by Wednesday. Pay me then."

"Man, there's not that much of a hurry. They've given us 'til next month."

"There's that much of a hurry for me, Ted. See you Wednesday."

David hung up the phone feeling relieved. Acquiring one kind of freedom sometimes meant compromising another. He felt it would be worth it. It had to be worth it.

He drove back to Bel-Air determined to get some work done. His own work. Time for the Tar Pits tomorrow.

He knew as he pulled into the drive that he wasn't going to tell anybody anything until he was almost out the door. A week is a long time to live with crosscurrents and persuasion. He didn't want anybody trying to change his mind.

David skipped up the stairs quickly, past Nicola's closed door and on up to his studio. Work to be done. He felt that at last he could breathe.

NINETEEN

Nicola let herself in the front door with difficulty. The key wouldn't fit the lock at first, her hands fumbled clumsily. Finally inside she stumbled a little and the door slammed behind her, echoing through the quiet house. I am a little tipsy, she told herself. No. I am drunk. She giggled. It was good that David and Barbara were in bed. Food, she decided, and coffee. But once in the kitchen the effort of making coffee seemed too much so she drank long gulps of Tab straight from the bottle and chewed hungrily at a piece of dry bread.

She had been at Pete Fletcher's condo in Westwood for most of the afternoon and evening, drinking straight vodka and making love on his circular water bed. Pete had finally passed out, which pleased Nicola. She felt that if she had spent anymore time on that crazy bed she would be seasick. And she wanted to be gone when he woke. Give him a chance to miss her. She didn't want him to take her for granted. He was getting interested in her, she knew.

I need more time, she said aloud in the kitchen. I need more time here. She would, she decided, call Ted Sharp in the morning, wheedle a little, lie a little, if necessary. It meant getting up before nine though, to catch him before he left the office. She squinted at her watch: ten minutes after midnight. He'd just be starting his shift at ten past eight London time. No time like the present, she told herself. She took another long drink of Tab then headed for the phone.

Ted Sharp had his usual early morning growl; she could visualize the scowl.

"Nicola. We've had two pieces from you. Where's the rest?" he barked, without any preamble or courtesy questions.

With an effort, she tried to keep her voice steady and sober.

"Well, that's the point. I'm working on some very exciting interviews . . ." she lied.

"What interviews? We didn't ask for interviews."

"Ted. I can get Georgia O'Keefe. She lives in New Mexico. And . . ."

"Who? Never heard of her."

"Ted! Of course you have. Ask Jeremy."

"Hold on a minute."

She waited. After a minute or two he was back.

"O.K, he says," said Ted wearily.

"And two others," said Nicola, praying he wouldn't ask their names. He didn't. "But the point is I need a little more time . . ."

"How long?"

"Three, four weeks?"

"Jeremy is not liking this at all. He is snowed under," said Ted, unable to keep a note of satisfaction from his voice. He loathed Jeremy. Nicola knew that was one thing working in her favor.

"He'll be fine when he sees the stuff."

"All right. But just get a move on, will you? If everybody took two months vacation a year . . ."

"It's not a vacation. It's a leave-of-absence. I'm only getting lineage, remember."

"Doesn't matter. You've got a job to do. Bye."

There was a click and then crackling before the line went dead. Nicola replaced the receiver slowly, breathing a sigh of relief. More time, she had more time. You will have to return someday, she told herself, then shrugged quickly, dismissing the thought, and headed back to the kitchen.

She felt desperately thirsty and drank greedily again from the Tab bottle.

"You look like an infant at a nurser," said David, coming quietly into the kitchen.

Nicola spun around, her hand on her chest.

"God, you made me jump. Didn't know anyone was up."

David was wearing a white T-shirt, now dusted with charcoal. His hands were black, his forehead smudged with a fingertip streak of gray.

"You've been coalmining."

"Working," he said shortly as he strode towards the sink. "New series."

He scrubbed at his hands. He seemed abstracted.

"And what about you?" he asked, over his shoulder. "Been partying? Or more your intimate evening *à deux*?"

"Partying *à deux*, I think you'd call it," said Nicola, falling into the big kitchen chair and stretching out her feet.

"Really?" asked David coldly. Nicola looked away, fiddling with a button on her shirt. It was hanging by a thread and seconds later she was staring at it in her hand.

"Looks like things got a little rough," said David in a harsh voice.

Nicola flipped the button as if it were a coin, tried to catch it and missed. It fell to the floor.

"You're being nasty, David. Hostile, as they say in California."

"Sorry, didn't mean to be hostile."

He turned. His look was so direct that Nicola felt exposed, and too drunk and too confused to deal with it.

"I'm having difficulty with this big brother role you seem to have slotted me into."

"Yes. Well, I suppose big brothers are allowed a little hostility."

He turned away.

"O.K. Now—food. Missed dinner."

He began pulling out items from the refrigerator and the pantry: peanut butter, cheese, dill pickles.

"You've been working all day?"

"Yep."

David was smoothing peanut butter onto thick slices of whole wheat bread. Nicola watched him.

159

"How come you know your way around this kitchen so well and I can never find *anything?*"

"I eat here a lot," said David, taking a hungry bite. "Usually around two or three in the morning. Want something?"

"No thanks."

"Might soak up some of the liquor."

Nicola stared at him angrily.

"I've not *had* that much liquor," she lied.

"Nicola, your eyes are glazed, your face is blotchy, and you have a definite pie-eyed look. You are crocked, baby."

Nicola started to speak, then shrugged.

"So what?"

"So what nothing. Have something to eat."

He handed her a chunk of cheese and a slice of bread. She chewed at it, watching him. He looked tired, but in a satisfied, sleepy way. A rumpled little boy after a hard and winning day of football. But so remote from her. She remembered, with the sense of nostalgia one gets when looking at a childhood photograph album, his arms about her. His hair on her face. His body linked to hers.

"Seems a very long time ago," she said to herself.

"It seems centuries ago." She had spoken too loudly and he knew what she meant. "But no reason to think of it, is there? No fucking reason at all."

"Don't be cross, David."

He groaned, put one small plate into the kitchen sink and turned towards the door. Nicola wanted to keep him there.

"When a lady is . . . crocked? . . . baby, then the next stage is to get sleepy."

David watched as she fumbled into her handbag and pulled out a thin, crumpled, hand-rolled cigarette. Grass.

"Into our fine, California ways, I see."

"Objection?"

"Why would I object. You carry that across town?"

"All the way from Westwood. At least five minutes by cab."

"Your . . . date . . . did not escort you home, then?"

"My date was in a coma."

"You affect him that way, too?"

Nicola smiled at him lazily, lighting the joint.

"Hey, mister. Want to share it?"

Nicola took a long, deep drag, then handed it to him. David stood very still.

"Look, if we get into this, I'm not sure my big brother act will hold up. You know that?"

Nicola took another hit and waited until the world began spinning. She saw only a shadowy figure before her. Tall, upcompromising—but not threatening. She stared straight ahead at the area around the knees of his Levi's where the cloth was beginning to thin. Threads were intercrossing, the cloth thinning. Threads connected and broke.

"Pretty knees you have in those jeans," she said.

"Come on, Nicola. Get yourself to bed." David replied irritably.

She looked up, beyond the threaded denim, but when she reached his face, a sad face watching her so closely that she felt he was almost inside her head, she cried out:

"What am I doing?"

"I don't know. I do know," said the voice, far above her, "that I have to go to bed and so do you. And I . . ."

There was a touch. The lightest touch on her shoulder. A butterfly touch. Gone immediately.

"David."

"I'm here."

She was lost. But something had to be said.

"David, when we first met, soon after, you said we should be friends. Something like that."

David nodded.

"Yes. We *could* be friends. That's what I said."

"Can we?"

There was silence. She tried to focus on him. His face was shadowed, unreadable, unknowable.

"Let's try," he said.

Suddenly, he was at the door, looking at her. Nicola held up the small remains of the cigarette.

"You won't share this?"

He shook his head.

"Sleep, love. Will you please?"

161

The door closed. Niçola ground the cigarette into the ashtray. She felt numb with the numbness of an observer, until, moments later, she began to feel the schizophrenic reaction one gets after staring a long time into a mirror. Is that me? Is that who I am? What I look like? I am that person. The feeling terrified her so much that Nicola had to sit up straight and shake her head vigorously before it would disperse.

I am losing my place in the world, losing my place. David had said to her that grief is always exhausting. For some reason, this came into her mind now and instantly she dismissed it. I am living a different life. I am experiencing a new way of life. I am a stronger person now. She did not know, then, that she was simply escaping, hiding—as the weak, not the strong, must hide.

TWENTY

Barbara had a business appointment. A goddamn *vital* business appointment she told herself as she watched David watching Nicola over the breakfast table. Nicola seemed unaware of his eyes or at least unbothered by his surreptitious scrutiny. She has bigger fish to fry, thought Barbara, with a worried mixture of relief and jealousy. She's got her father's fucking ambition if nothing else. Barbara had a remote fear that Nicola was setting herself up in competition—anything you could (once) do, I can do better. She flaunted her young body around the house, talked openly of her conquests. She had started going around with Peter Fletcher, the wild son of one of the big studio heads. He was worth a pretty penny, Barbara knew, good looking, too. He also had a reputation as a cocksman, which didn't do a young man any harm.

Nicola had been out with him last night and was looking pleased with herself this morning. The girl had extended her stay—now talked airily about going back to England 'sometime next month.' Barbara wanted her out of the house—fast. Not just because David was obviously intrigued by Nicola—he wouldn't be so stupid as to follow *that* up—but because her stepdaughter was getting on her nerves.

She couldn't just kick her out. She could make things as unpleasant as possible so that Nicola would leave of her own accord; but tactics like that would alienate David. He was a dummy when it came to being fucking straight with people. Soft as a half-cooked egg. And she didn't want to alienate him: she liked that firm, brown body in bed. Needed it, in fact. For the present, she was encouraging Nicola in her pursuit of the moneyed young men around. Let some jack-off take the girl off her hands. As for David—Barbara knew very well how to bring him back to heel.

"Well, kiddies," she said. "I gotta run. What're your plans for today?"

David, she knew, was sketching at La Brea Tar Pits. Some crazy idea. She waited for him to invite Nicola along. He did.

"God, does it mean walking?" asked Nicola, groaning. "I'm half-dead today."

"Serves you right," said David and added as she looked up at him and smiled, "you can sit on a bench and watch. The fresh air might clear your poor little head."

Nicola put her head on one side and considered this.

"Come on, make up your mind," said Barbara impatiently. "We've got one car today so I have to drop you off."

"All right," said Nicola ungraciously, getting to her feet.

Barbara, with a flash of anger, noted David's pleased smile.

She dropped them off just outside the park.

"Skip your meeting, and come with us," said Nicola, poking her head back into the car.

"Wish I could, sweetie, but I can't," said Barbara. "Back as soon as I can. Have fun."

She blew a kiss to David and drove off, watching them through the rearview mirror.

Two young people going to the park. Pretty as a picture. Shit, she thought. *That* won't go any further. Not David and Nicola Graham. I have been fucked around enough by the Graham family. Nick Graham. He had been about as faithful as any alley cat. To her. She'd just been somebody to have around, look after the kid, cook for him and his goddamn cronies. He had sex with her once in awhile; she

164

supposed he thought that would keep her happy. But she wanted much more than that. And always, she felt he was comparing her with Susan, his first wife, Nicola's mother.

"I'm not Susan," she had screamed at him, one heavy-drinking night. "I'm not a housewife, nor a goddamn mother. I want a proper life."

"You have a proper life, woman. What the hell is a proper life? You're alive. You breathe." He had paused. "Don't you?"

"I can't stay cooped up in here, day in, day out. Why don't you take me with you? Take me out in the evenings?"

He had looked at her as if she were stupid.

"Somebody has to look after Nicola," he said.

He was to say that often.

"You don't love me," she had screamed. "You don't give a shit about me."

He had come over to her then, held her.

"I love you," he said. "In my fashion."

Nick Graham. A big hulk of selfishness that women fell on their knees for. She had seen them at parties—sidling up to him, involving him in idiotic small talk, always ignoring the blonde woman at his side. His second wife. She was an American and could, therefore, be discounted. They had flattered him with compliments so inane that Barbara laughed out loud in their company. They had fluttered their eyelashes and took every chance to press his arm, touch him lightly with the touch of intention. Sometimes, later, he would laugh at them with her. They would verbally destroy these primping, sycophantic creatures together. Afterwards, regardless, she would find out that he had slept with them.

"Good Christ, woman, what does it matter? One organ pokes at another organ. It's meaningless. I was drunk, she happened to be there. Meaningless. I'm here, am I not? I'm here with you."

"You don't love me."

"I love you . . ."

"In my fashion!" she mimicked, screaming.

165

Once again, angered at the memory, Barbara stepped hard on the gas just as the light turned red on Santa Monica Boulevard. A chorus of car horns blared and Barbara gave a vulgar one finger gesture to anyone who might be watching. After that she felt better.

The Parisienne Gallery was on La Cienega and she could see the fat fag, Christopher, dozing over a newspaper as she parked the car. When she walked into the gallery he leapt to his feet, giving orders to his minions as if he were the busiest man in the world. He was deliberately keeping her waiting. The frog. Barbara picked up his newspaper while he raced about sweating, and she smiled. The frog had been doing the crossword puzzle and had actually managed to fill in two clues. With malicious delight Barbara filled in as many of the rest as she had time for. Christopher stopped his speedway act then and ushered her into his office. He grinned like an aged baboon and gave her a drink. Barbara downed it in one.

"Sorry to keep you waiting, sugar," he said, breathlessly. "Now on the phone you said . . ."

"I said everything necessary on the phone," said Barbara. "All we have to do is fix the date. Fill this up would you, Chris."

She handed him her empty glass. He gave his slimy little laugh as he refilled it.

"Now Barbara, there are problems. You know that. He's an unknown . . ."

Barbara waited for awhile, took her new drink, sipped it, and watched him.

"We all have problems, Chris," she said softly.

"Right on." His head bobbed with the words.

"Even little Mary has problems."

That stopped him as she knew it would. He reached for the bottle for himself. She was pleased at that: he didn't normally drink much.

"Mary?"

"Lovely girl," said Barbara. "Really. She's good people. But . . ." she paused delicately. "She's got problems like the rest of us. She must be a good wife, Chris . . ."

166

"She is."

Barbara smiled.

"She's lucky having you. Because, of course, she doesn't *know* she's got problems. You're good about that, Chris. Tactful."

He was sweating. He wiped his forehead with his hand.

"Barbara, I'm not sure I know . . ."

"Maybe I'm wrong." Barbara tilted her head, looked at him inquisitively.

"Maybe," said Christopher, smiling nervously.

"Maybe you're not so tactful. Maybe she's already met Tony. Little Tony. Sweet boy. Maybe they get along just fine."

Christopher stood, took her glass which was still half full, and turned his back to refill it. She guessed his hands were shaking.

"And shit, that reminds me," continued Barbara lightly. "When is it we have lunch? Mary and Angie and I—is it next week? I do believe it is."

There was silence for awhile. Christopher turned back and handed her the drink.

"She did mention something about it," he said. "Anyway, sugar—to work. Gossip is for the gals. Save that for your lunch. You know of course . . . you know that Mary doesn't like gossip."

Barbara met his frightened eyes and smiled.

"Of course. Who does? Now—we were about to fix that date."

"Yes," said Christopher.

Victory, thought Barbara, driving back to La Brea. Not the greatest victory of her career but worthwhile. Worthwhile. That slimy worm deserves a little pressure, she told herself. He should stay away from little boys.

She swung into the park and saw David and Nicola immediately. They were sitting on a bench and David was sketching Nicola. The girl was pulling a haughty British face and David laughed. Barbara felt a sharp pang. How young he looked. Sometimes when he was sleeping she would study his face and think he looked like a teen-ager.

A child. But he made love like a man, of that there was no doubt. He was good in bed. Not as inventive as Jeff, or let's face it, as downright bizarre as Jeff. But good.

She walked towards the young couple thinking that today's little meeting could not have been better timed.

TWENTY-ONE

Nicola slept late then took a long bath, heavily scented with some Estée Lauder oil Barbara had given her.

"I can't stand it, honey. You might like it."

Nicola had smiled and taken it. It was a pleasant scent, she thought. God, she was tired. She stretched back in the tub and as she raised her knees discovered another bruise on her thigh. He was a rough lover, dear Peter. Seemed to go out of his mind. Helped, probably, by those little capsules he sniffed. Amyl Nitrite? Nicola had taken one small sniff and hadn't liked it. A horrible hot flushing and the feeling that her flesh did not belong to her anymore. Melting into his body, becoming him. "I am Heathcliffe . . . ?" She smiled at this train of thought. Pete was no Heathcliffe but he was amusing. He also spent money with such ridiculous abandon that Nicola was at times both irritated and fascinated by his carelessness.

Pete Fletcher had never known refusal in his life, had never been snubbed or denied anything. It gave him a childish belief in his own ability to conquer anything and everybody. And beneath that, something dangerous—a wild quality, as if he wanted to kick down walls. He behaved badly in the best places and was forgiven. He was indulged. Nicola felt intuitively that if she dropped the super-cool front that interested him, he would drop her. She didn't intend him to do that. She wanted him. She wanted to be where he was, have the control and freedom that his wealth allowed. After that—she would see. She didn't see him as a lifetime proposition.

169

She got out of the bath and dried herself slowly. She was rubbing a soothing, scented oil onto her skin when she heard her bedroom door swing open. Instinctively, she reached for a towel to cover herself.

"Nicola!"

Barbara's voice. Barbara on one of her rare visits home for lunch.

"In here."

Barbara sauntered into the bathroom, gave Nicola a cursory glance, and began flicking at her hair in the mirror.

"Can you get your act together in fifteen minutes? I'm taking you out to lunch," she said over her shoulder.

Nicola paused, surprised.

"Of course." She knew she sounded ungracious but couldn't help it. "Why?" she asked.

"Celebration," said Barbara.

Barbara had smoothed an eyebrow with her index finger and now moved to the door, leaving as abruptly as she had come.

"But what are we celebrating?"

"Tell you later. I have to get the boy genius moving. And wear a dress will you, please. This is not a blue-denim lunch."

Nicola shook her head, bemused, as Barbara slammed out of the door. She studied her wardrobe and picked out a soft green silk dress and open-toe sandals. It was a simple outfit but she knew she looked good in it. Amused and curious, she made up her face carefully.

David was working on the La Brea Tar Pits sketches when he heard Barbara's footsteps and he cursed. He had nearly completed them, wanted to get them over to Ted Andrews that afternoon and pick up the cash. His own apartment front-money—he wanted it in his pocket.

Barbara didn't come all the way down to the studio but merely shouted from the top of the stairs.

"Put on your best gear, honey, 'cause you're coming out to lunch."

She turned immediately to go back downstairs.

"Can't do it, baby," David called. "Sorry."

Barbara stopped, turned, and came fully into the studio.

"Yes, you can. Because it is very, very important."

He put down his pencil and looked at her.

"Why?"

"Tell you there. Now, hurry. We're running late."

He stared at her. A strange look in her eyes. Triumphant? He sighed. What the hell, an hour or so wouldn't make that much difference. He would be out of here, out of all this, soon.

"Okay! But give me time to shower."

"Shower, sure. And wear that navy velvet jacket I got you, would you? This is dressy."

"Nope. I'll wear what I damn well please, thank you, ma'am," he said angrily.

"David, please."

She was *pleading* with him. He frowned. What the hell was this?

"All right, Queen Bee. All right."

Barbara, satisfied, marched out.

When the three congregated in the hallway Jeff already had the Cadillac parked outside the front door. Barbara strode out first, a small smile on her lips. Nicola and David exchanged glances as they climbed into the car.

"How smart you look, sir," said Nicola.

"Feel like a goddamn poodle straight out of the shampoo parlor," said David.

Jeff stopped the car outside the Hotel Bel-Air. Nicola had many times admired the flamingo pink hotel, reminiscent in style of a Spanish mission, complete with imitation belltower. She had never been inside before. Barbara led the way over a canopied bridge. A California sycamore twisted and lurched across the small stream beneath them.

"How pretty," said Nicola, admiring the scene.

On the other side of the narrow footbridge, the stream widened and two swans floated there like fluffy morning clouds. David stopped, leaning over the rampart of the footbridge to watch them.

"Come *along*, kiddies," said Barbara.

"Can we just look around for a few minutes," pleaded Nicola. "It's such a charming place."

Barbara consulted her watch.

"I've got one call to make. All right, I'll meet you in the dining room in ten minutes."

David and Nicola strolled down the path alongside the stream in silence. A slight breeze ruffled the leaves of the sequoia redwoods, the sun was warm on their faces. Nicola followed as David took a small path that led to one of the colonades of the hotel. A turn, and they were facing a square flower garden. In the center of this, what had once been a fountain, edged with blue Spanish tile, now held flowers and plants. The splash of color, more dramatic in the cool greens and washed pink of the hotel, gave the place an intimate, though open-air, feeling—rather like that of a secret garden in an elegant country house.

"A very nice place to stay," sighed Nicola.

"One day, perhaps," said David softly, "you'll be able to afford it."

She glanced at him quickly but he had walked away and was studying a green flower mural on an outside wall.

"As hotels go," he said when Nicola reached him, "it's somewhat more tasteful than that iced cake on Sunset and nicer by far than the glittering Wilshire."

Nicola nodded. She touched his arm briefly.

"Let's sit down and have a cigarette and breathe in the fresh green air of affluence," she said.

He looked down at her face, in shadow now, but golden where the sun had tanned it, the skin smooth and soft. The green of her dress blended perfectly with the background. He thought she looked very beautiful.

"Let's go meet Barbara," he said, "and find out what this is all about."

Barbara was already in the dining room, seated at a window table, a glass of scotch and ice in front of her.

"So, did you have to inspect the honeymoon suite too?" she snapped.

David looked at his watch.

"We've been exactly ten minutes," he said.

The table was set for four. Barbara motioned Nicola to the opposite window seat and patted the chair next to her for David, then, softening, she made a gesture to a waiter across the room. He arrived in moments with a bottle of champagne snugly tucked into its ice-bucket.

Nicola smiled.

"Barbara, what is this?"

"Wait," said Barbara.

The champagne was poured. Nicola and David both waited for Barbara to speak. She lifted her glass.

"We are celebrating a very difficult deal I've just put together," she said. "So here's to it."

Nicola and David sipped dutifully. David tried to hide his anger. He was wasting time here when he could be working, just because Mrs. Hampton-Norde had survived another business deal. She looked so pleased with herself that he finally snapped.

"Barbara, you're always making deals. So what?"

"So what?" she asked, raising an eyebrow. "This was an exhibition I just never expected to get."

So, she'd got one of the biggies had she? Nicola was looking at her with interest.

"Who's the painter?" she asked.

"Guess?"

"Oh, for Christ's sake, Barbara . . ." David swallowed his champagne in a gulp. At that point he couldn't have cared if she'd managed to arrange a Beverly Hills showing of the complete works of Rembrandt.

"David Leyton," said Barbara.

There was a look of harsh amusement on Barbara's face. David was stunned, staring at her blankly.

"Are you kidding?" he asked.

"Why should I kid?"

"My own exhibition?"

"That's what I said."

"But . . ."

David shook his head like a small dog, glanced at Nicola then looked back at Barbara.

"But, but, but . . ." she mimicked. "So what's wrong with that?"

"Christ, nothing is wrong with that. But when did you . . . ? How?"

"Been planning it for days," said Barbara. "A surprise, it was meant to be. More a shock?"

"Honey, this is marvelous," said David, believing it at last.

"How super!" exclaimed Nicola, though she was a little confused. Was David ready for a full exhibition? And how . . . an unknown painter? She looked hard at her stepmother. Barbara was smiling.

"When?" asked David.

"Four weeks from now. The Parisienne."

David's eyes were alight.

"How did you do it?"

"Same way I usually do it. You wanted it, right?"

David shook his head again, then reached over to hug Barbara.

"Good God, I'm virtually speechless."

"Have some more champagne; soothe your poor little voice box."

They were ready to order when the gallery owner came chugging breathlessly over to them.

"So sorry I'm late, darlings," said Christopher. "Got tied up. You know how it is."

"Of course we know how it is, Chris," said Barbara. "Now . . . this is Nicola, Nick Graham's daughter. You met at the opening, I think."

Chris nodded, shaking Nicola's hand.

"Of course, of course."

Nicola could not remember him at all.

"And David Leyton, of course you know."

"Indeed, indeed. An exciting moment for you, David."

"And thanks to you, Chris."

"Not at all," he said, settling himself next to Nicola. "Thanks to Barbara. She fought hard for you. But she's right, of course. Quite right."

Chris waved away the champagne and ordered scotch. He was sweating slightly and almost at once he began to inform David of the size of the gallery, the number of pictures needed, ways and means, prices and cuts. The waiter took their order and Chris continued about advance publicity and plans for an opening night. David listened intently, nodding. Barbara interrupted once in awhile. Nicola said very little to the three, contenting herself with enjoying the food and watching the other patrons in the dining room. She had heard such conversations many times before, at home in London.

After the meal, Barbara and David were eager to get back and begin the sorting and choosing of paintings. They shook hands with Chris at the edge of the canopied bridge outside the hotel.

"Thanks again, Chris," said David.

"Nothing, my boy, nothing. Let's aim for a success, shall we?"

"We'll have a success," said Barbara with bright confidence. "Have you ever known me to fail?"

Chris laughed.

"Not yet, darling. Not yet."

"Exactly whose show is this?" Nicola muttered to David. He looked at her hard.

"Mine," he said.

Back at the house, Nicola threw herself into a chair while the other two, in a panic of energy, consulted papers, studied lists of paintings, argued about pictures to be included.

Nicola half-listened to the conversation, feeling left out. She had heard such discussions as a child. She had felt left out then.

"Naked water lily series. Last year. Want those in," David's voice.

"All four?" from Barbara. "Surely not."

"Absolutely."

Nick Graham years ago had fought for an hour with a gallery owner. Nicola had overheard:

"It may not be tasteful to you, sunny boy. Whatever that soppy word might mean. But it's going on the wall. Understand? Or nix. Nothing. And I'll have your balls for bullets."

He had his way. It had been the most talked about picture of the exhibition. David knew what he wanted too.

"Bullshit!" he was saying now. "That *must* go in."

Replay, replay. Nicola took a deep breath, trying to clear

her head. She was experiencing an odd, numbing sense of unreality. Life on a carousel, round and round. She walked quickly to the window and opened it. Fresh air, warm fresh air. David and Barbara were ready to go.

"Shall I come with you?" Nicola asked.

Neither of them answered for a while. David was filling a briefcase with lists. Barbara looked up eventually.

"Honey, you'd be bored out of your mind. We'll be most of the time in Jerry's tacky attic—that's where the bulk of David's work is. You'd hate it."

Nicola nodded and went back to the window. A thick, yellow smog lay over the city. She closed the window.

"See you later," Barbara called from the door.

David shouted good-bye and then they were gone. Nicola prowled the room restlessly, irritated that the afternoon had been so disrupted but mostly feeling a disproportionate anger at David. At the word exhibition she had simply disappeared for him, had ceased to matter. But I shouldn't matter, she told herself firmly.

She picked up the phone and dialed Pete's number. Keep it cool now, she told herself. Don't gush, don't sound desperate. But she sounded desperate, even to herself.

"Hi, Englishwoman." He was surprised as she thought he would be. "Anything doing?"

"No. I was just bored. Thought I might enjoy hearing a nasty Yankee voice."

"Sweetheart, if I had the time I would talk to you for hours. But I'm tied up today—I told you."

He had. She wondered what a playboy could be tied up with. He had said something about accounts.

"O.K. See you tomorrow."

"Tomorrow," he promised.

A click and he was gone. You are going to blow it, she warned herself, if you start chasing him like that. She settled into an armchair and picked up a newspaper. She had not read a newspaper for days and the news stories seemed meaningless to her. She could not concentrate. She could hear noises from the kitchen, the clattering of pots and pans. Again, that frightening sense of déjà vu. She had sat in a large empty house before, listening to noises from the kitchen. Mrs. Jenson in later years. Barbara before. Always waiting for her father to come home. He was so often out—and so joyfully noisy on his return.

"And what have you been doing, little chicken?"

"Nothing much." The teen-age Nicola, given to long silent moods and stifling embarrassments.

"Nothing much? Good grief, child! All the great books to be read, all the marvelous music to be heard. Even that mind-dulling box over there," he pointed contemptuously to the television set, "and you have been doing 'nothing much?' Shame on you. But a remedy immediately. I shall beat you at chess and put you in your place."

She had beaten him. She suspected that he had let her win deliberately but it had cheered her up nevertheless. Nicola tried to push the memories away. Don't think ill of the dead and how could she think ill of him with so many happy memories. But memories based on quicksand? She had loved him. She had loved a fiction, she told herself. The man she remembered was not the man he was. But he had been amusing. He had been loving. Her mother died because of him. Her mother died because of him. A mantra.

She poured herself a gin and tonic and took it out to the pool. She would have a swim. A long, hard swim to clear her head . . . and her mind of memories.

TWENTY-TWO

"You're quiet, tiger."

Nicola looked up at Pete Fletcher and smiled.

"Sorry. Miles away."

They were having dinner at Moonshadows on the beach, after having spent the afternoon sunbathing.

"The sun makes me sleepy," she added,.apologizing.

Pete looked at his watch, waved to the waitress, and got out his wallet.

"O.K. Let's go. Let's go crash the party."

Nicola stared at him, surprised, then began to gather her belongings. Pete was already on his feet.

"What party?"

"Daddy's party," he said, with heavy irony.

In the Ferrari, she turned to him. He was smiling.

"At your home?"

She had never visited his parent's home. Pete had his own condo in Westwood.

"Sure."

Nicola looked down at her white jeans, now creased and splattered with sand. Her open-toe sandals were muddy, her T-shirt felt less than fresh after the day's running around.

"I'll have to change first."

"Bullshit," he said. "You're fine."

"Pete, please!"

"No time," he snapped.

She did not dare plead with him further.

When the car began ascending the winding twists and

turns of Chalon Road, Nicola combed her hair rapidly and tried to apply a little make-up. She wished he had warned her. She would have made an effort to look like the sort of girl a man took home to meet his parents. She knew that with proper preparation she could have made a good impression. She sprayed a little perfume behind her ears nervously.

The house was called Silver-Screen. It was a long, low, Spanish style structure set way back on the wooded hillside, protected by automatic gates. For this evening, a uniformed attendant checked passes at the main gate and, recognizing Pete, he grinned and waved his hand.

"Looks like quite a crowd," Pete called to him.

"And they're still coming in, buddy," said the attendant. Nicola looked behind. A silver Rolls waited for them to move on. She slid down a little in her seat.

The driveway outside the house was jammed with cars. The silver car following them wasn't the only Rolls it seemed. A young rent-a-cop stood to the right of the door, surveying the scene impassively. Sounds of chatter and laughter drifted through the wide windows. There was, too, the tinkle of glass and ice.

"The bash is for Thomas Craig," said Pete casually as they got out of the car. "You ever met him?"

Nicola stared at him. Craig was probably Britain's best known actor, and still, though aging and in poor health, doing fine work on both stage and screen.

Nicola had seen all of his films and a number of his stage appearances—particularly when he was involved in the Royal Shakespeare Company's productions at the Aldwych.

"*Sir* Thomas Craig?"

"That's the dude."

"Of course I haven't met him. I don't mix in those circles."

"You're mixing in those circles now, baby," said Pete.

Pete opened the front door with his own key and Nicola, hiding a little behind him, followed nervously. The guests had spilled out into the hallway and a number of faces turned towards them. Nicola felt numb with embarrass-

180

ment. The men wore dinner jackets, white tie. The women were in stunning formals that glittered and glimmered in the softly lit house. She felt, rather than heard, a pause in the conversation, an impression of indrawn breath, of disapproval, until an overweight older woman wearing a low-cut emerald silk swept forward with a cry.

"Pet-er! Dar-ling!"

"Hi, mom," said Pete, kissing her cheek. "Thought we'd drop by for a quick one. This is Nicola."

"Pleased to meet you, Mrs. Fletcher," said Nicola, extending a hand.

The older woman touched the offered hand very lightly.

"Are you British? How delightful," she said, not waiting for a reply. "Now, daddy's around somewhere. I'll find him. Have a drink."

She bounced away, smiling.

A young, blond waiter was at their side with a tray of brimming champagne glasses. Nicola took one.

"Get me a Rob Roy, would you," Pete ordered, and turned to Nicola. "Well, well, the gang's all here."

Nicola, after a few sips of her drink, had courage enough to look around. A number of faces she recognized, mostly from the older generation of Hollywood greats.

"Good Lord," she whispered to Pete when she spotted a matinee idol from the forties. "Jack Dempson. I though he was dead."

"Almost," said Pete. "Almost."

Nicola studied a group of women, gathered together in a gossiping circle in the center of the room. One of them she recognized from the society columns.

"So that's where Princess Margaret sold her jewels," she muttered.

Pete grinned, looking over at the baubles and beads that decorated the woman.

"Don't feel bad, tiger. Those are replicas. Insurance costs today mean the real rocks are safely in the bank vaults."

"Look real enough to me."

The waiter had returned with Pete's drink and he grabbed it quickly, turned to Nicola to say that he would be back in a minute and vanished into the crowd. Nicola, standing alone, felt uncomfortable. She edged towards the far window and looked out at the pool and gardens, her back to the room.

"Now, I *like* a woman who has her own style," said a voice behind her. She turned to find a short, balding man wearing proper evening attire appraising her.

"Not deliberately, I'm afraid," she said. "Didn't expect to be here or I'd be wearing a long frock, too."

"You look gorgeous," said the man. "Good enough to eat."

Nicola ignored that.

"I'm Nicola Graham." She held out her hand. He shook it.

"Josh Feldman," he said.

She had heard of him. A producer. One award-winning film a few years ago and a few recent ones that had bombed. He studied her carefully.

"Who'd you come with, sugar?" He asked finally.

"Pete Fletcher."

"Ahh," he said. "That explains it. Pete never did like to dress the same as the crowd."

"You know him?"

"Knew him years ago at the Estelle Harman workshop. Pete aimed to be an actor in those days." He coughed. "Didn't we all."

Nicola hid her surprise.

"He was a wild man in those days. Wild."

"Why did you give up acting?" Nicola asked, to change the subject.

"I was lousy. Just like Pete."

There was a stir in the room. The main guest had arrived. Nicola, not troubling to hide her curiosity as were so many of the other guests, looked over Feldman's shoulder to see Sir Thomas Craig and his redheaded young wife Caroline being greeted by Mrs. Fletcher. The actor was shorter, older, than Nicola had expected and he looked tired and ill underneath the practiced theatrical smile.

"Looks like he's got one foot in the grave," said Feldman, a note of sympathy in his voice.

"He looks rather . . . different . . ." said Nicola slowly.

"Expecting Big Daddy? The Prince of Denmark?"

Craig had played both parts brilliantly during his long career. Nicola glanced at Feldman, surprised.

"Something like that."

"You will learn, honey, that an actor is always somewhat less than the sum of his parts," said Feldman, chuckling at his own cleverness. Nicola smiled politely.

Pete was pushing his way back to her, greeting a few people on the way, having his back slapped avuncularly by his father's friends.

"Come say hi to the old man," he said, "then we'll split."

He ignored Josh Feldman's outstretched hand and pushed Nicola towards the middle of the room. Alvin Fletcher was a tall, slim, silver-haired man, soft-spoken, smiling. He greeted Nicola warmly.

"One of my favorite cities," he said of London. "Aren't you homesick?"

"Not at all. I like the California sun."

He laughed.

"Yes. Well, the British weather is another item altogether. You must meet your fellow countryman later. If we can get him away from some of the older ladies here."

Sir Thomas had been surrounded by a band of middle-aged females, long time fans and admirers. Caroline, twenty years younger than any of them, stood back a little, smiling indulgently.

"Won't be able to do that, Dad," said Pete. "We gotta run any minute now."

Alvin Fletcher frowned, disappointed.

"We're not really dressed for such a lovely party," said Nicola, by way of apology.

"That doesn't matter," said the older Fletcher. "Not at all."

"Excuse me a minute," said Pete, and moved across the room. Caroline Craig was now on the very edge of the group. Pete touched her shoulder and she turned and smiled immediately.

"Does he know her, I wonder," mused Alvin Fletcher. "Dear God, that son of mine knows *everybody*."

He was watching his son with such paternal pride that Nicola realized at once why Pete was as self-centered as he was. An only child, born late in a long marriage, spoiled and indulged. And still adored.

"Do ask Pete to bring you to dinner one evening. Janet will be delighted, I know."

"I'd love to come. Thank you."

"Mrs. Hampton-Norde is . . . your aunt?"

"My stepmother."

"Oh, that's right. Yes. I haven't met the lady, I'm sorry to say. Though, of course, I know of her."

Nicola wondered exactly what he knew.

Pete returned at the same moment as his mother came to join them, bringing with her an old lady dressed in black lace, her white hair held back with silver combs.

"My dear," said Janet Fletcher to Nicola. "This is Miss Maude Caulfield. She was in England for thirty years. She'd love to talk to you."

"Sorry, Mom. Sorry, Maude," said Pete abruptly, taking Nicola's arm and beginning to propel her away. "We're late and we gotta move. See you."

Even in the face of such obvious rudeness Alvin Fletcher continued to smile. His wife simply looked disappointed.

"What on earth's the hurry?" Nicola asked Pete when they were outside the house.

"No hurry. Just wanted to get out of there."

He jumped into the driver's seat of the car, opened Nicola's door from the inside and she got in.

"Why did you want to go knowing you'll get claustrophobic in three minutes?" asked Nicola, feeling cross.

"Wanted to take another look at his chick."

"Who's chick?"

"The knighted geriatric's chick."

"Caroline Craig? You know her?"

"Used to ball her once in awhile before she hit the big time," said Pete loosely. "Anyway, we did have to split. I told some pals we'd call in for a card game. You willing?"

"Of course," said Nicola. "Who are the friends?"

"Married couple," said Pete shortly. She waited for him to add more but he said nothing.

"Do they have kids?"

"Of course not."

Pete switched on the car radio so loud that further conversation was impossible. Driving the car too fast around the bends towards Laurel Canyon, he sang along with the mellow sounds of KNX-FM, tapping his fingers against the wheel. He seemed prepared to enjoy himself.

Nicola liked their house, a charming woodframe, but did not like the couple. She sensed something brittle there, a strange, cold relationship, a studied indifference. They were both physically attractive—she tall, blonde, a one time model; he taller, brown-haired, wearing tinted spectacles—but they rarely looked at each other. Though both were witty, they did not laugh at each other's sharp jokes, leaving the laughter to Pete and Nicola.

After just one drink Nicola helped Carol prepare sandwiches while Pete and Donald set up the poker table.

"I'm not much good at poker, I'm afraid," said Nicola in the kitchen. The girl turned.

"Don't worry," she said. "They both think they're better than, in fact, they are. You could make yourself a little cash tonight."

Nicola stared at her horrified.

"You play for money?"

It was Carol's turn to stare.

"Of course. What did you think?"

"Well, not with friends. Pennies, perhaps."

The girl laughed.

"Not pennies."

Nicola returned to the living room, found her handbag and counted her money. Thirty dollars in cash and the rest in traveler's checks. She put the checks back.

"I've only got thirty dollars," she said. "So I won't be playing too long. I didn't expect to be playing for money."

She tried to say it lightly but felt foolish.

"Put that away," said Pete, waving an arm impatiently.

She glanced quickly at Carol. Had the girl been joking? Carol smiled. Nicola put her money away and sat at the table. Then Pete pulled out a thick wad of bills, peeled off a number of them, and gave them to Nicola. Five hundred dollars. She pushed it back.

"Really, Pete. I couldn't."

"Don't be stupid," he said crossly. "I'll win it back off you."

Nicola took back the money. Carol, passing Nicola's chair, leaned down.

"You've got a lot to learn," she murmured.

To Nicola's surprise, Pete did win most of it back. But not from her. By two in the morning he had won a couple of hundred from Donald and a hundred or so from Carol. Nicola had more than doubled her money and had before her over a thousand dollars. She had watched with fascination as the bills changed hands and the pile of money by her left hand grew steadily. There was tension at the table: Carol chain-smoked, Donald bit his lip, and Nicola was soon damp with excitement. She had never won money before. Only Pete remained cheerful and at ease. He pocketed his winnings, smiling happily.

"Good game," he said. "Thanks for the hospitality, folks."

Yawning and stretching the four said good night. In the car Nicola glanced at Pete. He was smiling.

"Well," she said. "We played a 'blinder' as they say in England."

"You certainly did. Keep it up. We could be doing this more often."

She held out five hundred dollars to him: "Your loan."

He shook his head, waved it away.

"Keep it," he said. "I like women to be indebted to me."

Nicola put it in her purse with the rest.

"How about a celebration?" he asked, as they turned onto Sunset Boulevard.

"Now? Where?"

She glanced at her watch. It was 2:30 A.M.

"I know a party. Could be fun. You ready for a little fun?"

She nodded.

"Why not?"

The house, on a hill north of Sunset, was small and dark and seemed deserted. Faint rock music could be heard but no laughter or conversation.

"It must be over," said Nicola.

He laughed, "I'd say it's in full swing."

Pete opened the door and walked straight in. The light was blue in the hall, a soft pink in the room facing, and as Nicola followed him inside, the lights changed—to green and purple, to orange and turquoise. The guests merged into this kaleidoscope and most of them were naked or semi-naked. They were in groups of three or four, stroking each other; in twosomes writhing ballet-like on the floor; and there were some single bodies, propped against walls, eyes open and empty, staring into inner space. For Nicola, the shock was both visual and auditory—so little sound, so little laughter. Sighs, moans, a voice singing very softly and the gentle beat of the music in the background. Like a film with the sound turned down.

"Feel overdressed?" asked Pete.

Nicola smiled nervously.

"A little. But isn't it rather . . ."

"Don't worry. I'll get something to warm you up."

She stood against the wall and watched two young guys and a girl stroke each other rhythmically. Touch therapy. They were smiling but not at each other—just smiling. Pete returned and handed Nicola a glass of fruit punch. She sipped it gratefully, feeling she needed a drink before the inevitable disrobing.

"Take it slowly," Pete warned. "And look here—one for you, one for me."

He handed her a fat cigarette then lit it for her.

"Let's sit down and watch for awhile."

They sat on the floor. Nicola, kicking off her sandals, drew hard on the cigarette and held the smoke down as long as she could, just as Pete had told her. Minutes later she began to relax and she stretched out her legs lazily. In front of them, illuminated by the pulsating strobe lights, a young girl knelt before a standing youth. Her blonde hair flowed over his thighs.

"Pretty," whispered Nicola. "Pretty."

A little later Pete pulled at her T-shirt and understanding him she undressed quickly, helped him to undress. As she reached for him he held her away, a faraway smile on his face.

"Now, go play," he said.

Nicola, reacting like a child to euphoria, giggled.

"By myself. My little self?"

He smiled again, "With the others."

"Naughty girl going to play," whispered Nicola.

Like an infant she crawled towards the center of the room where a group of bodies made a stylish collage, their limbs intermingled. But a boy and girl grabbed her playfully before she reached the group.

"Here," said the girl. "Here."

They were young and, Nicola thought, beautiful. Both fair, with angel faces. They eased her onto her back and gently stroked her body, teasing her flesh, at first with fingers then with mouths. The girl slid her soft full mouth down Nicola's body until her lips found the crinkly pubic hair, then her teasing sharp tongue darted, darted again. Nicola sighed. The boy was stroking her face. He put a finger in her mouth, probed once or twice then replaced his finger with a full penis that pushed shyly between her lips. She welcomed it, circling it with her tongue to the same rhythm the girl angel played. Her flesh was melting. The lights flashed dimly behind her eyes. Only sensation left. She sucked greedily at the fleshy comforter in her mouth. The sharp dagger of girl-angel tongue had been replaced by a warm sword that probed then plunged, again and again. In her mouth a sudden flooding, love juices from the boy-angel. She swallowed, lovingly. Suddenly he had gone, her mouth empty but the warm sword still between her legs. Close to explosion and the lights behind her eyes . . .

"Sniff," said a warm voice.

She sniffed hard. Her body exploded into stars, vanished. She was falling off the edge of the world. Hands held her, arms were around her. She opened her eyes and in the apocalyptic light she saw beyond the still bodies, a

188

blurred, familiar shape. Pete. Still sitting against the wall, knees up. He held his penis in his hands and his hands worked feverishly. His face was contorted, his eyes watching her. She gazed at the wildly pulling hands with fascination. They jerked finally, then stopped. A blur, a painting. Hands. She passed out.

She was in the car. She was dressed but her sandals were on the seat beside her. Pete was rubbing her cheeks, then her hands. She groaned and looked around—they were still outside the party house.

"Ah, good," said Pete. "You're back." He started the car.

"What time is it?" Nicola heard her own voice as if from a distance. It sounded husky, as if she had a bad cold.

"Nearly six. You O.K.?"

"Yes. I think."

"Wow," he said. "You were really something. You must have really hit that punch."

"I did," Nicola said. "I didn't realize it was . . . Don't you, well, join in, Pete?"

"Don't much care for putting it in cats I don't know," he said. "Never know what they've got. And I love to watch. Boy, I enjoy that. And you . . ." he glanced at her affectionately. "You were worth watching, baby. You certainly were."

Nicola's memory ended with the angel couple. There must have been at least one other guy, she thought, because there was one in my mouth and one . . . and after that? She could not remember. She could not ask. She would never know.

At Barbara's door, she kissed Pete quickly and ran inside. She ought to bathe, she ought to at least shower, but all she wanted to do was sleep. She stood hesitantly by the bathroom door, then fell onto the bed and slept.

She woke at 11:30, her mouth dry, her head seemingly packed with surgical cotton. The events of the night before flashed through her mind, images on a screen that had little to do with her or reality. She put Pete and the party out

189

of her mind and wondered what to do with the afternoon. The day stretched before her, a long tedious space of hours to be filled. The house was quiet: David, she knew, would be at Jerry's house, sorting pictures; Barbara was probably at the gallery. She decided to go to see David, give him a little help with the work he had to do.

There was a pile of mail on the hall table and two letters for her. One was from Felix, the other handwriting was Jonathon's. She opened this first. She read through a couple of cheery paragraphs until she reached: "Have to tell you, lovely, that there are some very cross faces around here—Jeremy, Sharp—and many mutterings about replacement, and whispers of cards on the table. Don't hate me, but you should be sending more stuff. And you really ought to get back here before . . ."

Nicola stopped reading, folded the letter and tucked it into her handbag. She paused, then slid the letter from Felix in there too, unread. Lectures I don't need, she decided. Not this morning.

Maria was in the kitchen.

"Is Jeff around?" Nicola asked. The maid smiled, opened the kitchen door and called to Jeff. He appeared immediately, as if by magic.

"I'd like to go over to Jerry Womberg's house," Nicola said. "Do you know where it is?"

The man nodded. That same expressionless face.

"I'll be ready in about ten minutes," she said.

He gave an indifferent shrug and left.

"Doesn't say much, does he?" said Nicola to Maria.

The maid smiled as she poured out coffee.

"He is a quiet man," she said, then added softly. "But the señora—she like him."

Nicola looked up quickly but Maria had turned away, was busy at the stove. Nicola sipped her coffee.

The quiet man was, in fact, mute all the way to Jerry's house. He pulled into the drive of a vast, colonial-type mansion and simply stopped the car. Nicola looked at the enormous building. She thought it could probably house five families.

"Thanks," she said to Jeff when she was out of the car. He was already driving off.

Jerry opened the door himself.

"Heh—nice surprise," he said, smiling. "Come in."

The inside of the house was as opulently tasteful as the exterior. Nicola noticed a lot of French furniture, some antique lamps, good pictures.

"This is a lovely house, Jerry," she said.

He looked pleased.

"Look around as much as you like. I'll be back with you in a few minutes. It's just . . ." he glanced at his watch. "I've got ten minutes to phone a client."

"Go ahead," she said. "Is David still in your attic?"

"He certainly is."

"I'll pop up and say hello then."

"Straight up the stairs until you can't go any farther."

David had his back to her, and was so preoccupied with the stack of paintings he was sorting that he was unaware of her entrance. She crept up behind him and kissed the back of his neck. He started, smiled, then turned back to the stacked canvases.

"Hi there, beautiful," he said.

"Hi to you."

Nicola perched on a desk and watched him as he studied paintings, made notes, studied some more. He was frowning slightly but she sensed he was enjoying himself immensely.

"Almost there?" she asked.

"Almost."

"All these going in?"

"Not all."

"Can I help?"

"No," he said quietly, busy with his task.

Nicola kicked her heels against the desk. "Thank you, Nicola" she ended for him. David did not reply, she suspected he wasn't listening. She jumped down off the desk.

"I seem to be interrupting you."

David looked up then.

"No. No, you're fine. Stay where you are."

191

She roamed the room, looking at the pictures. She was impressed and rather surprised. The earlier paintings showed a young man's clear influences—echoes of de Kooning and Pollock. But the later ones indicated that he was finding his own voice—a power and a promise of things to come.

"Well, well, your own show," said Nicola. "Well done, our Barbara."

"She'll be paid," David snapped. Nicola looked at him, surprised.

"Edgy, eh? You expect to sell some, then?"

"Of course, I damn well expect to sell some."

Nicola, contrite, went over to him and hugged him quickly.

"Sorry. You'll be a smash hit. I'm sure of it."

He held her for a moment then released her and looked around the room.

"This has to work," he said. "It has to be the beginning."

"Beginning of what?"

"Everything."

Nicola was irritated by this.

"Everything," she said mockingly. "What the hell is everything for a painter?"

David had gone back to his work; she knew he was barely listening. She prowled the room aimlessly.

"I thought we might have lunch," she said after awhile. "Celebration, sort of—we haven't actually celebrated it yet."

"There's weeks to go. I'd prefer to celebrate afterwards."

"You're too busy for lunch?"

There was a pause. She watched as he scribbled on a large legal pad. Finally he glanced up.

"I promised to have lunch with Barbara," he said. "Join us."

"No thanks, I'll call Pete. No I won't, I'll call Alan."

"Call him from here," he said.

Which for some reason incensed her. He caught her by the shoulders as she reached the door.

"What is it?" he asked, looking down at her face. "You're angry. Why?"

She looked back at him and anger gave way to confusion.

"I am," she admitted. "But I don't know why. I don't know."

He kissed her forehead lightly, then her mouth. A gentle, friendly kiss. She rested her head on his chest and he stroked her hair. His gentleness recalled the soothing touch-therapy of the night before. But in contrast to that impersonal playground scene, this had the reality of daylight and Nicola lifted her head, wanting him to kiss her properly. He did, with an urgency that increased in moments. Nicola, pressed hard against him, felt herself aroused. Could feel that he wanted her.

"Make love to me," she whispered.

He released her quickly.

"Don't, for Christ's sake, play those games with me."

She stared at him.

"I wasn't playing a game."

"Make love to you here and now, right? Then you go off to lunch with Fletcher or Alan or some other fucking Bel-Air stud. Right?"

She did not reply for a moment.

"I hadn't thought beyond . . ." She stopped. A silence.

"Nicola, what are you doing? Do you know?"

She turned her back to him and tapped the edges of her fingers together as if thinking hard.

"All I know is that I wanted you to make love to me," her voice was very soft, almost inaudible. "I don't see that you should be offended by that."

"It isn't enough," he said harshly, choosing his next hard words deliberately, "a five minute fuck in someone's attic. Do you understand that?"

She turned to look at him, her eyes cloudy.

"Most men would be . . . happy."

"I'm not most men."

"No," she said. "No, you're not." She turned towards the door. "See you."

Halfway down the first flight of stairs Nicola turned. David was clearly visible through the open door of the attic. He had his back to her. He was already back at work, sorting his pictures.

Alan was free for lunch. Nicola, curled up in a velvet covered armchair in Jerry's lounge, had just replaced the receiver when Barbara was shown in by the maid.

"How long you been here?" asked Barbara, surprised.

"About ten minutes."

"Jerry around?"

Barbara, as if the house belonged to her, opened the doors of an antique French cabinet and pulled out a whisky bottle.

"He's somewhere in this incredible mansion," said Nicola. "But Christ knows where."

Barbara was now at the ice-bucket.

"You having a drink?"

"No, thanks. Oh . . . why not? Small gin, please."

Barbara with practiced expertise mixed the drinks.

"You seen wonder boy?" she asked over her shoulder.

"He's working away like a demon upstairs."

"Good. You coming to lunch?"

"No. Thanks. I have a date with Alan."

Barbara sipped her drink and studied Nicola thoughtfully.

"And what's happened to Pete?"

"Seeing him tomorrow." Nicola smiled slightly. "I just felt like a change."

"You're playing hard to get, you mean," said Barbara, raising an eyebrow.

Nicola smiled.

"Maybe."

"Don't overdo it. Pete wouldn't, I imagine, take lightly to being messed around."

"I know what I'm doing," said Nicola.

"I hope so. Why don't you invite Pete for the boat trip we discussed?"

"Might do that," she said.

Barbara set down her now empty glass.

"If Jerry turns up tell him I'm upstairs with David. See you later."

Nicola nodded. She stretched restlessly once Barbara had left the room then walked to Jerry's large window. The house had enormous grounds, two tennis courts, a large pool. But it was the garden that held the attention—a long, velvety lawn, geometrically cut, with borders and islands of flowers arranged so that colors balanced and complemented. There was an elegant Italian fountain, a few cherubs and statues. It was tastefully done but the affect was still overwhelming.

"Like my garden?"

Jerry came to stand next to her and looked out with pride.

"It's beautiful, Jerry."

"I like it."

"Do you work on it yourself, ever?"

Jerry laughed.

"Afraid not. I've got an excellent gardener. But—well, he follows my instructions exactly. I did design it myself."

"It's lovely."

Nicola turned from the window.

"Barbara's upstairs with David. They'll be down shortly. They're going out to lunch."

"Then if you're not joining them why not have lunch here with me. My cook . . ."

"Jerry I would have loved it. But I've just made a lunch date."

He looked disappointed.

"I am sorry," said Nicola. "We are rude, aren't we? Bounding into your beautiful house and hardly stopping to talk to you."

Jerry shrugged.

"I don't mind that. I've too much work to do really to stop and talk."

Nicola felt that her tactless remark had offended him and she touched his arm gently.

"Come join Alan and me. We're going to Scandia."

"Alan would love that I'm sure," he said, smiling.

"He won't mind."

"Of course he will. Thank you, dear, but I have a lot of work. It will be a short lunch for me."

The doorbell pealed.

"Alan," said Nicola. "I'd better go."

Impulsively, she kissed Jerry's cheek. Jerry smiled then turned back to his garden.

TWENTY-THREE

Jerry would remember Barbara's boat trip with intense humiliation and embarrassment. Afterwards, he did not blame Nicola but instead blamed himself for not learning from an earlier lesson. For Nicola managed to do exactly what her stepmother had done years ago, with the same coldblooded curiosity and a similar desire to use him to hurt others. Jerry had, for awhile, been concerned at the changes in the girl; had felt certain, for some reason, that the changes were conscious—a deliberate metamorphosis. He had not guessed that this metamorphosis would affect him.

Things began to go wrong for Nicola right away and Jerry felt sorry for her. They were ready to sail, Barbara was impatient to get going and David, Art, Angie, and he were gathered in a group on the deck of the boat. Nicola still stood on the quay, waiting for Pete. He was half an hour late. Nicola had telephoned his house but there had been no reply. Jerry prayed that Pete would come quickly. Nicola's face looked so pale and set as she stood alone on the quayside.

After forty minutes Barbara went down to her.

"Come on, honey. We're all ready to go. He probably got tied up."

Barbara had put an arm around Nicola's shoulders. The girl shrugged it off and walked swiftly up the gangplank. Jerry gave a last swift prayer that Pete might appear. It was not answered.

Nicola leaned back against the boat rail saying nothing.

197

"Men," said Barbara lightly. "They're full of promises, promises . . ." Nicola turned her back.

"They're also full of shit," Barbara added. "OK, cap'n, set sail."

The eighty-foot yacht had a three man crew and it was soon underway. The shoreline at the Marina receded and, with the fascination that any boat trip involves, they watched the land diminishing as they increased their distance from it. Nicola was watching the coast road, still searching for Pete's car.

"Who's for a champagne takeoff?" Jerry asked the group. He'd arranged for a couple of crates to be brought on board.

"Darling!" said a delighted Barbara.

Everyone except Nicola turned from the boat rail and beamed at him.

"In any case," said Jerry, smiling at David. "A celebration is in order."

"Of course," said Art. "Well done, David."

David smiled.

"Bit premature, but thanks."

Nicola turned then.

"Christ, he hasn't even done the bloody show yet!"

Art and Angie looked at her in surprise.

"Good luck toast, then" said Jerry quietly.

"The point, sweetheart," said Barbara, "is not that he *hasn't done*, but that he is *going to do* it."

"Big deal," said Nicola.

David was watching Nicola levelly. She caught his look then stared down at the floor, ashamed.

"Sorry," she said.

"Doesn't matter," said David.

"It shouldn't," said Nicola sharply and unexpectedly.

Barbara was annoyed.

"No squabbling, children," she said. "We run a happy ship."

She rang for the champagne but Nicola drank little of it. She stood at the boat rail, staring out to sea. It is tough, thought Jerry, to be stood up, but it is even tougher in public. He hoped Barbara would not bait her.

Barbara, in fact, played the grand hostess with style and seemed unconcerned at the girl's tense face or her silence. Nicola drank a great deal of wine at dinner but barely touched her food. She asked for brandy afterwards and Barbara ordered it without a murmur. Nicola kept the bottle by her side when dinner was over and filled her glass frequently as she sat flicking through a magazine. She refused to join the others in a card game. Jerry had no interest in cards either and after a stroll around the deck sat down next to Nicola. She did not look up from her magazine.

"Let me mix you a brandy-champagne cocktail, Nicola" said Jerry, seeing that her glass was nearly empty. "One of my specialties."

"Will it get me drunker, faster?"

"Very likely," he said, taking her glass. "Is that your intention?"

"Absolutely."

"I'll make it a strong cocktail."

He was pleased that she followed him to the bar to watch the process. He was proud of his cocktail mixing. David joined them, wiping his brow.

"I've resigned," he said ruefully. "My pride couldn't take any more. Accused of cheating, for Christ's sake!"

Jerry smiled. Barbara's angry voice carried clearly from the lounge section. She was holding her cards like weapons, pointing them at Art and Angie.

"There is some crap going on here," said Barbara. "There is some crap."

Angie and Art exchanged nervous looks.

"Barbara is losing, I imagine," said Jerry.

"She's lost two games, that's all. But two games in a row. That always makes her suspicious."

The two men grinned. Nicola looked impatiently at the half-mixed cocktail and Jerry got back to work.

"Nicola has decided to get pleasantly . . ."

"Anaesthetically . . ." Nicola interjected.

"Drunk. And I am creating my very special cocktail." Jerry added a splash more brandy.

David was looking at Nicola curiously.

199

"What's this, Nicola—to mend your broken heart?"

There was heavy irony in his voice and Nicola gave him a long look.

"Balls to you, David," she said.

Jerry poured the mixture into three glasses, then poured another one for Barbara who would scream if she were left out.

"Come on now, Nicola," David was saying. "You don't give a damn about Fletcher."

"Don't give a damn? How the hell would you know?"

"Now, now . . ." said Jerry, worried by this.

They ignored him.

"I know," continued David. "He's rich. Right? He's also a boring bastard. And thick as pig-shit."

"So? Who needs an intellectual?"

Jerry picked up Barbara's drink and began to carry it across the room.

"I know what you need," said David, in a lowered voice. To Jerry's chagrin he could not catch the rest. Barbara shouted with delight at her cocktail but turned immediately back to her cards. She was winning now. David was staring at Nicola angrily when Jerry began crossing the room to rejoin them.

"You've turned into a bitch," he heard David say.

"Why do you think that?" asked Nicola. "Because I won't love you forever?"

David turned on his heel and walked out onto the deck. Nicola stared after him, moved as if to follow, then stopped. Jerry joined her, wondering what the hell it was all about. He was relieved that Barbara was absorbed in her card game.

"Why are you two . . ." began Jerry, then stopped. It was none of his business.

"None of my business," he said to Nicola. She gave a rueful smile.

"None of mine either, really," she said obstrusely. "How about some more of that delicious cocktail?"

She drank a lot of it, then and later. When the card game was over, Jerry mixed another couple of shakers for them all. Then the inevitable drunken dancing began.

David and Barbara were wildly cavorting around the floor. There was a frenzied energy to David—his movements and his voice.

"Shake it, baby," he shouted to Barbara, "shake it."

Barbara dutifully performed an uncontrolled Eastern-style dance. Jerry looked away. Art and Angie, lying boozily and untidily on the sofa—she stretched lengthways, her head in Art's lap—shouted encouragement.

"She sure can shake 'em," said Angie, then promptly closed her eyes and went to sleep.

Jerry was holding Nicola in his arms, supporting her mostly, and moving slowly around the floor. She had wanted to dance but he suspected she had gone to sleep on his shoulder. She was not asleep, however. She lifted her head and looked over to see Barbara's dance.

"How elegant," she said, clearly and sarcastically.

Jerry looked down at her, then across to the dancers. Barbara, involved in her gyrations, had not heard but David's look to Nicola was poisonous. Jerry settled Nicola's head back on his shoulder. He was worried about her. She had drunk too much, she was behaving irrationally and she seemed to be spoiling for a fight.

"You're tired," he said to her gently.

"Ready for bed," she said. "Ready. All ready. Come and tuck me in?"

"I've not had much tucking-in practice."

"Help me get there, then," said Nicola peevishly. "Because I sure as eggs ain't going to make it by myself."

She let go of him suddenly and staggered backwards. He grabbed her.

"See?" she said.

Jerry put his arm firmly around her and began to lead her towards her cabin.

"Night you good people," he called.

"*Already*," said Barbara, whirling around to face them. "Are you crazy?"

"We ought to hit the hay, too, sweetheart," said Art to Angie.

"Honey, I'm comfortable."

"Bedibyes," shouted Nicola, as they left the stateroom. "Nice Jerry's going to tuck me in."

She turned for a moment and Jerry gripped her tighter. But she simply blew two kisses into the room. David, Jerry noticed, was frowning angrily.

Nicola's cabin was tiny. She flopped down on the bunk bed, closing her eyes.

"Help off with clothes," she said sleepily.

"You can do it."

"Can't."

He stood uncertainly.

"Please," she said. "Be a friend."

He clumsily tugged off her sweater. She was bra-less and Jerry looked away.

"Jeans," she said.

He struggled with her jeans. She was left wearing a small pair of panties.

"Don't go," she called. Jerry was half out of the door. He turned and looked at her helplessly.

"What do you want, Nicola?" he asked unhappily.

"Just a cuddle. Just a little comforting cuddle."

"I can't cuddle you."

"Of course you can. Don't be a prude."

She sounded as if she were going to cry. He came back into the room.

"Get under the sheet," he said. She did as he requested and Jerry sat on the edge of the bed.

"What's wrong?" he asked gently.

"I'm just a baby. Just a miserable baby. Lie down and cuddle me."

He paused, looking at her face, then lay down on top of the sheet and held her for awhile as one would hold a child. He thought she was falling asleep, her arms around his neck. But when he tried to remove her arms she moved closer to him and began sleepily to stroke his shoulder. Her hands moved down to his back.

She was pressing hard against him now and, unexpectedly, her hands were along his thighs, fluttering over his groin. With a jolt he realized that she was trying to seduce him. He wanted to sit up, move away, get out. But could not. Like a fly in the web of a spider, he was trapped. Trapped by a curiosity. *Could* she seduce him? Would his own body react? He had been able, years ago as a teenager, to fuck girls. Perfunctory sex though it was, and too fast. Later, when he had finally come to realize, accept, and half understand his sexual nature, he had not bothered to try. He knew a few bisexuals. He did not envy them. But was he . . . Nicola had undone his zipper, her small hand stroked him. Nothing. Nothing for minutes that stretched relentlessly. Nothing.

"What a shame," said Nicola, removing her hand. Her voice sounded normal, sober, and without a trace of warmth. It was then he felt the overwhelming mortification and shame. She was sorry for him, perhaps. She was using him, certainly. Why? To get at David? But why David? She had been pretending. Acting a part. He did his trousers up quickly. She was not the first actress to play the role. Years ago her stepmother . . .

"Cheer up, Jerry," said Nicola sitting up in bed. He was standing now. "It happens to all the fellas all the time."

"You know better than that," he said.

"Please sit down. Just for a minute or two. I don't want you to leave angry."

He was angry. But he sat down.

"Why?" he asked. "Why did you do that?"

She ignored the question.

"Have you tried it with girls before?" she asked softly.

"Not recently."

Barbara. That scene at the gallery. "When you get it up again Jerry, if ever, you can show me what I deserve . . ."

Years ago, Barbara, drunk like Nicola but genuinely so, had taken him to her bedroom. She had not known him long, he was recently her attorney and she had not known he was a homosexual. She had tried to seduce him and, like Nicola, failed. He had forgiven her in the bedroom, though he had been embarrassed by her laughter. It was when he came downstairs in the Bel-Air house that he understood. Her husband, Serge, had returned—as Barbara had obviously anticipated. He had divorced her afterwards—as Barbara had planned. She had married again, an old, respectable, very rich man. Jack Hampton. Hampton died and left her a very rich widow two years later. Just as she wanted. Jerry had been cited as co-respondent in her divorce from Serge which distressed him greatly. At the time he was building up a law practice. What distressed him further was that Barbara told many of her friends, and some of his, about the incident. He had never forgiven her for that. So why did he keep her as a client? Why socialize with the bitch? He never could work it out. Masochism, maybe. Or waiting for the chance of revenge.

He sighed. Nicola was watching him closely.

"What are you thinking about?"

"Nicola," he began with an effort. "You should go home. Before you destroy yourself."

"Destroy myself? I'm fine."

Jerry swallowed.

"When you arrived, there was an innocent fawn-like quality to you. Very attractive. You're losing that."

"So, it's lost," she said.

"Not lost entirely," he tried to be truthful. "There's still something about you. I still feel you don't belong here."

"I don't belong anywhere," she said.

Jerry got to his feet. He stopped at the door.

"Nicola, you must . . ."

"Don't tell me *must*," she said angrily and quickly turned her face to the wall. He left her.

Restless in his own bed, Jerry realized she had achieved one positive thing—she had dissipated, somewhat, his own guilt about her. Over the weeks, as he got to know and like Nicola, he had grown more uncomfortable about his part in Barbara's collection of Graham paintings. He had been to London, at her expense, only once. And that was years ago. He had met Nick Graham by appointment at his London club and had told the painter only one small lie: he had said the picture he wanted was for himself.

"Always pleased to sell to an American," Graham had boomed cheerfully. "Bring art and civilization to that barbarous country."

Jerry had grinned. It was impossible to take offense at the large, smiling man.

"I'm kidding, of course," said Graham. "The Land of the Free hasn't quite reached the barbaric heights of say, Orpington or Kew, or the gods protect us, Surbiton. The Lord help you all when it does."

Jerry, who had heard of these middle-class strongholds, smiled again.

"Have another drink," he offered.

"Of course. A double. And that's another thing I like about Americans. They know how to pour a decent drink."

Nick Graham had happily let Jerry buy lunch but he had sold him the picture for only sixty pounds. Barbara had sold it the night after the opening for $5,250. Jerry had been present at the sale and since then phrases like "defrauding Nicola out of her inheritance" had been buzzing in his mind. Now, hurt and humiliated, he pondered this—it was not legally true and it did not matter in any case. Nicola did not need any inheritance. She would achieve what she wanted as easily as her stepmother had always done.

He had thought previously that somehow they were all destroying her. A week or so later it was to cross his mind that, in fact, she came very close to destroying them all.

The gentle lulling of the boat plus the evening's alcohol had a soporific effect on Barbara. She fell asleep as soon as she hit the bed and began snoring loudly minutes later. David lay awake for what seemed like hours, listening to the sounds of the boat. That is, he *told* himself he was listening to the sounds of the boat while knowing, deep down, that he was listening for a clue as to whether Jerry had stayed in Nicola's cabin all night. Her cabin was on the other side of the boat, as was Jerry's. It was difficult to hear sounds so far away. And Barbara's snoring didn't help, nor did the whispered, drunken quarrel Art and Angie were having next-door.

David was tempted at one point to get some air on deck, stroll around the boat and meanwhile just check if Jerry's cabin door was open. See if he was in there. He dismissed the idea, annoyed with himself. What did it matter? She could fuck whomever she liked. But Jerry? Surely . . . ?

Either Jerry Womberg was a deep and dark horse, or Nicola was playing games. But why the hell . . .

He tossed in bed and Barbara stirred and cuddled up to him. Normally he would have stroked her properly awake and made love to her. For the first time in their relationship he moved away from her, to the other side of the king-size bed. Barbara began to snore again. David lay motionless, staring up at the flickering shadows on the ceiling.

He was awake again just after seven and got up immediately, leaving Barbara to sleep. He felt he needed a long shower; his head ached dully, his eyes were hot and itchy. He took his time in the shower, washed his hair, then strolled out onto the deck. Jerry Womberg stood, his back to David, staring out at the water. He looked very still, faraway in his thoughts. David stepped back, not wanting to disturb him, and went through to the dining area. Nicola was sitting there, reading a newspaper. David studied her for awhile. So they were both up. Did that mean . . .

"Hi," he said. "You're up early."

"It's not that early," said Nicola. "Anyway, what about you?"

"It's this healthful sea air."

"Something like that."

He sat down opposite her. The table had been set for breakfast. Nicola was sipping coffee.

"Where's Jerry?" David asked, casually.

She looked hard at him before replying.

"Well, he could be skin-diving, or fishing, reading, writing, sleeping, showering, fucking . . ."

"O.K. O.K." said David.

"How the hell should I know?" she asked.

"You might."

"He is, in fact, out on deck wondering whether to throw himself into the deep blue sea."

Before David could reply to this, a breezy voice greeted them.

"Morning, children," said Barbara. "And a pretty one too."

Barbara was smartly dressed in pants and a cream colored shirt, her hair styled neatly, her make-up perfect.

David marveled that within an hour she had transformed herself into this elegant creature and that, as ever, the excesses of the night before left no mark on her. She never suffered hangovers, she woke with little appetite for food but with a certain enthusiasm for the day. He smiled at her.

"You look good."

Nicola looked up from her newspaper, inspected Barbara's outfit, nodded and went back to her paper. Barbara raised an eyebrow. The crew began bringing in hot dishes which Barbara inspected.

"Looks fine, just fine," she said, then turned to Nicola. "Where's Jerry?"

Nicola looked up and from one to the other of them.

"Jesus Christ," she said. "Am I my brother's keeper? He could be skin-diving, swimming, fishing . . ."

"He's on deck," David interrupted.

"No, he's not," said Jerry's voice. "He's here."

Jerry, jaunty and smiling, said good morning to all three and settled himself at the table.

"Good, we can start eating then," said Barbara. "Art and Angie will not be joining us for breakfast for the simple reason that they both feel very sick. I told Angie it must be morning sickness."

Barbara chuckled and began to spoon crisp bacon onto their plates.

"This is some spread," said Jerry. "Yes, indeedy."

The hearty note was unconvincing and David felt a sudden sympathy for the middle-aged man so uncomfortably bearing their scrutiny. David glanced at Nicola, knowing his look was hostile. She looked back with wide-eyed innocence.

"Mm, delicious," said Jerry.

"Jesus, how can anybody eat like that first thing in the morning," said Nicola. She finished off her coffee in a gulp, then moved away from the table. The three watched her in silence.

"Fresh air for me," she said, strolling out towards the deck.

"Irritable bitch," said Barbara.

"She's only a child," said Jerry, eyes on his plate.

"A child, he says! You weren't treating her like a child last night."

"We talked for awhile."

"Talking, eh? Is that what they call it nowadays?" said Barbara. "I wouldn't have thought, Jerry, that you . . ." Barbara stopped, smiled to herself. "Never mind," she said.

David said nothing. He buttered some toast, sipped his coffee, then attempted some of the bacon, eggs, and pancakes. The food *was* good.

"God, it looks like the chimps' tea-party," said Nicola from the doorway. She gave a disgusted shrug and walked back out on deck. David watched the slight figure at the rail for a moment. They finished breakfast in silence.

TWENTY-FOUR

The week before his exhibition was due to open, David was suffering from last-minute nerves and having serious second thoughts. What if he wasn't ready? If he failed this time he'd find it difficult to get another chance. A guy from *New West* had come out to chat with him about the show. David had found himself stuttering and stammering, unable to think clearly or give any intelligent answers. He saw the man out with relief, consoling himself with the thought that artists were allowed a little eccentricity. He suspected the guy thought he was not so much crazy as stupid.

Maybe I am, he thought, lying back in the sun by the pool. Certainly Barbara is treating me like a child and Nicola is treating me like a crass moron and either I'm out of step or the rest are. He studied the group covertly. Nicola was sunbathing—topless. This, he guessed, was to annoy Barbara. Or embarrass Jerry. The attorney had joined them for the afternoon, bringing with him a young friend, Tim, who could have been, though it was not obvious, Jerry's lover. The first time David had known the older man to give anything like a public sign of his homosexuality. The two of them sat in deck chairs, reading newspapers. Barbara was giving them curious glances, hoping no doubt, thought David, that they will give a sign—clutch each other or hold hands. She had been surprised when they arrived, no doubt about that. Barbara was also looking at the almost naked Nicola with irritation.

"Let's go in, for God's sake," Barbara said eventually. "The sun is half down."

"Oh, it's lovely," said Nicola.

"Pretty warm still," added Tim, quietly. Maybe *he* was enjoying the view of Nicola's pretty breasts.

"Like hell, it is!" said Barbara, encouraged, as usual, by opposition. "It's getting cool. Come on. Let's snack on something."

"One quick dip," said Nicola.

She walked to the edge of the pool with everybody except Jerry watching her. She dived elegantly into the pool, swam to the end, then walked back, dripping, to her towel. David watched her sadly as she dried herself carefully, slowly, paying special attention to her breasts. Barbara, annoyed at this display, swept up towels and lotions in her arms and led the way to the house. Nicola, her towel draped casually around her waist, began to follow.

"Don't you want this?" David called, holding up Nicola's top. She turned back, looked at it.

"Why?" she asked.

David inspected it carefully.

"It's pretty," he said.

"But not as pretty as . . ." Tim murmured.

She heard this and she smiled before walking into the house. The men followed, Jerry lumbering behind. So Tim wasn't—or was he? David shrugged. It hardly mattered.

In the house, Barbara was already giving orders to the patently nervous maid while Nicola sat curled in a chair still topless.

"Ham, cheese, crackers, bread. Whatever you've got," Barbara barked. "*And* . . ." the maid's head bobbed back around the door.

"Get the fucking ice, would you. Pronto."

A real Barbara temper, but not caused by the maid. She turned to Nicola immediately.

"Put some clothes on, would you."

"Why?"

"Because I say so. And you're a guest in my house."

Even Jerry looked up in surprise. Nicola stared at her stepmother then walked slowly towards the stairs.

210

"Of course, madame," she said. "Delighted to oblige."

Barbara sighed when she'd gone.

"What the hell has happened to Pete Fletcher?" she asked nobody in particular. "Get that bitch out of my hair."

No one answered because no one knew. David had seen Pete around town a few times, accompanied as usual by some chick or other, but he hadn't spoken to him. He knew that Nicola had not seen Pete since before the boat trip. She had been moody and quick tempered since the trip, though she had a number of guys calling her, a few of them rich enough for what David imagined she wanted. She stayed out late most nights, or did not return home at all, and was beginning to look tired. David feared she would return to England soon. He did not want her to go. Not yet.

Nicola came into the room, wearing a sweater over her bikini, at the exact moment, Maria arrived with the food.

"Oh, gourmet eating," she said sarcastically.

They all ignored this. David poured drinks, Barbara frenetically carved ham and cheese, offering it to the men.

"One bite," said Jerry, "then we really have to go. Sorry, honey."

Tim chewed at a small sandwich.

"Nice," he said.

"Super," drawled Nicola.

"Will you cut that shit out." Barbara's voice was quieter than usual which made it all the more menacing.

"Why don't we all cut this out?" asked David quietly. "Christ knows what this sniping is about but it's boring as hell."

"Wouldn't want the little boy to be bored now, would we?"

Nicola's words were half lost in the scraping of a chair as Jerry got to his feet.

"We have to go, Barbara," he said. Tim stood with him.

"It's been very nice," he said. "Thanks."

"Stay a little while, you guys," said David, thinking that some male company, of whatever sexual persuasion, would be pleasant for a change. Besides, he liked Jerry. An intelligent man and a good talker. He hadn't had much chance to talk today.

"Really, we must go," said Jerry, regretfully.

"Leave 'em alone," said Nicola. "They're probably going out for a cozy little dinner together."

There was an embarrassed silence. David felt that he would like to smack her face. But Jerry smiled suddenly, straight at Nicola.

"Bye, all," he said, as he walked to the door. Tim followed.

"Bye, gentlemen," said Nicola.

Barbara jumped to her feet as the front door clicked.

"Shit," she said. "I wanted Jerry."

She bounced out after them.

"If she wants Jerry, she's welcome," said Nicola. "Poor little man. Interesting couple they'd make—the castrated and the castrater."

David looked hard at her.

"What the hell is wrong with you today?" he asked, expecting a flip, sarcastic reply. But she gazed back at him and sighed.

"God knows. I'm tired, I suppose. And cheesed off. And Barbara is getting on my nerves. Childish bitch."

"We're all childish. You, too."

"Thanks a lot," she said, stretching her arm to carve herself more ham from the cart next to her. "But I'm just a mite young. One would think with maturity . . ."

"That is, I guess, the whole problem."

Nicola looked at him inquisitively.

"She's jealous of you," he explained.

Nicola laughed.

"Jealous! For God's sake, she doesn't know I've even touched you."

"Maybe not. But . . ."

"Maybe? Have you told her?"

"Of course not," he replied, with impatience. "She's simply jealous of *you*. You're young, super-attractive. You've got it all to come."

"And she's had it?"

They laughed together and some of the tension ebbed from the room.

"Not really," said David.

"Not really, eh? The great stud speaks. Great in the sack is she? Give good . . ."

"No, not fucking really," Barbara's voice froze them both. She strode into the center of the room, pale with anger, the heavy lines sharp around her mouth.

"And as for touching him, *sweetie*, you can touch him all you want. I don't give a shit. But touch him out of my house."

David swallowed hard then went to the bar to pour her a drink. She had never demanded fidelity from him. That wouldn't bug her too much. But with Nicola? That would be different.

"Calm down, honey," he said, pouring a large scotch.

"In fact, get *out* of my house," she screamed at Nicola. The younger woman looked back at her without expression.

"Here." David handed Barbara the scotch. She took it, looking at him steadily.

"You too," she said.

"I'm not going anywhere."

"You're overwrought, stepmother darling," said Nicola. "Sit down and drink your drink."

Shocked by her clumsiness. David gave Nicola a warning look. She gazed back calmly. Barbara was predictably incensed.

"I said—get out!" she said, her teeth clenched over the words.

Nicola stretched her arm again and very slowly began to carve slithers of ham from the joint. The long knife made a tiny, scratching clink as it repeatedly touched the metal plate. Apart from their breathing, it was the only sound in the room.

"Later," Nicola said finally. "Tomorrow, maybe."

Barbara sipped her drink, fighting for control. David put an arm around her shoulders but she shrugged it off immediately.

"Sit down, Barbara," he said.

"I want her out—now."

But she sat down, sipped her drink, then turned to Nicola. Her voice, though still angry, was controlled.

"I want you to go and I want you to go immediately. You've been my guest here. You've eaten my food, drunk my liquor, fucked my friends. And you repay me . . ."

"Repay you!" Nicola shouted, her temper breaking. She stopped then, took a number of short breaths to steady herself and continued to carve tiny pieces from the ham.

"Why the hell should I repay you? You wanted me here. Add a little class to my father's exhibition. You asked me here."

"Class?" scoffed Barbara.

David, disgusted with both women, walked over to the window.

"Jesus. A couple of fishwives," he said.

"All right, I asked you. I wish I hadn't fucking bothered to ask you. I thought it might help the sales. But, shit, I didn't need you at all. Not at all. I've sold everyone of my goddamn pictures."

"They weren't *your* pictures. They were *his*."

"I own the damn things. I owned them," said Barbara.

A stunned silence filled the room. David, not sure what this meant, turned from the window. How could Barbara own *all* of Nick Graham's pictures. They had been in private collections. Or had they? He remembered when she was arranging the exhibition a few had to be transported from somewhere. On loan, maybe. She could have loaned them out at some point, and got them back for the show. Maybe.

Nicola, perplexed, was staring at Barbara.

"You own *these* . . ." she said, making a sweeping gesture to include the Graham pictures in the room.

"I am keeping these, honey," said Barbara, dangerously quiet. "These are pictures of me and I want to be reminded every damn day what a jerk I was."

Nicola looked away.

"You sold the others?" she asked, softly.

"All of them."

"How many in that gallery did you own?"

"Most of 'em."

Nicola, intent on carving at the joint, did not look up.

"He didn't give them to you," she said.

"Give them to me? He wouldn't give a child the time of day. I bought them, sweetheart. Paid for them. With my own little pennies I paid for them. And Serge's little pennies."

Nicola looked up at her stepmother then.

"You had people make offers for you?"

"You've got it."

"Agents?"

"Agents and others."

"You must have paid pennies for them, then." Nicola could have been talking to herself. Her voice was soft. "Because my father sold his pictures as he painted them. He always needed the money. He sold them to the first bidder."

"I usually got in first."

"Got somebody to get in first for you?"

"Right."

"And then you hoarded them," stated Nicola, nodding to herself.

David, trying to follow this, began to understand. But unclearly.

"What the hell is this?" he asked. "Will someone explain . . ."

"I'll explain to you," said Nicola, snapping with anger. She had jumped to her feet, still holding the long carving knife, and she waved it like a baton as she spoke.

"She bought them up. Deliberately. This cow here bought them up on purpose."

"So? I paid for them," said Barbara.

"She knew him. She knew him well. She knew he'd sell cheap to anyone. So she got herself a collection and hoarded them. Deliberately. There were never any available for shows," her voice was rising in anger. "All the early stuff just vanished. We couldn't trace them. But he never tried very hard. She knew that too. That's why he had so little exposure. Nothing."

215

"He *deserved* nothing." Barbara shouted. Nicola's voice was even louder.

"You cow," she screamed. "You kept them to destroy him. You . . ."

"Quiet down. Both of you. Now. Quiet down, please!"

David was ignored. The two women, white with fury, faced each other, blue eyes clashing against blue. David had never felt so helpless. Between men, the punches would have been flying and he could have intervened physically. Here, the violence hung in the air and words carried it.

"You couldn't destroy that sonofabitch," Barbara hissed. "He was made of . . ."

"You helped him destroy himself. That's what you did. And you think you're keeping these to remind you?" Nicola waved the knife towards the pictures. "Oh, no, you are not. You are not fucking well keeping . . ."

As she moved like a whirlwind across the room, David understood. She was at the first picture in a manic frenzy, before he reached her. Two long, slashing movements of the knife. The painting of a young woman, a young Barbara, was severed.

"Stop that!" screamed Barbara, hysterical now.

She reached Nicola as David did. The girl turned, her eyes bright, crazed, as she waved the knife towards them.

"Stay away. *Away*," she said.

"Nicola, for God's sake," said David, as calmly as he could.

He could grab her, but he feared she would injure herself with that gleaming weapon. Or injure Barbara. Reason with her. Reason with her.

She had moved, catlike, to the next, smaller picture in the room. One swift slash of her knife and the picture collapsed, hung at a crazy angle.

A sketch of a bluebell wood, a woman and child.

Barbara, choking, grabbed Nicola's arm but let go immediately when Nicola swung around with the knife.

"Come near me, bitch, and I'll slice through you, too."

216

Barbara, eyes wide with fear, backed away. David stepped in front of her, looked calmly into Nicola's eyes.

"Nicola. Calm down now, please."

Tears ran down her cheeks, but she held his gaze.

"*And,* I'd sliced through you," she said.

Behind her the destroyed sketch clattered to the floor. Barbara with a yell of anguish moved as if to grasp Nicola. David held her back, firmly.

"They're mine! Mine," she screamed at Nicola. "Do you know how much they're worth, you crazy, fucking bitch."

"They're worth nothing to you. You didn't pay for them. My father paid for them."

Nicola circled the room like an animal, still holding the knife in front of her.

"Nicola, I'm going to take that off you. Give it to me now." His voice sounded steadier than he felt. He wondered if indeed she had snapped, if she was truly crazy. The wildness in her face, those brilliant eyes. She stopped circling for a moment, looked at him, then began again.

"Give it to me," he continued. "Then we must all sit down quietly and . . ."

"Where are the rest?" she whispered. "The hall. Of course. The pictures in the hall."

She sped around so fast that David thought she would stumble. He automatically reached forward to check her fall. Then, in confusion, he realized that Barbara had grabbed her first. With horror he saw the knife rise. With one vicious movement Nicola buried the knife in Barbara's shoulder.

"No!" he cried out.

Barbara had fallen to the floor, blood soaked her yellow dress, was melting into the carpet. She lay perfectly still. Nicola stood, frozen, looking down at her. David moved the girl away and knelt down by Barbara's body.

"I've killed her!" she shrieked.

The knife had fallen onto the carpet. The wound bled Barbara's bright blood. He felt her pulse. Still there. Her flesh warm. He tore off his shirt and began to staunch the flow of blood. Nicola had sunk into a crouching position on

217

the floor and she rocked backwards and forwards, whimpering.

"Killed Barbara. Killed Barbara. Killed."

The whimpering chant continued as he got to the phone. To his relief, he immediately got hold of Barbara's doctor and came back to the unconscious woman, bleeding less now, on the floor.

"Killed, killed, killed," the chant continued.

"She's not dead," said David clearly.

Nicola, still rocking could not understand.

"Nicola," he said loudly.

The blank face turned to him. The eyes burned in her pale skin.

"She is not dead."

Nicola frowned at him.

"Barbara is alive," he said. "The doctor is coming. It's all right."

Nicola, sinking her head back onto her knees, continued her rocking but the chanting stopped.

"Nicola." He waited until the head lifted and her eyes met his. "Go upstairs now, wash your face, and rest in your room awhile. Do you hear me?"

She looked quickly at Barbara, shuddered violently, then nodded. Shakily, she got to her feet.

"Go along now," he said.

She walked unsteadily to the door, her face averted. He heard her slow footsteps on the stairs.

Barbara stirred. Her face was gray, making the blonde hair unnaturally bright. He moved a strand of it away from her forehead. And waited. At last, the sound of a car. The doctor.

He was a friend of Barbara, a bustling, efficient man, and in a few minutes he had tended the wound and given the now conscious woman a sedative and a pain killer.

"You must rest," he said. "And don't move that arm. Now—I should ask you how you managed to sustain such a wound. It's not serious. But . . ."

"You don't have to ask," said Barbara, weakly. "Do you?"

He sighed.

"No."

Between them they settled her in bed and almost immediately she fell asleep. It was only after he closed the door to the doctor that David began to tremble. A sudden, unmistakable reaction. He looked down at his hands, amazed. He had asked for a couple of sedatives from the doctor, saying they were for himself. He had intended to give them to Nicola and he wondered if he should take them himself after all. He shook his head. He would have a very stiff drink instead. Then—he must see Nicola.

She crouched on a chair by the window, gripping her knees so tightly that two fingernails snapped. She didn't notice. Minutes before, she had vomited violently into the bathroom sink and a stale taste still clung to her mouth. He had told her to wash her face. She could not wash her face yet. She must see the doctor arrive. She waited. It seemed hours before a car pulled into the driveway. Nicola craned her neck to see a man enter the house. A middle-aged man, carrying a bag. The doctor.

The click of the front door. Voices. Silence for a while. Later, voices on the stairs, fumbling and then, unmistakably, the sound that, tense like a spring, she had waited for, the sound that would release her—Barbara's voice. Quiet, but most certainly Barbara. The voice rose slightly, a complaining note, an impatience in it. Barbara alive. Nicola put her head in her hands and sobbed noiselessly, the tears dripping through her fingers, dampening her neck and the front of her sweater.

She waited until she saw the doctor leave, then stood stiffly and went into the bathroom. Her face in the mirror was greasy pale, streaked with tears. She studied it for awhile, her mind spinning.

"What happened to me?" she said aloud. "How could I?"

She washed her face thoroughly. Like Lady Macbeth, she thought, a washing away of sins. Then she returned to her window seat and watched the night sky. A clear night, stars visible. The trees etched against it looked threatening.

She shivered, told herself she must pack, must get back to England no matter how. Once there, she could think it all out. She could not untangle her thoughts now.

She had sat so long in the gradually deepening darkness that when the light was turned on suddenly it dazzled her. She turned, frightened, to see David, his face pale too, his eyes dark. He came swiftly across the room and put his arms around her. The warm contact brought the tears threateningly close again and she swallowed hard.

"How is she?" she said into the softness of his shirt.

"She's resting. She'll be O.K. There's nothing serious."

"The doctor?"

"He won't say anything."

"Will she . . ." Nicola swallowed again. "Will Barbara do anything about it?"

"No."

He released her slightly and looked down at her face.

"She asked me to book a flight for you tomorrow. I've done that."

His eyes were dark with pain. She looked away.

"I'd rather go tonight."

"You need rest first."

"I won't be able to . . . rest."

Nicola looked back at him: the dark, thick cap of hair, a tendril or two now fallen over his forehead, the brown eyes that were often smiling searched her face sadly.

"I've hurt you," she said.

He looked at her for a long time.

"Yes. But I think you've hurt yourself more."

"We say good-bye then?" she asked, in a small voice.

"Do you want me to come with you?"

The question like a bridge between them.

"No," said Nicola. "This is your world. With her."

"No. It's not."

"It is, David. God, it was nearly mine. What happened to me? What happened to all of us?"

He stroked her hair for a moment.

"I don't know," he said. He had rested his head against her hair and his voice came to her muffled and sad. "I could have loved you. Did. Do."

Nicola pulled away, turned to look out the window.

"You loved the rest of it more."

"No."

"You did," she said softly. "But so did I. I wanted . . . Christ, who knows? Why did I . . . God, I wish we had . . ." her voice trailed away.

"We still can."

Silence in the room for a few moments until Nicola turned to face him again.

"And your exhibition?" she asked.

He flinched slightly but his eyes held hers.

"That matters," he admitted. "It is important. But I think you are more important."

"You think?" she asked and for the first time came the ghost of a smile.

"Good-bye David. I am sorry. I'm sorry for all of us."

He looked at her hard, kissed her lightly on the forehead then moved to the door.

"Rest, if you can," he said. "I'll see you in the morning."

She turned away so that she would not see him leave and, at the sound of the door closing, held her fist to her mouth to hold back the tears. She listened to his footsteps going down the stairs, then moving around downstairs. In the quiet house she could even hear the clink of ice as he poured himself a drink. There was no sound from Barbara's room.

Nicola pulled out her suitcase and began to pack hurriedly. When this was done she switched off the light and took her place at the window again to wait until the house was silent.

An hour or so later she heard David's footsteps again, they hesitated outside her door, stopped for a moment or two. Nicola sat rigidly, her heart pounding. The footsteps faded. She heard the click of Barbara's bedroom door. Silence settled on the house. She waited longer, looking frequently at her watch. Half an hour . . . an hour. She could not wait too long, there would be few taxis around later. She would walk down to the Bel-Air gate she decided and wait, or phone if she could find a booth. Or perhaps pick up a cab coming back through Bel-Air.

At last she felt ready. The sound of her heartbeat seemed to echo through the house. Her hand, holding the suitcase, was sweating and she held the case tightly, high from the floor lest she bump the bannister or the stair. She moved slowly, fighting an urge to run. At the bottom of the stairs, she listened. Silence in the house, crickets outside, and a car somewhere far away. Her breath was coming fast, there was a tightness in her chest. Slowly the door opened with a muted whine. The cool air was welcoming and filled with the scent of mown grass and pine. Noiselessly, she closed the door, picked up her suitcase, and tiptoed along the crunching gravel path. She glanced upwards—no lights in the house. She was almost free.

A dark shape emerged so suddenly that she nearly screamed. She dropped the suitcase, her flesh prickling. Jeff stood in front of her, his face shadowy in the darkness. She thought he was going to block her way, instead he picked up the suitcase.

"LAX?" he asked, quietly.

"Pardon?"

"To the airport?"

"Yes," Nicola whispered, trembling in the eerie darkness.

How had he known? How could he know? She did not dare refuse. It was easier just to follow him to the Cadillac. He walked like a cat, soundlessly. If he took her to the airport, then she was safe. If he had other ideas . . . Too tired to deliberate, she followed him.

He opened the front door of the car, motioned her in. Like a robot, she obeyed. He took her suitcase back to the trunk of the car. How could he make no sound? Her skin felt clammy and cold, unreasonable fears flooded her. He was some sort of spook—all knowing, all seeing—or a murderer. Murderer? The word itself haunted her.

Then he was there beside her, starting the car. He drove it very slowly so that it made only a slight purr. At the end of the drive he picked up speed. Nicola sat stiffly, gripping her hands together, staring out the window, reading street signs—Bel-Air Gate, Sunset Boulevard, San Diego Free-way, Century Boulevard Exit. A sign saying LA International. The airport. She relaxed. She glanced nervously at the young man beside her.

"How did you know?" she asked.

Jeff looked at her, then back at the road.

"That I would be leaving then?"

"I knew," he said.

"But how? I was supposed to leave tomorrow."

She did not think he was going to reply. Eventually he glanced at her.

"I watch," he said. "Listen. I know most things."

"Do you . . . sort of *guard* Barbara?"

Jeff was quiet for awhile, considering this. Suddenly, he laughed harshly.

"Guard?" he said. "Shit no. I plan on living there someday. Proper living."

Nicola frowned.

"But how . . ."

He shrugged his shoulders as if to loosen them, lifted one hand from the wheel.

"I know what goes on. That means sometimes I know too much. About her. And she likes me. She likes what I do."

Nicola looked at him, startled.

"With her," Jeff explained. "Sexually."

"Sex . . ." Nicola looked away from him, trying to place this knowledge to fit the disorder of her thoughts. "Is that why you always seemed to be watching me?" she asked.

"I watch everything," he said. "Everybody. I thought you and Leyton coulda got it together. Tried to help that a bit. Might've worked. For me."

"And you would have just moved in? She'll find someone else, surely?"

"She won't need anybody else when she's got me," said Jeff, confidently. "And shit—she's running out of steam."

Nicola stared at him, shocked.

"My God," she said.

He looked at her face and whatever he saw there must have amused him. He grinned. Nicola, shaken, looked away. She rested her head on the cool glass of the window and waited for this journey to be over. At last they reached the airport. He didn't say another word. She thanked him tonelessly. He dropped her suitcase onto the sidewalk outside the British Airways terminal and quickly got back into the car. She watched the car disappear before walking tiredly into the building.

TWENTY-FIVE

She saw him standing at the window, the lithe young body tense, watching something, and she tried to call out to him. But the sedative had been a strong one: she felt packed in cotton wool, hidden away in a drawer. She felt herself floating back into the depths of sleep and heard a sound that made her force open her eyes. The sound of a car driving away. David was dressing quickly, a black, swiftly moving form against the gray darkness of the bedroom. He passed once through a shaft of moonlight. The door opened and closed again.

"David?" she called, too quietly.

He was gone. With an effort, she pushed herself into a sitting position, slapped one cheek hard with the arm that did not ache. The pain in her shoulder began again. A door slammed, another car started up. Sounded like the Mercedes. Where was he going? Then she knew. Two cars. Nicola in one. Had Jeff driven her away, taken her out of this house? He would. He was loyal, he would get her to that goddamn airport before she knew what hit her. And David? He had gone with her, of course. A lovesick calf chasing a fucking rainbow. Her eyes heavy, she fought sleep. He would be back, Barbara told herself. He *must* come back. She wanted him. An exhibition she had fucking well fought for, he wouldn't give up a chance like that for a neurotic little bitch obsessed with her sonofabitch of a father.

For Barbara, the evening's tragedy was not her wound—she knew she would soon get over that—nor the sudden violence from Nicola. Barbara had been frightened but she had been involved in too many scenes of temper to be worried about violence. No, she mourned the slashed paintings. They had been worth one hell of a lot. That bitch. But David . . . He hadn't taken his clothes. A last good-bye? The dummy. But if he didn't come back . . . he would. He must. There were others who wanted her. Jeff would service her. She smiled at the expression—it applied. And that little friend of Womberg's . . . Tom? Tim? He had looked at her. A look she recognized. Jerry as the cuckold once again. That old attorney didn't have sense enough to know when he was being taken for a ride. Look at Nicola, the bitch. Twisting him around her little finger. He should have seen her tonight. Wildcat. Mad woman. Just because she thought her dear little daddy had been ripped off. Nicholas Graham *deserved* to be ripped off. And she had begun that process the night she left him.

Barbara had been halfway through her second bottle of wine when Graham returned that night, fourteen years ago. She had expected him to be late: he was visiting Terry Lampton, an actor friend in Brighton, and she suspected he would catch the last fast train, thereby ensuring a bar and a few en route nightcaps. But it was almost one in the morning when she finally heard his key in the lock.

She remained with her feet up on the coffee table until he came into the room, then she sat up straight, staring in disbelief. Over his arm dangled a blue knapsack and by his side was a young girl. She was fair, slender, wide-eyed. The girl, looking at her, smiled tentatively.

"Barbara . . . this is Anna. Anna, my wife Barbara."

The girl said "hello" softly and when Barbara did not reply but continued to stare hard at Nick Graham, the girl too, looked up at his face.

"Anna," said Graham, "is our new *au pair* girl."

"Our *what*?" Barbara hissed through her teeth.

"She's from Belgium," Graham continued, "from . . ."

"Le Zoote," said the girl. "It is on the water."

"Le Zoote by way of Soho?" asked Barbara, her face white.

"Le Zoote on the water, and she loves children," said Graham, matter of factly.

"She is a *child* herself," said Barbara, an anger so tight in her chest she could hardly speak.

"Also, she likes to cook."

"You do?" asked Barbara, for once, directly to the girl.

"Yes."

"You can make coffee?"

"Of course."

"Then—through that door is the kitchen. Make us coffee, please. Black."

"Don't be so . . ." began Graham, but the girl, after a moment's indecision, walked into the kitchen and closed the door behind her.

Barbara immediately jumped to her feet.

"What the hell are you playing at?"

Nick Graham pushed a hand through his gray mane of hair and shook his head slowly. She realized that he was drunker than she had first thought.

"No cause for alarm, my dear."

"Don't 'my dear' me, you bastard."

"She's an *au pair* girl," he said tiredly. "Help out in the house. Play with Nicola. Take her out more—the theater, and so forth. She needs more of that."

"So she's for Nicola. And for you. What about *me*."

"You complain incessantly you don't get out enough. Well, now you can. We both can, together if we please."

"Where did you find the little whore?"

Graham's temper snapped.

"Watch your tongue, woman! She's no whore. I met her on the Brighton train this afternoon. She was going to look for a job there and we chatted for awhile and . . ."

"You took her to Terry's with you?" Barbara was incredulous.

"Of course not. She looked around the Lanes and went to the pictures and we arranged to meet at the station. I thought you'd be pleased, damnit."

"*Lying* bastard. I want her out of here. Out!"

"Dear Christ, woman. You bitch about spending your whole life in the kitchen and now . . ."

"Tomorrow, she goes."

Graham shook his head and yawned.

"Really, I am not going to listen to this nonsense at this time of night. Get the girl some blankets so she can sleep on the sofa. Tomorrow, we'll sort out the box room and . . ."

"Tomorrow that cunt will be out of here."

He was heading for the door, one hand waving dismissively. But Barbara reached the door before he did and after an indrawn breath, swiftly, viciously, she slapped his face.

Graham's eyes flashed anger for a moment but this faded into tired irritation. He pushed her very lightly on the chest, away from him.

"Enough," he said, turned and went upstairs.

Barbara, breathing deeply, heard the door to Nicola's room open and close again as he checked, as he did every night, on his child. Then his footsteps were on the landing towards their own bedroom.

She stood, trembling and uncertain for awhile, then entered the kitchen. The girl stood waiting, with three cups of coffee steaming on a tray. She was uncomfortable but there was no fear in the blue eyes as they met Barbara's. For the first time, Barbara looked properly at her face—the fine bones, the soft curve of the mouth, the clear blue eyes, and she felt at once a cold chill and the beginnings of pain. For the face was so very like the many photographs she had studied, secretly, upstairs in the attic. The album of wedding and honeymoon pictures. The woman holding a tiny newborn. Susan: Nicola's mother. She took a long, harsh breath.

"I'm going to call a cab for you," she said. "Right now. I'd suggest you go to Victoria Station again. There'll be trains to Brighton all night. I don't want you here."

The girl, unflinching, looked back at her.

"I do not think I want to be here, thank you," she said quietly.

Barbara's hands trembled as she dialed the taxi company. The girl picked up her knapsack and stood in the hallway by the front door. Barbara poured herself a large scotch and sat in an armchair watching the girl. The minutes ticked by slowly. In the silence, Barbara could hear her own breathing and the night sounds from upstairs. Nicola murmuring in her sleep, Nick turning over in the bed. At last, the sound of a car. The girl opened the front door very quietly, then closed it behind her. Barbara heard the cab door slam shut and soon the vehicle moving away. She listened until all sound of it faded, until she was certain that the girl had vanished into the night and then, abruptly, shaking violently, she began to sob.

When the sobs had subsided she poured herself another drink then looked at her watch. It was two-thirty in the morning. She had to decide what to do.

Barbara sat downstairs, sipping scotch, for two hours, then, her head reeling, she climbed the stairs to the bedroom. A bedside lamp was still on. Balancing unsteadily, she studied Graham's sleeping form for a minute or two.

"Bastard!" she muttered. "Bastard!"

Then, with a sudden pouncing movement, she yanked the bedclothes off him and shook him as hard as she could.

"For Christ's sake . . ." he began.

"I'm leaving. I'm going back to the States."

He opened his eyes, frowned, then closed them again.

"Save your big scene 'til tomorrow," he said. "We'll discuss it then."

"But I'm going now. Tonight."

"Don't be ridiculous."

"I am going now!" said Barbara, fumbling in the closet for a suitcase.

"Be quiet, woman. You'll wake Nicola. Tomorrow we'll talk about it."

Barbara was not listening to him.

"And don't think sweet Little Orphan Annie or whatever her fucking name was will comfort your poor little heart and warm your cold little bed, because Little Orphan Annie has gone back to wherever she came . . ."

At this, he sat up and stared at her.

"She's what?"

"I kicked her out," said Barbara, piling clothes into a suitcase.

He got out of bed and came to her, grabbing her arm angrily, turning her to face him.

"You did what!"

"Kicked her out. Good riddance."

"In the middle of the night! You push a young girl out in the cold? You selfish, small-minded *bitch*, you . . ."

For a moment she thought he would strike her but he suddenly let go of her arm, sighed and turned away. He climbed back into the bed and lay watching her.

She turned on him.

"What do you think I'm made of!" she screamed. "You think I could stand that under my own goddamn roof? Isn't it bad enough outside the fucking door? I would give you twenty-four hours, you sonofabitch, before you were fucking her."

There was a small silence, then Nick Graham's voice, steady, sensible.

"Twenty-four hours? I fucked her all this afternoon in Brighton's most charming Ship Hotel."

It was the last thing he said to her. With that, he turned over, his back towards her, as if to sleep. Stunned, Barbara stared at him, then snapped shut her suitcase. He did not move. His breathing was even. She left the room, tugging the suitcase behind her.

Downstairs, she called the cab company again, then sat down for a few minutes to work out how much money she had. It was not much. She had enough for cab fare to Heathrow and a little left over. Her air fare would have to be on a credit card. Once there, she would have to sell some of her jewelry. She pondered for awhile then, quickly, took down the two smallest Nicholas Graham sketches that hung in the lounge and slid them into the bottom of her suitcase.

Six hours later she was on a Pan Am flight back to the United States. She had a story prepared for customs—as his wife she took the sketches everywhere—they were gifts—but her one suitcase was not opened. The sketches went with her to California . . . and later to Bel-Air. They were the start of her collection. A collection she had continued for fourteen years. And had so recently told him about.

She had written the letter impulsively, after an evening of heavy drinking, lonely drinking, in the lounge that held his pictures.

"So, why aren't you painting any more, old man?" she had written. "Must be two years since I added to my collection. Yes, I have most of them. Can't decide whether to burn one each year on our wedding anniversary or simply store them all in a damp, dark basement away from the light of day and admiring eyes. Oh, poor deprived youth. Not to gaze on a Nicholas Graham. Not in your lifetime, in any case." She had waited with nervous excitement for his reaction—half expecting him to storm the Atlantic. Deep down she wanted that. She wanted to see him again, if only to enjoy his anger. Once, it occurred to her that he might notify the press, enjoying the limelight as he did, and she trembled at the thought of seeing her name splashed across the *L.A. Times* in this connection. But there was no response. Nothing. Until a month later when she read that he had killed himself.

Dead? That big brute dead? It seemed impossible. In her Bel-Air bedroom, sinking back into a drugged sleep, Barbara felt something she had not felt for a long time, had not ever expected to feel again: a sense of loss.

TWENTY-SIX

On the San Diego freeway, David cursed the California speed limits and prayed for a glimpse of the black Cadillac. Jeff's few minutes start meant he could be miles ahead. David hoped he *was* taking her to the airport, but where else would he take her? He wondered how Nicola had arranged for Jeff to drive her. And when.

David had been lying restlessly next to the sleeping Barbara when he heard the soft click of the back door. He had gone to the window more out of a need to move, to do something, than real curiosity. He had expected to see Jeff strolling around the garden. He did that often. Instead, he saw Nicola with a suitcase, then Jeff. Without thinking David had dressed and jumped into the car. He could not bear to see her go without speaking with her further. He could not bear to see her go at all.

Her ashen face a few hours ago haunted him.

"What happened to me? What happened to us?"

He had no answers. Barbara, over the years, had perpetrated a plot of revenge against Nick Graham. That he understood. But . . . He shook his head, trying to clear it. Nicola.

No sign of the Cadillac as he pulled up outside the British Airways terminal. She would choose that, surely? But no sign of Nicola either. He parked the car and walked quickly into the terminal, searching faces. None of them Nicola. At last, he saw her. She was huddled on a bench, staring at a magazine, her suitcase beside her. A few people milled around, there was an echo from the loud-

233

speaker—an airport in the small hours of the morning, brightly lit and half empty. A place for sadness.

She stared at him blankly when he reached her. He sat down next to her on the bench and took her face in his hands.

"I want to come with you."

"You can't."

"I want to." He smiled. "Not maybe. Not I think. I know. I know for sure."

Nicola did not smile.

"Your exhibition?"

"You matter more."

She sighed.

"I can't let you do that. I won't."

"You must."

"You'll regret it. You'll hate me always."

He touched her cheek.

"How could I hate you?"

She shrugged.

"It happens."

"I love you," he said. "Do you . . ." He could not finish the question, he was scared of the answer. But the blue eyes had softened.

"Yes, I think I probably do," she said. "I wouldn't have been so hurt and furious when you rejected me otherwise."

"Rejected you?" he looked at her in surprise. "I've never rejected you."

"In the attic. When you were sorting your paintings."

He frowned, thinking back, then remembered.

"But I was working!" he said, and at the significance of this they looked at each other and both smiled.

"See," she said. "I told you."

"That's not really a rejection."

"No, perhaps not."

He smoothed a curling wisp of hair from her cheek.

"Will you let me come? Will you take me on, finally?"

She looked down at the floor, curled one small foot and stared at it.

"No, to the first part," she said. "Possibly yes, to the second. But not yet."

He felt an acute disappointment.

"What do you mean?"

"I don't want you to come now. Anyway, how could you? No luggage, no passport."

"I was hoping you'd wait here. There can't be a flight until the morning?" He raised an eyebrow.

"No. The first is 12:45. T.W.A."

"You're in the wrong terminal."

"I know. I just feel more comfortable here. I'll go to the right one nearer the time."

"Look," said David, taking her hand. "I just raced after you. On the way here I figured I could find you, talk to you, then go back and pick up my things. We could take a flight together."

He squeezed the small hand tightly, willing her to agree.

"No," she said. "I want you to go back, do this exhibition. Stay with Barbara until . . . she's better. Then, if you want to come to England, I'll be there."

It was logical, it was sensible, and David knew that he would do it. He wanted the exhibition. He wanted Nicola. He would eventually get both. But he didn't want her to see him acquiesce so easily. He must not lose her. He loved her, he knew that.

"No," he said firmly. "I'm coming with you."

She was smiling.

"Don't be silly," she said. "You know my way is best. You've already agreed. I was watching your face."

He looked into her eyes. Yes, she knew. She had read his thoughts. He grinned back at her.

"You're spooky," he said.

"You could say that. Now—shall we find some coffee?"

"Let's go someplace else. It's a long time till midday."

"Where?"

"There's a place pretty close by," David said casually. "The Airport Marina."

"Is it a coffee shop?"

"It's a hotel."

He waited, heart pounding, for her reply.

"Shall we buy my ticket first?" she said.

In the T.W.A. terminal she purchased her ticket and

with a pang he watched her tuck it carefully into her bag. As they were walking towards the car she suddenly let go of his arm and stopped.

"David . . . shouldn't you go back. Barbara . . ."

"Fast asleep. And I'm staying with you until it's time for you to leave."

She made no further protest until they were inside their hotel room.

"I feel this is wrong," she said, looking away from the double bed that dominated the room.

"Of course it's not. I love you," he said, coming to hug her.

"I've done so many wrong things recently."

"Don't think about that. I'll order us a drink."

She looked tense and tired. David, longing to hold her, make love to her, checked himself. Let her relax a little first. They sat on the bed, holding tightly to each other's hands, until the drinks finally arrived. Nicola sipped hers then put it down immediately.

"I don't know that I want it really," she said. She rested her head against his shoulder.

"God, I feel strange. Drained. Unreal."

"You're exhausted. Let's get you into bed."

He helped her to undress and the simple action of lifting her sweater over her breasts aroused him totally. He kissed her hard, holding her tight against him. Within seconds they were lying across the bed and a little while later David made love to her as gently and as tenderly as he could. She cried out at last, clinging to him. His reward.

Afterwards she lay sleepily in the crook of his arm.

"God, I do love you," he said.

"I don't know why you don't hate me." Nicola's voice was low. "I've been so crazy."

"I tried to," he admitted honestly. "For awhile, I tried to."

"Did you . . . love . . . Barbara?"

He shook his head.

"Not love. Nothing like love. I liked her, I suppose. She fascinated me. So tough, so uncompromising. I guess too . . ." he paused, trying to get it right, "I was curious because she is so disliked. People are frightened of her. I wanted to show her that I wasn't. Something like that. I can't say I fully understood her."

Nicola sighed.

"I don't understand her. Or myself. I think I hate her. I must or I wouldn't have . . . I'll try not to hate her. Will you feel guilty about leaving her?"

"No. She'll find someone else."

"Will she? Jeff said . . ."

Nicola stopped and David tilted her chin so he could see her face.

"Jeff? What did Jeff say?"

There was a long pause. Nicola seemed to be tussling with something.

"She sleeps with Jeff occasionally," she said, finally.

He edged up onto one elbow and looked down at her amazed.

"Jeff! How do you know?"

"He told me."

"Jeff? Good Christ."

"Does that upset you?"

He shook his head.

"No. Not at all. It makes it easier . . . not to leave her," he added hurriedly, seeing Nicola's face. "Just easier not to feel guilty."

Sbe smiled.

"Yes," she said.

He lay down again, cuddled her against him.

"Try to get some sleep."

"I'll never sleep," Nicola murmured. But after awhile her arms around him, she relaxed. She breathed softly, a tiny frown creased the sleeping face.

At boarding time he took her to the gate, held her tightly, then watched the slender figure disappear. She had been dry-eyed, very quiet, and thoughtful all morning. He had her address in his pocket and her promise. That was all. He felt that was enough. He drove back to the house feeling dazed by the rush of events and the lack of sleep. Barbara would question him, of course, and he would tell half the truth. He had stayed with Nicola at the airport until her flight was called because he felt she should not be alone in her distraught state. That information would have to suffice. He would get through the next week, he would stay until the end of his exhibition. Then he would leave. Nicola. Nicola. On the now busy freeway, he began to whistle.

TWENTY-SEVEN

Felix had taken her key and came hurriedly into the apartment clutching a large pile of newspapers and magazines and a bottle of wine. She was sitting close to the fire, wrapped in a blanket and she smiled blearily at him.

"How do you feel?" he asked.

"Much better," Nicola lied. The cold was in its third day, the runny stage. Felix had insisted she stay indoors on this chilly London evening. He put the wine on the table and dumped the papers on her lap.

"All the American papers I could lay my hands on," he said. "Couldn't spot much but I haven't read them properly. There's a bit about the show in the top one."

It was a local Los Angeles magazine. She opened it quickly.

"David Leyton . . . innovative . . . sculptural configurations that contain video monitors . . ."

"Good Lord," she said aloud! she hadn't known about *those*.

" . . . strong composition . . ."

The reviewer wound up by saying that the artist's "involvement" was immature but it would, he was certain, develop. Nicola was not too sure what he meant by that.

"Not bad," she said to Felix who was opening the wine.

She fumbled through the other papers, stopping every minute or so to blow her nose. There were a few two-line mentions that the show had opened, an advertisement in the *Los Angeles Times* and that was all.

"Hardly raves," she said, taking a glass of wine from Felix. "But not bad for a start."

He took the magazine and read the review carefully.

"Funny language you people use," he said. "Like legal jargon. Created to confuse."

She laughed:

"My little reviews aren't like that. I wouldn't know how."

"You'll learn," he said, sourly.

"Grump."

"Me? I'm all sweetness and light."

"You are. I used to think I was."

He looked at her quizzically. Nicola had told Felix a little about her experiences in Los Angeles but not in detail, not the things that worried her most—the loss of reality and personality. Jekyll and Hyde. She did not know where to begin.

"When can I meet your girl?" she asked, to change the subject. Felix had met a young music student while she was away and was exhibiting the usual Felix signs of infatuation.

"Soon. Promise. You'll like her, she's a sweet lass. It's ironic," he said, grinning. "You tell me to go find myself a redhead, so I find a blonde. And you come back a redhead."

"I'm growing it out."

"Good," he said. "It's hideous."

They sipped their wine. Nicola sneezed. Felix picked up a newspaper then threw it down in disgust.

"Can't be bothered to pick through all that," he said. "When's your fella coming out?"

She paused.

"Not sure. His letter said . . . when the exhibition's over. When everything is tied up. It should be soon."

"Will you live here? In this apartment?"

"Yes," said Nicola. "I suppose so. We won't be able to afford much else. We may go back to California eventually. It could be a good place . . . Oh, Christ, Felix!"

He stared at her, surprised.

"What is it? Don't you want him to come?"

"God, yes. I do. I do. But—I can't explain. I feel that everything is a replay."

"A replay?" Felix was frowning.

"Yes. I feel unreal. It frightens me. My mother and father, you know, artist and wife. Poverty of sorts. I didn't want that in Los Angeles. I wanted to replay Barbara. God. How? Why?"

"You're not making any sense," said Felix pleasantly. "Begin again."

Slowly, candidly, with long pauses, she told him all that had happened in California. The parties, the men, her desire to live as Barbara had—on some man's wealth. She stumbled over Pete and the party then told Felix about Barbara's statements about her father, her mother's death, about David, and finally, she told him about stabbing Barbara. That last incredible scene.

He listened carefully, patiently, and when she had finished they had also finished the wine.

"Your stepmother sounds like a bitch," he said at last. "She could have been a catalyst for some of that in you."

"In me? I didn't know I had it in me. Look, love, I thought of myself as a particular sort of person—not an evil person, at any rate. And Felix, the terrible thing is I enjoyed some of that. Enjoyed it. I became a 'why not?' Remember we used to talk about the 'why not' people. I used to be a person who needed reasons. Good ones."

Felix was silent for awhile.

"People can corrupt others," he offered. "As power can corrupt. And absolutely, etc. But look, I don't know. I can't imagine you—but then I wasn't there. I need to think. Stay warm. I'll get some more wine."

Before she could protest, he had disappeared through the door. She read the review again. Was David pleased with it? His one letter since her departure was full of love but he had confessed he was edgy about the exhibition.

"I feel that if I fail, I fail you too," he had written. Nicola smiled and flicked through the other newspapers. No mention of Barbara in the social columns. David had not mentioned her. Nicola had written to Jerry—a letter of apology—and had received a sweet letter in reply. He had not mentioned Barbara either. Felix returned, carrying two bottles of wine.

"Just in case," he said. "Besides, I'm thirsty."

He took off his coat, opened the wine in silence. He was frowning, still puzzling out what he wanted to say. When they were settled with a large glass of wine each, he looked over at her.

"First of all, forget the replay bit. That's nonsense. Your life will be unique as every life is. So—you marry, live with, whatever, an artist as your mother did? But David is not your father—he's not even like him by the sound of it—and you are not your mother. Besides, you are living in different times, in a different world. So forget that.

"As for the rest . . ." he paused, sipped his wine. "Montaigne believed that the traveler takes himself wherever he goes . . ."

He stopped again, looked hard at her.

"So that was . . . the real me."

"No!" snapped Felix. "A part of you. Temporarily, if you like."

"Jesus Christ."

She rested her head on the back of the chair.

"You survived, love," said Felix.

"Dear God, but only just! God knows what might have . . . And you know, they almost fired me here. Ted Sharp stood up for me for some reason. Jeremy still treats me as if I just crawled out of the Gorgonzola."

"Deserved, perhaps?"

"Of course. Of course. I'm not saying . . ."

"You got lost for awhile," said Felix. "That's all."

They sat for awhile in silence, watching the flickering fire. Eventually, they began to talk of other things: of her job which she would start again on Monday, of Felix's girl, of David's chances of success in London. After awhile they talked of old friends and of films to see, books to read, just as they had always talked. Later, when Felix left, a little unsteadily, Nicola returned to her chair by the now dying fire and sat for a long time, staring into the ashes.

TWENTY-EIGHT

It was a grey, leaden-sky day. A blustering wind rattled the bedroom windows as Nicola, hands shaking nervously, tried to apply mascara to her lashes. It smudged clownishly. She took four deep breaths and tried again. Her hands were steadier but her heart was still bumping out a tense rhythm. It had been a month since David's last letter.

"You must be prepared," Felix had said carefully a week ago, "for the possibility that perhaps . . ."

"He might not come?"

"Yes. If his work is so important to him. If he has enjoyed a measure of success . . . well . . ."

"He'll come, Felix."

A sure voice. But her friend's words only echoed the ones in her head. David's work was important to him. She was . . . she had believed, she was important too. She tried to tell herself that she might never see him again. It was too chilling a thought to believe.

Then, yesterday morning, a telegram. Just the date, the time and the flight number, signed—love, David. At first, her euphoria had caused her to dance—the old shuffle-train tapdance she had learned as a child. Later, the doubts began. He could be coming only to tell her he must go back. To say good-bye properly. He had, she knew, a certain amount of honor. He might feel a gesture of that sort was necessary. He would not leave her hanging.

As she dressed to meet him, she thought that she must look beautiful in case this was the last time. She studied herself. Brown velvet pants tucked into her new, leather, knee high boots, cream silk shirt, a short fur jacket. A cold weather outfit for a chill, dark day.

The henna dye had faded and her hair was regaining its natural fair color but the ends still curled. Alan, at Sassoon's Bond Street salon, had spent two hours trimming and straightening and had adapted the curl to form a modern "shake." It suited her, but she longed for it to grow out, wanted her old, gleaming long hair back again.

She was at Heathrow an hour too soon. She lingered in the coffee bar over a cup of foul coffee, then studied the paperbacks in W.H. Smith's. At last the loudspeaker crackled with the information she had so long awaited. His plane had landed, passengers were disembarking.

She stood a little way back from the jostling, excited crowd of families and friends who leaned on the ropes that sectioned off a thoroughfare for arriving passengers. After long minutes, people began to emerge from the exits from customs. Blinking, yawning, tugging heavy suitcases: the British identifiable by their peeling skins and sensible coming-home macs and jackets; the Californians, tired under their tans, wearing light denims and double-knits, carrying carefully matched luggage.

Twice, Nicola's heart jumped as the figure of a tall, dark-haired man could be seen dimly through the glass doors, then sank again as strangers emerged into the light. He would not come. She had known he would not come.

Then, he was there. The figure, even through the glass, instantly, surely recognizable. Taller than the others, the hair just a fraction longer, falling over his forehead. The doors opened. Under the clear light he was browner, healthier—energy vibrating from him—than she remembered. He did not look tired from the flight. He put down his suitcases and searched the faces. He was here. He saw her. And smiled. The smile she had not forgotten.

Nicola, with a rare disregard for manners, pushed people aside and elbowed her way towards him. He had his arms around her and his face in her hair in seconds.

"My God, I have missed you," he murmured. She nuzzled his cheek.

"I was so scared you wouldn't come. I can't believe you're here."

"I'm here."

She wanted to ask him—for how long? For always? But could not.

He stood back and looked at her, touching her hair gently.

"And I need coffee. Urgently. The liquid they served on that plane was dishwater."

"Just wait," she said, leading him to the coffee bar, "until you taste this."

He pulled a wry face when he took his first sip of Heathrow coffee.

"Now I understand why the English drink tea. Is it as bad as this everywhere in the country?"

"Mine is better."

He grinned.

"Thank God."

He was staying, then. Was he?

"Tell me everything . . . the exhibition, Barbara, Jerry . . ."

"In detail—later. In a nutshell: the show went fairly well . . . a start; I met a few British dealers too . . . have one to see here."

Her heart leapt with hope at this.

"Barbara . . . has been surprisingly stoic. But then she's a sturdy lady. I moved out the day after you left. Stayed with Jo-Jo. Jeff, as you predicted, moved in. But she stood by me over the exhibition—I'm grateful to her for that."

Nicola made a face. He stroked her cheek.

"Don't worry about Barbara. Incidentally," he reached into a small attaché case and pulled out two pieces of paper. "She sent you this. I think it was meant to be a kind gesture, though I'm not sure."

Nicola studied the two ragged sheets then slid them together.

A sketch of a bluebell wood. A woman and child. Her eyes filled with tears. She could not wait longer to know.

"David . . . are you staying? Are you here to stay?"

He stared at her.

"I'm here to *marry* you, dummy."

Nicola looked into the warm brown eyes.

"Good," she said.

MORE
BEST-SELLING FICTION
FROM PINNACLE

BEST-SELLING MOVIE BOOKS FROM PINNACLE

☐ **41-177-4 CAN'T STOP THE MUSIC**
by Bronte Woodard and Allan Carr   **$2.50**

Now, the biggest musical comedy extravaganza of the Eighties—*Can't Stop the Music*, starring the #1 international singing sensation Village People, Valerie Perrine and Bruce Jenner—can be yours for keeps with this exciting photobook, complete with over 150 action shots from the hit movie, *plus* a full-color souvenir photo album!

☐ **41-056-5 THE HEARSE**
by Henry Clement   **$2.25**

An emotionally distraught schoolteacher is driven to the edge of madness by a macabre hearse, in this supernatural thriller starring Trish Van deVere and Joseph Cotton.

☐ **40-712-2 SURVIVAL RUN**
by Robert Hoskins   **$2.25**

A weekend orgy in the desert becomes taut with terror when six lost teenagers unwittingly stumble upon an international drug-smuggling ring, in this suspenseful motion picture starring Peter Graves, Ray Milland and Vincent Van Patten.

☐ **41-148-0 ZULU DAWN**
by Cy Endfield   **$2.50**

Proud, unyielding Zulu warriors defend their homeland in one of the bloodiest massacres in African history—now a major motion picture starring Burt Lancaster and Peter O'Toole.

Buy them at your local bookstore or use this handy coupon.
Clip and mail this page with your order

◉ **PINNACLE BOOKS, INC.—Reader Service Dept.**
271 Madison Ave., New York, NY 10016

Please send me the book(s) I have checked above. I am enclosing $_____ (please add 75¢ to cover postage and handling). Send check or money order only—no cash or C.O.D.'s.

Mr./Mrs./Miss _____

Address _____

City _____ State/Zip _____

Please allow six weeks for delivery. Prices subject to change without notice.
